Send in the Clowns

(And Abe Lincoln Too)

D1516095

Mark A. Albright

NEWMAN SPRINGS PUBLISHING
320 Broad Street
Red Bank, NJ 07701

First originally published by Newman Springs Publishing 2018

ISBN 978-1-64096-293-4 (Paperback)
ISBN 978-1-64096-294-1 (Digital)

Printed in the United States of America

To Flo Albright (1927–2017) and Clint Albright (1925–2011),
or as I called them, Mom and Dad.

Prologue

In the beginning, God created the heavens and the earth. Then a whole bunch of other stuff happened, which brings us to the start of this story.

First, let me talk about the narrator of this tale a bit—me. I was selected to write this book because I had just finished *Fifty Shades of Grey* (reading it, not writing it) and had plenty of time on my hands. I know all the people involved, but I'll be writing as the all-omniscient author. That's the one who knows what they say and what they think but who is not ever actually involved in the action—kind of like my life in general.

This is a story of murder and deception and humor and sex (not in that particular order). It is a story of a couple of comedians, a best friend, a femme fatale, an evil wealthy guy, some other less important people, and oh yeah, some clowns. Plus a cameo appearance by Abe Lincoln (but not the vampire-slaying Abe Lincoln). It is a story that takes place in New York City—the city that never sleeps but could probably use a good nap every now and then.

And it is the story of brothers. There have been many famous brothers over the years—Wright, Smothers, Grimm, Doobie—who have worked together with varying degrees of success. One lesser-known set of brothers was the Dickens Brothers, Charles and Larry. Not many people have heard of Larry and with good reason.

Only a handful know that Charles Dickens had a cynical brother who helped write his famous lead paragraph for "A Tale of Two Cities." Charles began by writing, "It was the best of times. It was the best of cities." It was his brother, Larry Dickens, the one with a dark side, who came in and added, "It was the worst of times. It was the worst of cities."

The combination of brotherly writing worked to make the first paragraph one of the most famous opening leads to a book ever and captured the ambivalence of the times in which they lived. However, when Larry tried the same technique at the end of the book, it was not as successful. Charles wrote, "It is a far, far better thing I do than I have ever done before. It is a far, far better rest that I go to than I have ever known." Larry added, "It is a far, far worse thing that I do than I have ever done before. It is a far, far worse rest I go to than I have ever known." Luckily, Charles caught that change before it got to print, and the rest is Dickens history.

The moral of the Dickens story is this: brothers, in moderation, can be quite helpful.

Logue

Chapter 1

S uch was the case of the Darwin brothers, Dan and Carl. When they were together, some of the time, it worked well. When they were together too much, well, they were just together too much.

Onstage together, working as a comedy team, everything clicked. Carl gave Dan the courage to be himself Dan kept Carl from being himself too much. Carl, at forty-four, was the outgoing one, the fearless one, the one who saw opportunity around each corner. Dan, three years younger, was the introspective one, the cautious one. Dan also knew opportunities were around the corner, but he also knew that lurking there along with the opportunities were lots of bad things. And since the bad things were often disguised as opportunities, Dan didn't rush in where fools feared to tread.

Dan had always wanted to be a comedian, but it was only when Carl joined him onstage that he got the courage to actually do it. Dan had moved from his hometown of Little Rock to New York to become a comedian since Little Rock was not the place to be if you wanted to be discovered. It had taken a real act of courage for him to make the move to what can be a really cold, hard city if you don't know anyone.

Dan had to work a variety of odd jobs along the way to make enough money to eat, and that was about all he'd made. He had ventured onto stage a couple of times by himself on open-mike nights,

7

but it had always been a gut-wrenchingly hard thing to do. He had no trouble coming up with material, but each time his name was called, it was as if his legs had gone numb and he couldn't move. And it never seemed to get easier.

Carl had moved to New York several years prior to Dan to be some sort of investment adviser. He had made plenty of money and had taken up stand-up comedy, partly to help out his brother and partly to prove he could do whatever his brother did. If he suffered stage fright, it was never apparent. Just having Carl by his side gave Dan the confidence to finally relax enough to actually be funny.

On the surface, they seemed more similar than different. They had similar looks, both over six feet tall with dark hair and blue eyes. Carl, at six one, was a little shorter than his younger brother and spent more time trying to dress better and look better. It was only upon closer inspection one could see the differences. They weren't so much like night and day as like dusk and dawn. If you don't know which direction the sun is, dusk and dawn look pretty much the same. Only time can tell you the difference.

The easiest way to sum up their differences was their views on their respective divorces. Dan had been divorced once and never really gotten over it. He was still trying to learn the lessons of the first marriage before attempting a second. Carl had been divorced three times and couldn't wait to try marriage again, or at least the preliminaries to marriage, which he said were the real fun.

"You're lucky," Carl had said to Dan. "Women love guys who've been divorced once. They believe the second time is the charm for men. With three divorces, I either have to lie about how many times I've been married or lie about the reasons for the divorces. The first time, you can say you were both too young. The second, you can say you married on the rebound and she wasn't the right one. But by number 3, well, somehow, it's gotta be my fault."

Not that lying was out of the question for Carl. After all, if the cause was just (that is, women, money, etc.), well, sometimes the truth was a subjective thing. As for Dan, he had some inner voice that just kept him from lying. Oh sure, he could tell some woman her hair looked nice or the dress didn't make her look fat when it didn't and it did. But for the big stuff, he just felt compelled to tell the truth.

All of which had led to Dan being in the mess he was in right now. After all, if he hadn't ever told the police what he had seen, he wouldn't be on the wrong side of one of the most powerful men in show business in the New York area: Hilton J. Jamieson.

And at such a bad time—just when the Darwin brothers' comedy careers had started to take off. Jamieson was to New York entertainment what Harvey Weinstein was to Los Angeles before his career seemed to take an unexpected downturn. Jamieson wanted to make sure that didn't happen to him.

Jamieson was determined to see that the Darwins' career never got out of the starting gate. He didn't really have anything against Carl, but since the brothers were a comedy team, he had to punish Carl as well in his attempt to intimidate Dan into not testifying. Objective observers would say that murdering a woman was Jamieson's mistake, but the way he saw it, it was Dan's being the only witness to the murder that was the mistake. And since he couldn't take back the murder, the only remedy was to take away the witness, or at least make him not be a witness anymore.

After years of going from dive to dive in the New York City area and parts beyond, Dan and Carl had finally gotten a more or less permanent gig (since a permanent gig in show business is an oxymoron) at Louie Shinn's House of Laughing Hyenas on the Upper East Side of Manhattan. They were the hosts every night except Fridays and Saturdays, when Louie had bands come in. Dan and Carl had tried to get Louie to change the name of the place since (a) the bands weren't trying to get laughs and (b) it was just a stupid name. But Louie liked it, and it was his place—end of discussion.

On Sunday through Thursday, Dan and Carl emceed comedy nights at the House of Laughing Hyenas. They came out and warmed up the audience and introduced three or four other comedians being featured for the night. If the other comedians were somewhat established, there might only be two, and the Darwins' warm-up routine became little more than an introduction. They had parlayed that gig into some others in more comedy clubs, as far away as Atlanta and

Chicago. And after one of Colbert's booking people had seen them, he had talked to them about being on his show. He didn't promise anything, but after he came back and saw them a second time with a few others, he said he thought they were ready.

But since Dan had agreed to testify against Jamieson, those other gigs had one by one dried up, and someone from Colbert had even called them to say they changed their minds. No one would say so, but the Darwins knew it was Jamieson and his people who were behind the cancellations.

Chapter 2

On this particular Thursday night, three weeks before Christmas when our story begins, the featured comedians weren't any more well-known than Dan and Carl. In fact, probably less so to the regulars at the Hyena House, as it had become known.

Like most bars and restaurants in the real-estate restricted Manhattan area, the Hyena House was not big. There was a small bar area when you entered that people crowded into until they went past a curtained doorway into the entertainment area. When it was really packed, you could fit about eighty people in there, and there was barely room between the tables for the servers to squeeze through. And the dressing room area was little more than a large bathroom.

As usual, Dan had prepared some material and was trying to get his brother to memorize his part before they took the stage. And just as usual, Carl just wanted to wing it. It was what Carl did best, and truth be known, it was what Dan did best also, but he would never want to rely on it.

"Come on, would you at least look at it?" Dan pleaded.

"I did," Carl said. "I got it, I got it. It's good. We do the opening deal, ad-lib some, then the other stuff, and then you get to do your joke about statistics or minorities or something."

"Yeah, it really sounds like you got it. Whenever you say you've got it, that's when I worry."

"You worry whenever I say anything. Just trust me, bro. Have I ever let you down?"

"Only when I've counted on you."

"Ooh, that hurts. Too late. It's showtime."

ANNOUNCER: And now, the comedy team that never leaves the field until all the outs are recorded and all the laughs are in—the Darwin Brothers!

(*Dan and Carl walked onto the stage to applause from a rather lively crowd. Carl, per status quo, enjoyed the applause a little more enthusiastically than Dan.*)

DAN: Wow, hard to believe he wrote that intro all by himself. Hi, I'm Dan Darwin, and this is my brother, Carl. We'll be your comedy hosts this evening. Now, you understand, as comedy hosts, it's really just our job to warm up the audience and introduce the other comedians. So we can't really be hysterically funny like we want to be, 'cause that wouldn't be fair to the other comedians. We can't wear you out laughing so you have nothing left.

CARL: I think we're safe so far.

DAN: Yeah, remarkably so.

CARL: Hey, I've got an idea, let's go into the audience.

DAN: No, not yet.

(*Carl took his microphone and headed into the audience.*)

DAN: I'll just wait here.

CARL: You're not still scared, are you?

DAN: Not scared, just prudent. I'll wait here.

CARL, *to the audience*: He's just a little scared—excuse me, *prudent*—because of "the incident."

DAN: You swore you'd never talk about that again.

CARL: I did? Hmm, I don't remember that. (*To the audience.*) You see, one time, my brother came into the audience and got a little too friendly with this woman in the audience, or what seemed to be a woman …

DAN: Hey, in my defense, he was a really good-looking man.

CARL: That's your defense?

DAN: He was dressed like a woman, looked like a woman. How was I supposed to know?

CARL: The Adam's apple, hands the size of boat paddles could have been clues.

DAN: Who looks at a woman's hands or throat the first thing?

CARL: I bet you do, now.

DAN: That's true.

CARL: Anyway, we have a standing bet. I maintain that anyone in the crowd has the potential to be funny, we just have to bring it out of them.

DAN: Actually, what he says is that anyone in the crowd can be made fun of.

CARL: Po-ta-to, po-taw-to. (*To Dan.*) Are you just gonna stay up there?

DAN: Oh yeah. And I'm not helping you.

CARL: Why not?

DAN: You know why.

CARL: Okay, okay, my brother's gonna pout until I let him tell his joke. Okay, go ahead.

DAN: How about that women's march? Wasn't that something? (*Some applause and cheers.*)

CARL, *chanting:* Yes, we can. Yes, we can. Yes, we can.

DAN: Actually, that's not the right slogan.

CARL: Okay, what is it?

DAN: This is the "me too" movement.

CARL, *chanting again:* Me too. Me too. Me too.

DAN: I hate to correct you again, but really, that's what the women would say.

CARL: What would the men say?

DAN: Uh, I don't know. I guess "We're sorry for being such bastards."

CARL, *chanting again:* We're sorry for being such bastards. We're sorry for being such bastards. That's not much of a slogan.

DAN: Not really, no.

CARL: Well, at least I went to the march.

DAN: Yeah, but you said you were going 'cause it's a good place to pick up girls. Not sure that was the real spirit of the march.

CARL: I told you I didn't really mean it.

DAN: Yeah, but then you told me you hooked up with a woman you met there.

CARL: Just because I say something, then say I don't mean it, then something happens which indicates I might have meant it—that doesn't really mean that I didn't mean it when I said I didn't mean it.

DAN: You can say that again.

CARL: I'm not sure I can.

DAN: Probably just as well. Before you get started down there with the audience, how about a statistical quiz?

CARL: Boy, do you know how to get a crowd revved up?

DAN, *ignoring him*: Does anyone here know the only minority group which is statistically overrepresented in Congress?

(*Silence from the crowd.*)

DAN: Really? Anybody?

CARL: I think they're thinking, which is always exciting.

(*A woman finally yelled out, "Men!"*)

DAN: That's right! Get that woman a drink. See, men are actually a minority of the population, but they have a vast majority in the Senate and the House.

CARL: I think they get it.

DAN: I guess it's not really a funny observation.

CARL: Not so much, no. Can I get started now?

DAN: Can I stop you?

CARL: No. Are you really not coming down into the audience?

DAN: No, I'll just be up here, getting ready for action—girding my loins, so to speak.

CARL: Okay, well, you might want to wait and do that backstage. I don't think the audience wants to see that.

DAN: No, girding my loins means … never mind.

CARL: All right, well, I'll find somebody to talk to while my brother is doing something I don't want to know about with his loins. Okay, let's start with these two attractive women here, who, by the way, have normal size-hands and no Adam's apples. (*He said to the closest one to him, a short-haired woman in her late thirties.*) Hi, what's your name?

SUE: Sue.

CARL: Okay, that's not funny.

SUE: Sorry.

CARL: Where are you from?

SUE: Right here, Manhattan.

CARL: Mmm, okay. Zero for two. Job maybe?

SUE: I work at a museum.

DAN: Wow, this just keeps getting better and better. You want to pay up now?

CARL: Hey, museums can be funny, I bet.

DAN: Yeah, *The Marx Brothers Go to the Museum* is one of my favorite movies.

CARL: What about that movie with Ben Stiller?

DAN: *Night at the Museum*?

CARL: Yeah, what about that?

DAN: Hadn't seen it?

CARL: Yeah, I know, me neither, but that's bound to be funny.

DAN: Hadn't seen it.

CARL: I heard you, but come on, Ben Stiller, he's always funny, isn't he?

DAN: Hadn't seen it.

CARL: Okay, I think that's been established. (*To Sue.*) Have you seen it?

SUE: No.

CARL: Okay, thanks for your help. What about the movie where the monster attacks the museum?

DAN: *The Relic*? Yeah, that was a laugh riot.

CARL, *to Sue*: Ever seen any monsters at your museum?

SUE: No.

CARL: Okay, which museum do you work at?

SUE: The Museum of Natural History.

CARL: Oh yeah, I guess the monsters would be at the Museum of Unnatural History. (*Some laughs from the audience.*)

DAN: Five minutes, one laugh, not bad.

CARL: You want to do your statistical representation joke again?

Dan: No, I think they got it the first time.

Carl: Let's see, what do I know about museums? There's only two jobs I can think of at a museum. There's a curator, and uh, I guess, the guards. That's it. I'm out. Are you either of those?

Sue: No.

Carl: What do you do?

Sue: I'm exhibits admissions coordinator.

Carl: Did Dan help you with your lines?

Sue: No, I'm just naturally boring, I guess.

Carl: All right, I'll bite. What does an exhibits admissions coordinator do?

Sue: When exhibits or anything else are delivered to the museum, I check them in and sign for them.

Carl: Oh, that sounds important at least. Not funny, mind you, but important. So when a big exhibit comes in, you have to check and make sure it's say from the Byzantine era and not the uh … (*Looked to Dan for help.*)

Dan: The Ottoman era.

Carl: The Ottoman era?

Dan: Yeah, that's the period when footstools were invented.

Sue: Actually, we have experts whom I call in to make sure the exhibit is actually what it's supposed to be and that everything is there. I don't really know the difference between Homo erectus and uh …

Carl: Homo non-erectus? Wow, I don't want to date you.

Dan: Or maybe you do.

Carl: Yeah, good point.

Sue: I'm married anyway.

Carl: Okay, well, that's not necessarily a deal breaker, but we'll get to that in a moment. Let me see if I've got this straight. When stuff comes into the museum, you sign for it, but if it's important stuff, somebody else actually checks on it to make sure it's right.

Sue: Yeah.

Carl: So if it's unimportant stuff, you can sign for that by yourself. Like old bones that nobody really cares about?

DAN: Chicken bones.

CARL: Yes, the not-so-famous chicken exhibit.

DAN: That's from San Diego, I think.

CARL: Yeah.

SUE: Do you guys really need me?

CARL: Not so much. So the job description on your job says "Must be able to sign own name."

SUE: Pretty much.

CARL: Okay, good gig. (*Sue started to sit down.*) Wait a minute, you're not through.

SUE, *standing back up*: Sorry, I was hoping I was.

CARL: So you're married, huh? Is this your wife here (*motioning to other woman*)?

SUE: No, she's married too. Not to each other. We're just friends. Would it be funnier if we were more than friends?

DAN: Not funnier. But a helluva lot more exciting.

CARL: Yeah. So this is, what, girls' night out?

SUE: Yeah, something like that.

CARL: So what are the guys doing tonight?

SUE: They're at a sports bar, I think.

CARL: Bet you wish you were there with them, huh?

DAN: The old "sports bar" story.

CARL: Yeah, just so you know (*making quotation marks with his hands*), "sports bar" is what husbands say when they're going to a strip joint.

SUE: Bet you wish you were there with them.

(*Carl applauded as the crowd laughed.*)

CARL: See, I knew you could be funny. Score one for my side. Okay, you can sit down now. (*Carl went to the next table, where a man and a woman are seated. He asked the woman to stand up.*)

CARL: What's your name?

LUCY JO (*in a strong Southern accent*): Lucy Jo Hanover.

CARL: All right, now we're talking. Lucy Jo Hanover from …?

LUCY JO: Columbia, South Carolina.

CARL: Really? I thought maybe Brooklyn (*turning to Dan*), South Carolina? Got anything for that?

DAN: It's the Palmetto State.

CARL: Palmettos. They're bugs or trees or something, right? I got nothing for that. Anything else?

DAN: Oh yeah, that's the home of the South Carolina Gamecocks.

CARL: Okay, that's more like it. (*Back to Lucy Jo.*) Is it really the home of the Gamecocks, as in cocks that are game, as in ready to go?

LUCY JO: Yeah boy, woo-woo!

CARL: No more calls, we have a winner. So is it true, all the cocks there are game?

LUCY JO: Every single one of 'em. Game—and big.

CARL: All right then. This your husband you're with?

LUCY JO: Yes, sir.

CARL, *lowered his voice in a confidential tone*: So he from South Carolina too?

LUCY JO: You betcha.

CARL: And he, um, stacks right up there with the other Gamecocks?

LUCY JO: He's the gamest and biggest of 'em all.

(*Carl applauded and shook the man's hand.*)

CARL: Come on, a round of applause, everybody. Stand up, sir. (*As he did, he towered above Carl.*) What's your name?

DEREK: Derek Hanover.

CARL: Congratulations, sir. Your wife says you're the biggest and best in the whole state …

DAN: And apparently she speaks with a lot of experience.

CARL: Easy for you to say from up there on the stage. In case you didn't notice, Derek's kind of a big guy here.

DAN: Yeah, so I heard.

CARL: So your wife seems pretty proud of you.

DEREK: She's been drinking a little too much.

CARL: Just about the right amount, I'd say. I think somebody's going to get lucky tonight.

DEREK: I just hope it's me.

Chapter 3

The brothers continued their interaction with various members of the audience with fairly good success. Dan hoped that Carl would make his way to the back of the audience. He noticed an absolutely stunning-looking woman who came in after the show started and sat at a table by herself.

She seemed to be having a good time, but she just didn't look like the kind of woman who ever went anywhere by herself. She had blond hair with an innocent but yet somehow knowing face and a body that looked anything but innocent. If you don't understand how a body can look anything but innocent, then you're probably not a guy.

And in a short, white, barely there dress, she didn't seem to care if other people noticed. She looked like a young Pamela Anderson, although there's nothing wrong with the older Pamela Anderson.

Dan was distracted as they finished up their comedy act and introduced the next comedian. He just knew some French-looking pretty boy model or a big, muscular athlete was going to show up and sit down with the dream girl. Either that, or she would get up and leave. But she was still there as they exited the stage.

"Did you see her?" Dan asked Carl as they got off stage.

"Of course, you think I'm blind?"

"Why didn't you go over to talk to her?"

"I couldn't think of a thing funny to say to or about her."

"Well, drooling and stuttering is sometimes funny."

"Yeah, well, you want to flip for her?" Carl asked.

"I already did. Hey, you've got a girlfriend. Give me a chance."

"Oh yeah, I forgot. Go ahead and hit her with your best shot."

"Yeah, I just got to figure out what that is."

"You go on out there, be yourself, and I'll come out and bail you out in a minute."

Dan began to leave then stopped, "Hey, wait a sec. That was too easy. How come you gave up so quickly? What am I missing here?"

"Nothing, bro," Carl shrugged innocently. "I'm just being nice. Like you said, I've got a girlfriend."

"No, that's not it. It's got to be something else." He paused to think. "I got it. You're letting me take first swing at her 'cause you know I've got no shot. She's too young for me. Too hot."

"I don't know what you're talking about. Of course you've got a shot at her."

"There's something else I'm missing," Dan said, pausing again. "Not only do I not have a shot at her, neither do you. That's why you're not wanting to try. You know we'd both strike out. She's not in our league."

"Hey, anything can happen. Britney Spears and that Federline guy?"

"But she's really not in our league, right?"

"Not even close. At least not now. When we're famous, babes will be lined up at our door. But why wait? Knock 'em dead. Hurry, before she gets away."

"Thanks."

As Dan exited the backstage area and went into the comedy room, she was no longer there. He was disappointed, but Carl had been right. Why didn't he have the instincts his brother had when it came to women? His brother knew instinctively whether a woman was available and, more importantly, attainable. Dan was constantly tilting at windmills and coming up with nothing but wind. Well, he guessed he would wander into the waiting area/bar area. The only other place she could have gone was the bathroom, and that was one windmill he wasn't ready to pursue.

He trudged dejectedly into the bar area, and there she was at the first seat at the bar, looking right at him.

Oh my god, what do I do now? he thought.

A girl like this, although young, had undoubtedly heard all the lines in the world. Maybe he would just walk by and pretend to be looking for someone else. After all, he was sure to get shot down, and who needed that?

"You looking for me?" she said smiling before he could compose himself. Damn, she was even better-looking when she smiled.

"Uh … looking for you? I … uh … don't know … mmm … well … uh … what?" Dan finally stuttered out.

"Wow, you're really good at this," she said, her smile turning into almost a smirk now. Even smirking she looked good.

"Yeah, I'm … uh … known for being … uh … fast on my feet with the ladies," Dan tried to get control of himself, or as much as he could with a girl like this. Since there was no open seat next to her, he just stood next to her. "Why would you think I was looking for you?"

"Call it a hunch. I sort of thought you noticed me while you were onstage."

"Yeah, well, you're kind of hard not to notice. We don't get that many drop-dead gorgeous women who come in here by themselves. In fact, there's not many women that look like you that drop in on New York City, and it's a big city. What's your name, by the way?"

"By the way, it's Shyanne."

"Really, like the city in … uh … Wyoming, I think?"

"Sort of, but not spelled the same. It was a little play on words by my mom. Seems I was conceived in Cheyenne, but she thought it would be more fun if she spelled it S-H-Y-A-N-N-E. I think she thought I might turn out to be shy. Then it would be like I was shy Anne."

"But you didn't turn out shy?"

"What do you think?"

"Um, I don't know. I just met you."

"I don't think shy girls dress like this."

"Not usually, no. So what is a girl like you doing in a nice place like this?"

"Well, that's just mean. And here I thought you were somebody I wanted to meet."

"Sorry, that was just a new line I was trying out. Wait a minute, you said you wanted to meet me?"

"I did, before I found out you were mean."

"Okay, *did* is past tense. Let's go back in time," Dan said, snapping his fingers as if he was magically transporting them back. "Why do you want to meet me?"

"You never heard of a comedian groupie?"

"To be honest with you, no. Never. Not once. Believe me, I've dreamed about one, but it doesn't seem to happen in real life. Singers, athletes, actors, even politicians, they all have 'em. And rock stars, who are not the same as singers, forget about it. But comedians, no. And the funny thing is, women always say sense of humor is one of the first things they look for in a man, but trust me on this, it ain't what they look for in a man first."

"Maybe you're just not that funny."

"Well, that was just mean. And here I thought you were somebody I wanted to meet. You know, you're not that funny, either."

"I know, but I don't really need to be since I'm drop-dead gorgeous and all."

"And modest too. Do you need me to sing a few bars of 'You're so vain'?"

"No," Shyanne said smiling. "I was only quoting this cute guy I just met."

"Where is he? I'll kill the guy, stealing my lines like that."

Shyanne laughed.

"Not funny, huh?" he said.

"You're starting to grow on me."

"Kind of like a fungus, huh?"

"Ooh, hopefully not. You seem to enjoy setting yourself up though."

"It's a gift I have."

"You know, once you stop stuttering, you're not half bad with the witty banter."

"Kind of half witty. Banter's my middle name."

"And what was the first name again?"

Dan extended his hand to shake hers. He thought about kissing it to seem gallant, but decided against it. She shook his hand, and just her touch sent a bolt of electricity through him.

Be careful with this one, Dan thought.

"Dan. Dan Banter Darwin. And you?"

"I think I already told you. It's Shyanne." She raised her voice. "Shyanne. Are you really a half-wit?"

"No, I meant the last name."

"That's all, just Shyanne."

"Oh, like a rock singer, or a stripper."

Shyanne acted offended. "A stripper!"

"Yeah, you know, strippers have just one name sometimes, like London or Raven or Destiny or Mercedes or Angel or …"

"Sounds like you have some experience in the field.

"I've just heard things, read books."

"You read books about strippers? That's sadder than if you actually had known them. It seems like reading about strippers, you might miss out on the best part."

"Sounds like you might have some experience yourself."

"No, no, just a good imagination."

"Damn, that should have been what I went with. Imagination, not reading."

"You can use that the next time you try to pick up a girl and insult her by thinking she's a stripper."

"I'm sorry about that. I didn't mean to offend you."

"You didn't. I get that a lot."

"Shocking."

"Don't push it."

"So I didn't blow it yet."

"Not yet, but the night's young."

Carl walked into the bar area and spotted them.

"Oh good, you found her," Carl said grinning.

Dan rolled his eyes and covered his face.

"Thanks, bro," he said.

"So he was looking for me?" Shyanne said smiling. "He said he wasn't."

"No, my bad. It was that other girl he was looking for. The chunky girl with the patch over one eye."

"Well, don't let me stop you," she said.

"It's okay," Dan said. "She already left … with a pirate, apparently."

"And I just hate being second choice."

"I doubt that's ever happened."

"You might be surprised."

Carl was still standing there and didn't seem in a hurry to leave.

"Shyanne, this is my brother, Carl," Dan said. "Carl, Shyanne. Carl was just leaving, I think, I hope. He just came by to screw up my life."

Carl reached and shook hands with Shyanne. Dan wondered if he felt the same electricity he had.

"I can stay if you need me to," Carl said.

"No, I'm fine, or at least I was."

One of the servers, Charlotte, entered the bar area and saw Dan.

"There you are," she said. "Mr. Shinn needs to see you. He says he needs to talk to you."

"Now?"

"He seemed to think it was quite important."

"Does he need me too?" Carl asked.

"No, he just said Dan."

"Shyanne, promise me you'll wait here. Please," Dan said.

"I'll stay here with her 'til you get back," Carl said.

"Yeah, like I'm going to leave her here with you."

"No, if you can't trust your own brother, who can you trust?"

"Yeah, okay."

"Do I get a say in this?" asked Shyanne.

"Yeah, sure. Can you stay just a minute?" Dan pleaded.

"Okay, but don't take too long."

"I just hope he's not firing us."

Dan grudgingly left the goddess with Carl and headed to Louie's office. He knocked.

"Come on in," Louie yelled.

"Hey, Louie, anything wrong?" Dan said as he walked into Louie's small overly furnished office.

"Nah. Sit down. Just wanted to talk to you about something."

"Okay."

"It's this fuckin' Jamieson guy."

"Is he pressuring you too?"

"Well, not directly. But he had one of his goons come in here."

"What did he say?"

"Oh, he tried to be subtle about it, said he was working for somebody, he wouldn't say who, but the basic gist of it was, it might be better for my business if you guys didn't work here anymore, some shit like that."

"Ah, Louie, I'm sorry. What did you say?"

"I told him to tell Jamieson to go fuck himself. He said he never said who he was working for. I said, well, whoever it was, tell him to go fuck himself. I didn't need any help running my own business."

"Thanks, Louie. But I don't want you to get hurt by this."

Louie scoffed. "Ah, hell. I've been running up against guys like Jamieson a long time. They want to run the whole world. I never asked for their help in opening this place. In fact, I worked my whole life making sure I didn't have to suck up to guys like Jamieson. This place ain't much, but it's all mine."

"I can't believe the guy. He doesn't give up."

"Yeah, that's why I wanted to talk to you," Louie said, more serious than he usually was. "This just confirms what you thought. He definitely knows you're the star witness—in fact, the only witness. He's been strong-arming guys to keep you two from working. Now I don't give a shit, but not everyone's like me."

"That's for sure."

"Are you sure you wanna go through with testifying against him? I mean, even if he's convicted, he's not going to let it go. He'll probably get some white-collar jail where he keeps on running things from his cell, like some kind of mob boss. I mean, this is America, guys like Jamieson don't get punished."

"You mean, they can get away with murder?"

"Do the initials OJ mean anything to you?"

"So what do you think I should do?"

"I think you have to consider what's best for your career, and if you cross Jamieson, you may not have a career beyond this place. I know this is a good place for you, but I also know you have a dream of going someplace bigger and better someday."

"You're the best, Louie. What would you do?"

"Me, I'd say fuck Jamieson and tell the truth. But that's me. You gotta do what you gotta do."

"That's what I'm going to do then."

"What?"

"I'm going to say fuck Jamieson and tell the truth."

Louie gave one of his big larger-than-life grins. "That a way, kiddo. Give him hell."

"But what about you? You going to be all right?"

"Fuckin' a, bubba."

"Fuckin' a, bubba" was Louie's way of saying "You can say that again" or "Right on" or, in this century, "That's what I'm talking about."

Louie continued, "I told that prick that came in here, somethin' happens to my place, like an 'accidental' fire or something, I was gonna tell the cops right now that Jamieson had threatened me and they should look at him as suspect number 1."

"What did he say?"

"He said he had no connection to Jamieson and he had made no threats."

"And?"

"And then I got out of my chair and headed for him, and he scurried outta here with his tail tucked between his legs like the little chickenshit he is."

"Way to go, Louie."

"Yeah, fuckin' a, bubba."

"Yeah, fuckin' a, bubba."

Dan gave Louie a high five and started to leave the office.

"One other thing, kiddo," Louie said as Dan was leaving. "Watch your ass. So far, this guy's just resorted to intimidation. But we know he's not above murder, so watch your ass."

"Okay, Louie."

It was hard to believe, but he had actually forgotten about Shyanne for a minute, what with the talk of being murdered and all. But now she was back front and center of his cerebral universe (and possibly other areas) as he hurried back to the bar area.

Much to his dismay, he saw Carl standing there sans Shyanne. But Carl didn't look unhappy. The bastard probably was glad he had missed his chance.

"What the hell did you do?" Dan asked, about to get mad. "Where is she?"

"Hey, don't get your panties in a wad. She said she was going to wait for you at that restaurant down the street, Rio Lobos. She said if you were nice, maybe you'd buy her dinner."

Dan was surprised. "Really? You're not just playing one of your little tricks on me?"

"No, but that would have been a good one."

Even though this was the best news he had heard in a while, the annoying responsible gene in his mind kicked in.

"But what about the rest of the night here? We've got some more guys to introduce."

"Hey, I can do it. I'll do the rest of the intros and clear it with Louie. You've done it for me before."

"But you still think she's out of my league?"

"Oh yeah, totally."

"But I should still go, right?"

"Yeah, 'cause the thing is, when you got a once-in-a-lifetime chance, you take that chance, even if you've got no chance."

"Okay, that makes some sort of sense, even though it sounds like you're Yogi Berra. All right, I'm going."

"So get gone."

"All right," Dan said, still hesitating.

"One other thing, bro. Just so you know, I think she actually likes you. I gave her all my best stuff and got nowhere. For whatever reason, she seemed to prefer you."

"You hit on her?"

"Big picture, here, Danny boy. She turned me down and wants to see you."

"What about you saying I could trust you?"

"No, what I said is, if you can't trust your brother, who can you trust?"

"So the answer is no one?"

"Yeah. Sorry, bro. She's beautiful. I'm weak. After a few seconds with her, I forgot I ever had a brother. What can I say?"

"Yeah, I know what you mean."

"Hey, Danny, be careful with this one. She could hurt you."

"But I should still go."

"Oh yeah. Now go in there and win one for the Darwins."

"Yeah, Mom and Dad would be so proud."

"Well, I wouldn't think about them when you're trying to score."

"I won't."

"Or me either."

"Don't worry about that."

Chapter 4

With that, Dan bundled up and headed to Rio Lobos, thinking along the way why would you name a restaurant River Wolves and remembering he didn't like Mexican food. And it was colder than God intended it to be. It was one of those December nights where the wind blew between the skyscrapers of New York and it felt like your bones would start to break just from the sheer cold.

Not that any of that really mattered. He was going to see the girl of his dreams, the once-in-a-lifetime shot where he had no shot. For her, he might eat Mexican food. Hell, he might become a Mexican food connoisseur. And he'd walk through the seven levels of Dante's Hell (or was it nine?) to get there. If she was even still there. Maybe when he got there, there would be a note telling him to follow her someplace else. He wondered how long he would follow her from place to place looking for her. Maybe forever.

He wanted to call Simone, his best friend, on his cell and tell her he was about to have dinner with an incredibly hot woman. Simone had suffered through enough of his bad times; she deserved to share in some good news. And Simone was always there for him in the bad times. But he didn't want to jinx it. After all, if Shyanne wasn't there, there would be plenty of reasons to call Simone then.

But when he got to Rio Lobos, he found Shyanne was there, already at a table, drinking a margarita and acting like it wasn't her first.

"Wow, you're actually here?" he said to her.

"Have I ever lied to you?"

"No, but my brother has plenty. Besides, now that I think about it, you did tell one lie already. You said I was cute."

"Okay, but that's just a little white lie. You're not that bad."

"Oh, thanks."

"There you go setting yourself up again. I say you're cute, you say you're not. I say you're not bad, you act hurt."

"Yeah, I used to be schizophrenic, but I'm over that now."

Dan then started carrying on a conversation with himself in two different voices:

"No, you're not.

"Yes, I am.

"No, you're not.

"I am too. Now leave me alone. I'm talking to the pretty girl."

Shyanne laughed and shook her head.

"You know, you really are funny. In a borderline crazy, be-careful-of-this-guy kind of way. But you are funny."

"Thanks, I think. Did you already order?"

"Just this frozen margarita, which is quite tasty." She took a seductive sip through the straw, or probably just a regular sip that Dan thought was seductive. "Do you want to order some food?"

"Well, I'm not really that hungry, but if you want to eat, I'll order something too."

"You don't like this place?"

"I don't really like Mexican food," Dan said.

"This is Cuban."

"Oh well, that's different. I loves me some Cuban food. I mean, their cigars are great, so the food must be good."

"Speaking of which, you mind if I smoke?"

"Cigars?"

"No, just cigarettes, or as I call them—smoky treats."

"No, I don't even mind if you smoke cigars, I guess. In fact, you could light up a big doobie right now, as far as I'm concerned. But you can't legally smoke in restaurants in New York anymore, but what the hell, I like living on the edge, so go ahead."

"Well, I thought if nobody objected, I might get away with it. Besides, you'll rescue if me if the smoking police come in, I'm sure."

"I'll be right behind you."

"That's how I like it," she said, smiling knowingly.

Wow, Dan thought, *this girl was too bad to be true.* She took out a cigarette and handed him the lighter.

"Oh, you want me to light it for you?" Dan asked, somewhat surprised.

"Yeah, I know it's old-fashioned, but I just like for a man to light my smoky treat for me?"

He lit it for her. "Yes, and smoky treat is such an old-fashioned term. You probably just want me to aid and abet you."

"I'm not going down alone."

"Oh good, that's the way I like it," he said, trying to match her knowing look but not succeeding.

"You want one?"

"No, I don't smoke."

"Not even after sex?"

"Check, please!"

"No, not yet. Let's not be premature."

"You say that word like it's a bad thing."

"Oh, it is."

"I wouldn't know."

"Of course not, Mr. Marathon Man."

"Ah, so that's why you're interested in me? You heard about my nickname?"

"Heard about it? I just made it up."

The waitress came by. She glanced at Shyanne smoking but didn't say anything. This was not one of New York's finest establishments. Dan ordered a margarita. Shyanne ordered something to eat Dan had never heard of, so he ordered the same thing. There was a moment of silence while Dan tried to figure what was up with this woman. This was either going to be the luckiest night of his life or the biggest letdown. He knew he should wait for some more margaritas to kick in, but he forged ahead anyway.

"So you never did tell me what you were doing there tonight all alone?" he asked her. "Not many women will go into a club by themselves."

"You want the truth?"

"Not necessarily."

"I got stood up."

"Okay, I said not necessarily the truth, but you can do better than that."

"No, really."

"Boyfriend, fiancée, husband? Feel free to lie some more at this point."

"Actually, it was our first date. Or supposed to be. My girl friend fixed me up with him. But it was me that suggested the comedy club. I thought I'd see if he had a sense of humor. I guess he did, since the joke seems to have been on me."

"So he hadn't ever seen you?"

"No."

"That figures."

"So the only reason someone would go out with me is because of the way I look?"

"No, but not seeing you is the only reason someone would break a date with you. That, or some sort of serious car wreck. I'm talking broken bones and lopped-off body parts."

"Oooh, you know how to make a girl hungry. Actually, he called while I was at the club and said he was running late because of work and asked if we could we meet later."

"What did you say?"

"I told him sure, and then I left and came here. You only get a chance to stand me up once."

"I'll make a note of that. Trust me, if I ever stand you up, there'll be some missing body parts as the reason."

"If you bring that up again, I'm going to make you eat my food too."

"The la lapallooza, or whatever it was we ordered."

"I knew you didn't know what it was."

"Of course I did. What are you talking about? The la lapallooza here is to die for."

"It's la polliosa," she said, pronouncing the double Ls like a y, which made her sound like she was from Havana.

"Okay, so I may not know how to say it. But you have to be impressed I ordered it anyway."

"I'm impressed with how easy you are."

"Thanks," he said as if truly flattered. "I can take orders with the best of them."

"Actually, I like a man to treat me nice when I'm good and take charge with me when I'm bad."

"I can do that too."

"You'll do whatever it takes, huh?"

"Oh yeah."

She laughed. "Your honesty is refreshing. Usually a line like that sends guys into macho overdrive."

Dan made his voice go deeper. "Those morons. They just don't know how to make their women behave."

"Yeah, like that."

Dan returned his voice to normal, "Was that all that was? A line?"

"I guess you'll have to find out."

"Check, please!"

"Still not time."

"Damn!"

"Patience, my dear Danny boy. Knowing when a woman is ready is like knowing when a fine soufflé is ready to take out of the oven. You eat it too early and it's cold on the inside, you wait too late and it's all rubbery."

"Are we still talking about food, I hope?"

"Food. Women, everything."

"Rubbery women, mmm, that's pretty appetizing."

Two margaritas apiece later, the food still hadn't arrived. Dan was worried it was going to hit midnight and his Cinderella was going to change back to a cleaning woman, or at least realize she was out of his league. Of course, the more he drank, the more it seemed like they were at least in the same ballpark. He had that good, cocky buzz feeling, and she was just pretty well drunk. It seemed like the perfect combination to Dan.

"So how long does it take to make this la lapalooza?" Dan asked, not bothering to try to pronounce it right. "It must be like a woman where you have to cook it a bunch or it has cold feet or something. Is that what you said?"

"Yeah, close enough," Shyanne was slurring her words now. "I'm pretty much not anymore hungry anyway. I think I may be drunk," she whispered the last line as if she didn't want anybody to hear.

"I don't think you need to whisper. I think everybody can tell you're drunk."

"No way!" she said very loudly.

"Yeah way. How many of those have you had?"

"Enough to think you are definitely cute and funny and sexy as hell."

"About the right amount then. But I'm glad you're not driving."

"So would you be mad at me if we skipped the la lapalooza and I invited myself back to your place?"

"Extremely mad, but I'll get over it." He paused for a second. "Okay, there I'm over it. But why not your place? My place is kind of messy."

"Because you told me you lived twelve or thirteen blocks from here, and I live all the way up on Eighty-Third Street."

"Okay, well, that's not that much further in a cab," Dan said.

He really hated having a woman like this or a woman like anything in his place without some serious advance time for straightening up. The place wasn't so much dirty as just like a hotel room that hadn't seen maid service in a week. It was times like this he wished he had taken Simone's advice and hired a maid.

"You don't understand, Danny boy, I have this physical condition that when I get ready for …" she lowered her voice to a whisper and said "sex," then returned her voice to normal, "I only have a limited amount of time before I just can't wait any longer. So time is of the, uh …"

"Essence?"

"'Xactly."

"Ch-che …" Dan started to say, then looked at Shyanne.

She nodded.

"Check, please!"

Chapter 5

He helped her out, handing the waitress some amount of money he hoped would cover the drinks and not be too much but not really caring. They got outside, and he started to walk.

"Can we get a cab, please, huh, can we?" she said.

"Sure, but it's not that far."

"Cabs are quicker if we can find one. Did you forget about my condition?"

With that, Dan bolted into the street, walking right in front of a cab, trying to ignore them. The cabdriver stopped after cursing at him in a language that appeared to be of another continent.

"Hey, it's an emergency," Dan yelled. "I have a woman in a condition."

The cabdriver said he was on the way to pick up another fare but to hurry up and get in and he would take them first. At least that was what it seemed like he said. They scrambled into the back, with Shyanne talking nonstop. It seemed drinking loosened her tongue as well as her morals. Not that Dan was complaining. But when she started talking about what great sex they were about to have, Dan was a little embarrassed by the cabdriver being there.

"Okay, we're almost there. Why don't we talk about it when we get to my place?" Dan said to Shyanne.

"Are you trying to tell me to shut up?"

"Well, I was trying not to, but yeah, I'm taking charge now."

"*You're* taking charge? *You're* taking charge? You don't know how to take charge!"

"Oh yeah," and with that, he leaned across the cab and kissed her hard. She kissed him back but in a way as if she was resisting.

"Well, if you think that's going to shut me up ..." she started, and he interrupted her by kissing her even harder.

This time she really kissed back hard. Their tongues seemed to be waging their own battle of wills.

"Okay, this is where you say to go," the cabdriver interrupted, stopping the cab.

Dan pulled out some more money and threw it to the cabbie as he and Shyanne hurried out of the cab. He had never thrown money in his life, and now he had done it twice in ten minutes.

"Well, I always sometimes wanted a romantic kiss in the back of a New York City cab," Shyanne slurred as they made their way to the door of Dan's apartment building.

"Okay, well, that wasn't it, but maybe one day. Right now, I don't think either one of us has romance on our mind. You want me to read a sonnet to you or something?"

"Not so much, no.

"That's what I thought."

He helped her walk the steps to get to the front door, almost picking her up to speed her along. He punched the entry code to the building with one hand while holding her with his other arm. He wished he lived on the first floor instead of the fourth. He was no longer worried she was going to get out of the mood, just that she might pass out.

After the longest elevator ride in history, they finally were inside his apartment. They began kissing again as he moved her toward the bedroom. He pulled away, with difficulty.

"Hang on, wait right here. Let me put some clean sheets on the bed," Dan said, hurrying into the bedroom. He had just ripped the sheets off when she said, "Hurry," or "I'm waiting," which he took to mean "hurry." With that, he just said, "Fuck it," threw the sheets on the floor, and hurried back to find she was standing there in nothing but her panties and was fondling her breasts. He had wanted to undress her himself, but when he saw her like that, all he could say under his breath was, "Oh, sweet Jesus, thank you."

"I'm sorry, did you say something?" she said smiling. She obviously knew what effect her body had on men.

"Just a small prayer and a silent commitment to start going back to church again."

"Well, let's see what you got, Danny boy," she said, starting to strip his clothes off. Somehow when she said "Danny boy," it was sexy. Of course, she could have called him "gator face" at that point and it would have been a nickname he liked.

As they both took his clothes off, they were kissing and groping each other like a couple of teenagers, only with a little more expertise. Okay, not really, about the same.

"Ooh, Danny boy, I'm likin' what I'm seein'. Size does matter. Don't let 'em tell you different."

Dan had never liked multitasking, but he was managing quite nicely to do several things at once. It's funny what motivation can do. Because Shyanne was only five four, Dan was having to lean down to get to her, so he briefly picked her up to make it easier to kiss her and grab all the important parts.

"Oh yes, carry me into the bedroom, throw me down on the bed," she whispered lustfully. That hadn't been what he had intended to do, but it was now. "Take charge, you big animal, there's nothing I can do to stop you."

Dan thought there was probably plenty she could do to stop him, but he wasn't planning on stopping. When he threw her on the bed and began to jump on top of her, she turned over, arched her butt up to him, and shook it slowly from side to side.

"I've been a bad doggy, do me doggy-style," she said in a little girl voice. As he prepared to enter her from behind, grateful she wasn't keen on foreplay right then, she said forcefully, "I said I've been a bad doggy. Slap my ass."

Dan hesitated slightly, and she said somewhat forcefully for a little girl, "Spank me, Master Danny boy."

Dan thought that never had a master taken orders so well. He had only playfully swatted a girl's butt before, but she seemed to not want playful. So he slapped her hard.

"Oh yes, sir, thank you, master, harder, sir," she said, still using the little girl voice.

Man, this girl knew all the right moves to drive men wild. So Dan continued to ride her, slapping her ass when he could and somehow managing to think he wished he had a camcorder, not only because no one else would ever believe this, but he wasn't sure he would either. He even started yelling to her, "Who's your daddy?" as he slapped her ass. That was a phrase he had never used in his life or even liked. But every time he said it, she said, "You are, Master Danny boy."

Dan thought the "Master" part didn't really go with "Danny boy," but the whole thing seemed so surreal it didn't matter. It was as if part of him was there having the time of his or any other life and part of him was watching himself have the time of his life.

He knew whatever happened from here on in, he could die a happy man. And at this point, he was no longer worried about her passing out, but there were a couple of times when he thought he might. Man, this being a master was hard work.

He had never been an expert at knowing these things, but it seemed she came several times before he climaxed. He thought that was probably a good thing. He fully intended to have another round with her as soon as he could physically do so. He collapsed beside her, still breathing hard, and enjoyed the feeling of her flesh reassuring him that what had happened was real. God, she even smelled good after hot, sweaty sex.

But after a minute of cuddling, her eyes started to close. He was talking to her as she puckered her lips as if to kiss him. He gave her a quick kiss and realized she was out like a light. But that was okay; that one had taken a lot out of him. He was feeling a little tuckered out himself. He was glad to know his heart was in good condition because he was sure it had never received that kind of workout.

Chapter 6

The next thing Dan knew, he was dreaming, but of course, he didn't really know he was dreaming until after he woke up. He was in a comedy club; only it wasn't the Hyena House. He was onstage, and he was naked. He had had similar dreams before; sometimes he was in front of the audience naked, sometimes in his underwear, and once even in a girl's underwear. That last one was one dream he had never wanted to have interpreted.

But in all his other similar dreams, he had been embarrassed and ill at ease about being naked onstage. This time, though, he was sitting nonchalantly on a stool as if he always performed naked. And his penis was a microphone, or the microphone was his penis; he didn't know which. There was even a knob on it which he could turn and adjust to make whatever size he wanted.

Wow, he thought in the dream, *this could be handy.*

And the women in the audience were cheering instead of laughing, some even throwing dollar bills onstage.

At that point in the dream, he thought he heard a phone ringing; then a few seconds later, a woman in the audience started calling to him, "Danny boy, Danny boy, wake up." No, dammit, he didn't want to wake up. Finally, the woman was touching him and telling him to wake up.

He opened his eyes, and the voice was that of Shyanne's. And there she was. Never had he woken up from such a good dream to find the reality even better. But then he wondered, in his groggy state of consciousness, had all of it just been a dream? After all, Shyanne had on her bra and panties and was sitting on his bed. Maybe he had just passed out or something.

"Hey, lover boy, time to get up," she said sweetly.

Okay, the "lover boy" was a good sign; maybe it hadn't been a dream. Also, the sheetless bed seemed anything but dry. Had they really just done it on a sheetless bed? Oh well, he wouldn't have cared if they had done it on a bed of rusty nails. Well, maybe a little bit.

"I need to go home and get ready for work," she said. She started to put her dress back on, and he noticed her butt still had red marks on it.

"Oh, Shyanne, look at your ass."

"Yeah, somebody got a little carried away."

"Well, if I got carried away, you were the one who took me to the edge and tossed me over."

"Hey, I'm not complaining. It was fun. And today when I'm sitting down and my butt hurts a little, it'll remind me of last night. But now it's time to go, and I don't want to be out on the street by myself. So throw some clothes over your unmarked butt, and let's go."

"Okay," he said, looking for something to put on. "So I'm not in charge anymore?"

"No, that was then. This is now."

"Now we're back to being equal?"

"Well, I wouldn't ask for too much if I were you."

"Good, I don't know if I could take being in charge like that all the time. Shyanne, I have to tell you, I've never been like that before. I mean, it was great, but I've never been a real macho kind of guy. I've always treated women with respect."

"Do yourself a favor, and don't analyze it. It was what it was. I believe in equality of the sexes in jobs and pay and life in general, but when it comes to the bedroom, that equal stuff doesn't get it done. One or the other has to take charge. I prefer it be the man, that's all. Wasn't it good?"

"Oh yeah, god, yes. Best time of my life."

"Well, good then. That's all that matters. Have you got some old sweats or something I can put on instead of this dress? It's going to be cold out there."

"Yeah, sure. Now, why are we leaving again?"

"I have to be at work at six thirty."

"Where do you work?"

"Saks Fifth Avenue. You know, Christmas crowd and all, we have to get started early."

"Wow, Saks, huh? What do you do there?"

This was the kind of question he usually asked on a first date—before sex, not after. But there hadn't been a lot of small talk last night.

"I'm a cosmetologist."

"Oooh, impressive. What is that?"

"I help women pick out makeup and try it on and show them how to put it on.""

"That sounds like you get to work with the rich and snooty."

"Yeah, it's a job. Are you about ready?"

They both threw on their coats and made their way to the street, this time in a little more orderly fashion.

When they got to the street, she asked, "Are you going to do that little taxi trick again?"

"No, I only do that when I've got a woman in some sort of condition with me. You're not in that condition now, are you?"

"No, easy, tiger. I'm just wanting to go home and take a shower and get maybe thirty minutes' rest before work."

They had to walk a couple of blocks to the Cordair Hotel to find a cab. The wind was blowing enough that their walk was mostly in silence. Finally, they made it into the relative warmth of the cab. Shyanne told the cabdriver to go to Eighty-Third and Columbus—which is how most New Yorkers direct cabbies, an intersection rather than an actual address. Even in sweats and a heavy coat and at four in the morning, Shyanne still looked awfully good to Dan. What with her hurrying home like this, Dan started wondering if this was it. After all, it had been the best night of his life, but she acted like that was the way sex was all the time for her.

"Can I ask you something?" Dan said.

"Sure."

"I mean, not to look a gift horse in the mouth or anything ..."

"I hope I'm not the horse in this analogy."

"As a matter of fact, you are, but don't take it as a bad thing. I was just wondering why me, why last night?"

"Why not?"

"So is that it for me?"

"What?"

"Just 'slam-bam, thank you, man.'"

"You're so insecure. You must have been hurt by somebody real bad."

"Well, yeah, but we'll talk about that another time. Or not. You going to give me a phone number, or do I just wait for you to show up at the comedy club again?"

She wrote down a phone number on a matchbook.

"That's my cell. Okay, you've got my number, you know where I work, and you're about to see where I live. Do you feel any better now?"

"Yeah, so I should call then?"

"Sure. I'll be going in to work soon, so you might want to wait till later."

"Yeah, I wouldn't want to seem overanxious anyway."

"Yes, you wouldn't want me to get the impression you liked me or something."

They were at her building now. Dan paid the cabdriver, and they got out. He turned around to tell the cabbie to wait on him, but he had already driven off. He walked her toward the front of the building, then she led him toward an alleyway.

She looked down the alley, didn't see anyone, and told him, "My place is actually closer to the door in the alley. I don't use it if I'm alone, but since I've got you to protect me ..."

He looked down the alley warily.

"I do have you to protect me, right?"

"Oh yeah, sure," he said, but not before observing that the door was only about fifteen feet from the start of the alley. You can be chivalrous without being stupid, right?

She went to the door, punched in a code to open it, and then turned to him.

"I can make it from here. Besides, my place is messier than yours."

"Oh lord, do I need to call the Department of Health?"

"You are funny, my sweet Danny boy," she said with a softness in her voice. This time "Danny boy" sounded not so sexy as caring. It was a name he would always cherish and never let anybody else use.

She hugged him and gave him a kiss, a much sweeter kiss than the ones last night. He reluctantly let her go.

"Danny boy, I really had a great time too, and I hope this night, well, it was special for me too."

"Yeah, no problem. But why does it sound like it's all over?"

"No, I didn't mean to. I'm just saying, the night's over, but the memories can last as long as we want."

"Okay," he said, getting an uneasy feeling about her mood.

They hugged again, and this time she held on as if she didn't want to end it.

"Bye, darlin'," he said.

"Bye, Danny," she said. As she opened the door, she held up a card. "And, Danny boy, just so you know, I took one of your business cards while you were still asleep. I like the card by the way. 'Dan Darwin—Comedian.' Are the phone numbers on there still good?"

"Yeah."

"Night, Danny boy."

He stood there, on the outside, watching her walk away. Okay, she had his phone numbers, that was good; he knew where she lived, that was good; where she worked, that was good; she had some of his clothes. But somehow he still had a bittersweet feeling. Like he might never see her again.

As Shyanne walked to the elevator, she could feel Dan watching her, but she didn't want to turn around. She didn't want to see his face right then. Everything had gone as planned. It had been easy. He had been easy. But there was one thing she hadn't planned on. She hadn't thought she would actually like the guy.

Chapter 7

As the elevator door closed, Dan turned and headed toward the street, not wanting to linger too long in a New York alley so late at night and not needing to act brave anymore since Shyanne was gone. He didn't know what might happen in a dark alleyway in New York, but in his wildest dreams, he couldn't have foreseen what happened next.

Coming down the alley from the street was a black stretch limo, and before he could get to the street, the limo had angled in sideways, blocking his path.

What the hell was this guy's problem? Dan thought.

Probably some drunk wealthy kids out for a late night of getting into trouble. He turned to look how far it was to the other end of the alley in case the kids decided to get out of the car and harass him.

As he did, his heart skipped a beat at what he saw. At the far end of the alley, three shadowy figures were running toward him. It was too dark in the alley for him to make out anything about them, but he sure wasn't going to head toward three unknown people running his way.

He turned back to the limo, figuring he would rather confront whoever was in there than the alley people. His heart went up into his throat at what he saw. Piling out of the limo were three clowns, and none of them appeared small or happy to see him. Damn, why clowns? All these years later and he still had a visceral reaction to seeing clowns.

To make it worse, one of the clowns was the biggest person he had ever seen, clown or otherwise. At about 6'8" and well over 350 pounds, he didn't look like somebody Dan wanted to cross paths with, in or out of clown costume.

He turned back around toward the other end of the alley, and the three running figures had gotten close enough to him that he could see they were clowns also. Before he could say "Hey, Rube," he found himself surrounded by clowns. He had already awoken from one dream earlier, and he hoped this was somehow a variation of his old nightmare. But as he checked all his senses, he realized this was no nightmare.

As they circled him like velociraptors, Dan was backed into the wall of the apartment building. None of them appeared to be armed, but with the giant clown there, who needed guns? He knew this wasn't the right time to think this, but he wondered where they got a clown suit to fit this guy. Was there some sort of store that specialized in clown clothing for the hefty? Focus, Dan, focus.

"Okay, wh-wh-what do you clowns want?" was all Dan could come up with as he tried not to let them know how terrified he was.

"We'll tell you what we want," said the second largest of the clowns, which was like saying the second smartest person in a group which included Albert Einstein. "We want you to tell us the truth. Did you order the code red?"

As he said that, he and the big one advanced toward him while the others fanned out to keep him from running.

"What?" Dan said as the nightmare kept getting stranger.

"Is it safe?" Clown Number 1 said.

Dan thought he was smirking at him, but how could you tell with a clown?

"Do you feel lucky, punk?" Clown 2 asked.

Dan realized now all three questions were lines from movies. He decided to attempt an answer to the last one.

"I did a few minutes ago," Dan said. "Not so much now."

"Don't try to be funny, Mr. Comedian," Clown Number 1 said.

The big one grabbed him by the coat collar and picked him up.

Dan had hoped somehow this might be a case of mistaken identity, but the comedian reference assured him this was not a random act of clowns gone bad. Apparently Jamieson was no longer content with subtle efforts at intimidation.

"Okay, guys, you're here to scare me," Dan said. "Job well done. I think I may have already wet myself. So tell Jamieson, mission accomplished. He doesn't want me to testify, I won't testify."

"Who said anything about Jamieson?" the big one growled, lifting him a little higher.

As Dan was lifted in the air by the clown, he suddenly felt as small and helpless as he had thirty-seven years ago.

"Calm down, big guy," Clown Number 1 said. "We may not have to kill Mr. Darwin after all. So you may be smart as well as funny?"

"Yes, sir," Dan said meekly.

"Maybe we'll just rough you up a little," Clown Number 1 said. "Then again, our orders were kind of vague. So who knows?"

With that, he motioned to Bozilla, who tossed Dan like he was a sack of Bounce laundry strips into a nearby heap of snow and slushy ice still leftover from the most recent snowstorm to hit the city.

Dan picked himself up and rubbed his left temple, which appeared to be bleeding from where he had landed on a piece of ice. But otherwise, he seemed to be okay, although a little sore. He was just relieved to no longer being held up in the air by the clown.

"Big guy, go get him," Clown Number 1 said. "And, Mr. Darwin, just for the record, we have no connection with this Jamieson person you referred to."

"Of course you don't."

As the big clown headed over to Dan, a bra came floating down from the sky like strange manna from heaven, followed closely by a pair of panties. Nothing can apparently break a group of clowns' attention like women's underwear raining down. They all looked up, as did Dan.

Above them, from a third-story window, was Shyanne leaning out, or at least her face and uncovered breasts were leaning out.

"Oh, I'm sorry, guys," she said smiling. "I seem to have dropped my panties and bra. Could one of you get them for me?"

While the clowns tried alternately staring at Shyanne while picking up her underwear, Dan looked around, figuring this might be his best chance to escape since he was now a few feet away from the clowns. One of the smaller clowns (possibly gay) had stopped looking at Shyanne long enough to notice Dan was trying to escape. He tried to get in front of Dan, but Dan swallowed his revulsion and fear of clowns long enough to grab the clown by his red hair and throw him aside. Man, that felt good.

And then when he thought the night couldn't get any stranger, it did.

The door to the apartment building opened, and out came Abe Lincoln—or, more likely, a guy made up like Abe Lincoln, complete with stovetop hat and scraggly beard. Dan was now only a few feet from the door and decided to make his move.

"Abe, hold that door open," Dan said, bolting toward the open door, and he heard Shyanne's voice from above saying, "Run, Danny boy."

Abe looked confused but did as he was told. As Dan raced into the open building, a shot suddenly rang out, and Abe grabbed his chest and fell over. Dan looked quickly back to see the big clown with a gun in his hand.

Dan started to reach down to grab Abe when another shot rang out. At that point, he decided Abe was on his own and slammed the door close behind him. Inside the apartment building, he saw the clowns headed toward the door. He didn't know whether they had the code to get in or not, but he didn't wait to find out.

Dan went racing down the hallway, stopped at the elevator, and briefly thought about trying to find Shyanne's apartment. No, he didn't want to put her in danger. He looked to his right and saw another long hallway with an "Exit" sign at the end. He ran as fast as his forty-one-year-old legs would take him. As he did, he reached for his cell phone to call 911, took it out of his pocket, and discovered it must have been broken when he was thrown into the ice.

He hadn't heard any signs of the clowns entering behind him. As he got to the exit on the far side of the building, he knew they could be outside waiting for him. He just hoped those big clown shoes would slow them down. He opened the door and looked out. No clowns, no limo. Should he stay, or should he go? He went.

He went like the wind. He ran the streets of New York, with blood running down his face and his legs already feeling the pain of not enough running in the last few years. He was looking for the nearest building he could duck into or a cab or a police car or any car he could flag down. Any car that wasn't a limo.

The only cars he saw were a couple of cabs, and neither of them appeared ready to stop to pick up a running, bleeding man. He continued running and looking behind him. Whatever direction the clowns had gone had apparently been a different one than he did.

As Dan ran, he realized the slush he had been thrown into had soaked through his clothes and he was literally shaking from the cold. He finally saw a couple of people out walking, but before he could think about asking them for help, he saw a doughnut shop with its lights on.

Dan tried to slow down a little as he entered the doughnut shop so as not to alarm anyone in there. It looked like the place had just opened. The only two people there were a man and a woman who appeared to be of Indian background, the kind of Indians who spoke with a British accent and might say, "It is bery, bery good to be in America," not the kind of Indians who might say, "America not so good since white man come, take our land." Dan thought that joke wouldn't work now that they were referred to as Native Americans.

The man was at the counter, straightening up and apparently inventorying the doughnuts. The woman was in the back cooking. The man had apparently been in New York long enough that a bleeding, wet, shivering man hurrying into his shop didn't faze him.

"Hi, my name's Dan. I need to use your phone to call the police."

As he said the word *police*, he glanced out the door and saw a black limo driving past. He immediately dived onto the floor, almost at the feet of the man. He looked up and made the shush motion to the man, thinking that even if the man didn't speak English, he would know the hopefully universal sign to be quiet.

"Did the black car keep going?" Dan whispered to the man, still from the floor.

"I see no black car," the man said. "We want no trouble here. Perhaps you should go."

Dan peeked out and didn't see the limo outside. He stood back up and went slowly to the door. No sign of a limo driving or clowns running. He turned his attention back to the man.

"No, I'm not going to cause any trouble," he said. "I just saw a man get shot, possibly killed. If you won't let me use the phone, can you tell me where the nearest police station is?"

"There's one two blocks up on Seventy-Ninth Street," the man said. "Would you like to buy some doughnuts?"

"No, I don't want any doughnuts. I just saw a man get shot. The last thing I'm thinking about is food. Well, okay, maybe just one."

At that point, the woman apparently heard the commotion, saw his condition, and hurried to the front.

"What happened to you? Are you all right?" she asked.

Dan told her his name and some of what had happened (leaving out the clowns and Abe Lincoln part). She said her name was Lapi, and she apologized for her husband being rude. She got some clean cloth towels, cleaned the cut, and put a Band-Aid over the cut. She then asked Dan if he would like to sit in the kitchen area to stand by the oven and warm up. Dan hadn't realized, but he was still shivering from the combination of being wet and cold and being shot at.

Dan thought there's the difference in men and women. The man was not so much concerned with Dan's health as he was with making a profit. The woman was the nurturer, taking care of the stranger. He didn't think it was an accident that the Good Samaritan in the Bible had been a woman. No, that wasn't right; he was a man. Oh, well, it was a good point, except for that.

He realized he should probably dry off a little before going out in the cold again. Besides, the limo might still be around. As he sat there drying off with the rich aroma of doughnuts all around him, he remembered he hadn't eaten anything last night. And after all, not even Homer Simpson liked doughnuts more than Dan. So he bought three doughnuts and some milk from the man, whose name was Ramasam. After the purchase, Ramasam seemed to like the stranger much better. He told Dan he could use the phone if he wanted.

Dan went toward the phone then decided that the police would probably just hang up on him if he told them a bunch of clowns had just shot Abe Lincoln and were now chasing him. No, better to do this in person.

He thanked the Indian couple as he left and headed toward the police station. As he did, he tried to collect his thoughts as he kept a constant watch around him for any black cars. Why had this happened? He could understand the threat part, but why clowns?

He thought back to that attempt he had made at writing a TV pilot about a man who was afraid of clowns, but went on to become part of a crime-solving clown team. But the only people Dan had shown the script to were Carl and Simone, who had both told him it was too unrealistic even for TV. Talk about a kick in the gut.

He knew Carl and Simone wouldn't have shown Jamieson the script, but how could Jamieson have known about his fear of clowns? It couldn't be a coincidence. He was thankful Shyanne must have looked out her window and used her greatest weapons to distract them. But why was Abe Lincoln there, and why did he open that door just at the right time? Again, he pictured Shyanne leaning out the window, and he briefly forgot about the clowns.

Okay, focus, Dan, focus. His mind's tendency to go off in a hundred different directions was helpful when trying to be creative. But for real-life decisions, not so much. He knew the police were not going to believe him. They had almost laughed at him when he told them about the Jamieson murder. They would really get a kick out of this one.

Whenever confronted with situations like this—and he had to admit there had never been one exactly like this—he went back to basics. His mom had always taught him if there was a choice to be made, do the right thing, and this was way before Spike Lee. Sometimes you didn't know what the right thing to do was, but this time he did know. There was a chance the Abe Lincoln guy could still be alive, and even if it meant being made the fool, that was what he had to do. He had to tell the police.

Chapter 8

He found the police station and headed inside. He breathed a deep sigh of relief that at least for now he didn't have to worry about gun-toting clowns.

The policeman at the front desk appeared to be in the waning moments of an overnight shift. He didn't look like he was going to be thrilled to hear Dan's story, or anybody's for that matter.

"Can I help you?" he said in a voice which suggested the last thing in the world he was trying to do was to help Dan.

Dan swallowed once and cleared his throat. Well, here goes nothing.

"Yes, I was roughed up and a man was shot."

Without lifting his eyes up from the crossword puzzle, the policeman said, "Okay, when did this happen?"

"About an hour or so. You see I was …"

"Hang on," the policeman interrupted. "You need to talk to a detective." He finally glanced up at Dan and looked him over. "Have a seat please."

While Dan sat down, the cop called to someone. No one appeared for a few minutes. He had a feeling this was not going to be like those cop shows where a whole staff of brilliant cops was going to be out on the streets looking for clues in a matter of minutes. Apparently, possible killings were common enough that it was no real cause for alarm. Just wait until they heard the part about the clowns, and the victim. *That would get them motivated*, Dan thought. Even when thinking, he still thought in sarcasm.

Finally, a man in a cheap brown coat and tie appeared. Dan guessed if he was a plainclothes detective, that was about as plain as one could dress.

"Hi, I'm Detective Sanders," the stocky man said. "You want to report someone being killed?"

"Well, actually, I said someone was shot. He may have been killed. He was definitely shot."

"Yeah, okay," Sanders said. "Come on back."

After they got back to the detectives' area, Sanders sat down at what must have been his desk and Dan sat on the other side. There were only two other men in the office, which Dan was glad about since he was sure his story was going to have all of them laughing. Dan thought about how he could tell the story to make it seem believable, and there wasn't any. No matter what he said, when he came to the clown part, his credibility would be gone.

"Okay, what you got?" Sanders said with the enthusiasm Dan would have for a telemarketer.

"All right, it started last night when I met this great-looking girl and we had the most incredible, toe-curling, heart-stopping, mind-blowing sex in my lifetime," Dan started off. This part of the story didn't actually have to be told, but it was something he would enjoy telling to anyone he could. He noticed Sanders wasn't writing anything down. "Don't you need to be taking notes or something?"

"You fucked some broad's brains out, I got it," Sanders growled.

"Okay, well, you certainly took all the romance out of it, but I guess that's about it. Anyway, we fall asleep, we're at my place, she wakes me up around four or so and asks me to take her back to her place."

"You got a car?"

"No, she just didn't want to travel alone late at night by herself."

"Okay. Is she the one who got shot?"

"No, no, I'm coming to that," Dan said, hurrying up the telling of the story.

He quickly told Sanders about the limo driving up and being surrounded by six guys. He didn't mention yet they were clowns, trying to make his story somewhat credible. When he mentioned the six guys knew who he was, Sanders stopped him.

"And who are you?"

"I'm the only witness to the murder committed by Hilton Jamieson," Dan said, hoping again to gain some trust with Sanders before he had to tell him the whole truth. "His trial is coming up in a few days."

"Yeah, I heard about that," Sanders said, showing a modicum of interest at last. "So these guys were trying to intimidate you into not testifying, you figure?"

"Yes, sir."

"Were they armed?"

"Well, I didn't think they were, but I found out they were later."

"So if you didn't see any guns at the first, how were they threatening you?"

"Kind of their manner, menacing, you know?"

"All right, other than this menacing manner, what else did they say or do to threaten you? You said they asked you some questions. Were they threatening questions?"

"No, they were just nonsensical questions from movies."

"Nonsensical?"

"Yeah, they wanted to know if I ordered the code red, was it safe, and did I feel lucky, punk."

"Okay, I don't get any of that, but go on."

"That's what I meant by nonsensical. Anyway, the big one—and he was the biggest person I had ever seen—picked me up, and this other guy who seemed to be in charge told him maybe they wouldn't have to kill me. They could just rough me up a little. Then the big one threw me into a pile of ice and snow. That's how I got the cut on my face," Dan said, hoping the cut would lend some credence to his story. Sanders looked at his face, seeming to notice for the first time it was cut.

What a detective he must be, Dan thought.

"All right, when does the shooting come up?" Sanders said, quickly losing interest.

"As I started to pick myself up, a bra and a pair of panties came floating down from the apartment window of the girl I had sex with. All the guys were looking up at her leaning out of her window, and

I started to run away. As I did, the door to the apartment building opens up, and this guy's coming out. I yell at him to keep the door open, and as I get to the door, a shot rings out. The guy holding the door grabs his chest and falls over."

"So what did you do then?"

"Another shot rang out, so I went on inside and I closed the door."

"So you think the guy was dead?"

"I don't know. He may still be there for all I know."

"Okay, we'll get somebody over there to check on him," Sanders said. "Can you describe any of these guys that threatened you? What did they look like, how were they dressed?"

Dan hesitated. This was it, the moment he would go from being a borderline nutcase in the detective's eyes to a certified one. He was about to become the clown. Hmm, Dan just realized the irony. To tell about the clowns, he must become one of them. He wondered if the detective would appreciate the irony.

"Yes, sir, they were, um, clowns, sir."

"Clowns?"

"Yes, sir, they were dressed as clowns."

"All of 'em?"

Dan thought that was an odd question, wondering why some of them would be clowns and some of them would be in suits, like they ran out of clown costumes or something. Or maybe some of them were dressed like Spiderman, or Spidermen.

"Yes, all of them were dressed as clowns," he said flatly, deciding this was not the time for jokes.

Although Sanders had raised his left eyebrow considerably at the first mention of clowns, Dan had to give him credit for not laughing. But at this point, he did signal the other two detectives to come over.

"All right, let me get this straight," he said, obviously for the benefit of the other two detectives. "Six clowns surround you and threaten you and shoot at you, hitting another man. What time was this?"

"Probably about four thirty."

"And what did the guy who got shot look like?"

"Abe Lincoln."

"Abe Lincoln?" Sander said smiling.

"Yes, sir."

Sanders looked to the other detectives.

"Hey, guys, we already solved that Lincoln murder, didn't we? It was that Booth guy that did it though. I don't remember anything about clowns being involved."

"I don't either," one of the other detectives said, trying to keep a straight face. "But we can check. There may have been a conspiracy. I never did buy that lone gunman story."

"Yeah, me, neither," Sanders said. Then looking back to Dan, he said, "Wait a sec. I think I may have a mug shot. Is this the guy who got shot?"

With that he took a $5 bill out of his wallet and showed it to Dan. Dan smiled, knowing he was going to be the butt of these guys' jokes long after he was gone.

"Good one, sir," Dan said. "But I didn't say it was the real Abe Lincoln, he was just a guy made up to look like him."

"Yeah, there's a lot of demand for Lincoln impersonators these days," Sanders said. "All right, Mr. Darwin, you said you hooked up with a woman last night. Before I put out an APB on a limo full of clowns who just shot Lincoln, can you tell me, was there any drinking involved in last night's activities?"

"Yes, more on her part than mine. I'm not drunk if that's what you're getting at."

"No, of course not. Are you aware of the charge for filing a false report?"

"Listen, guys," Dan said, looking at all of them, hoping to find a sympathetic face, "I know it sounds ridiculous."

"Oh, good, 'cause you were acting like you didn't," Sanders said.

"I knew you probably wouldn't believe me. I barely believe it, and I was there. I even thought about not coming in. But these clown guys chased me and shot at me. And there's a chance you could do something to help this Abe Lincoln guy."

"Well, I'm sure the Secret Service is already over there, him being a former president and all. But we'll send somebody over to check on Mr. Lincoln."

"Again, I'm not saying it was really Abe … Oh, never mind. Just so you know, though, the cops didn't believe me at first when I told them about Jamieson killing that woman. And now they not only believe me, they're basically relying on me to put him away."

"I'm feeling real good about our chances on that case now."

"I know. But I did my duty. I came in, told the truth. You don't want to believe me, I understand. I'll be on my way. I could use some sleep."

"No, no, no. Please stay. I forgot you were a big hotshot witness on an important case. That changes everything. So can you describe these clowns for my official report?"

"They were clowns. They had paint on their faces, rubber noses, weird-colored hair. And one of 'em was really, really big."

"The one who picked you up and threw you into the snow?"

"Yes, that one."

"Anything else unusual about them?"

"Other than being clowns and all? No. That was pretty much it."

"Okay, before I shut down all the major roads out of the city so these clowns don't get away, let me consult with my colleagues and see if they have any questions. Fellas?"

The short dumpy one did his best to look serious. "Yes, I've got one. Mr. Darwin, is it?"

"Yes."

"You sure the car was a limo and not a Volkswagen? It seems like I always remember clowns all piling into a little bitty VW."

At that point, the detectives couldn't restrain themselves any longer and were openly laughing and smiling. Dan smiled with them. He endured a few more questions about what size shoes they were wearing (very big) and were any of them armed with those flowers that shoot water (not that he noticed). They especially got a kick out of him being a comedian. Mercifully, they finally let him go with mockingly serious assurances they would do everything they could to apprehend this group of clowns on a crime spree.

Chapter 9

As Dan left the police station and started looking for a cab, he noticed it was about six thirty. It had seemed like he had been in there forever, but it was really just about forty-five minutes or so. What had happened was about what he had expected. Who would believe such a story? Did it even happen? Did any of last night really happen? Had a totally hot woman really had amazing sex with him, taken him back to her place and left him there to witness clowns gone bad? And witness the second killing of Abe Lincoln?

Maybe this was just a series of bizarre dreams. But the cold of the early morning certainly seemed real. And the rancid smells of the cab seemed all too real. Well, there was only one person to go to in this situation—Simone. She had been his best friend for the last seven years, and she was the one person in this crazy town, this world gone mad, he could count on. He still remembered it like it was yesterday the first time he had met her.

This would be the part of the movie where some weird music would play accompanied by hazy images seemingly shot through gauze so the audience would realize it was a flashback. But since this is a book, you can just say Dan remembered the first time they had met like it was yesterday.

*****

It was toward the end of his married days when he realized it wasn't really working out, but he didn't know exactly what to do about it. Nothing really bad had happened. She hadn't cheated on him; he hadn't cheated on her. She didn't have a drug problem; he didn't have a desire to slip into her clothes and go down to Soho. It was just a slow realization that they weren't really meant for each other.

He was still struggling to make ends meet doing stand-up comedy where he could and a bunch of odd jobs to pay the bills. It seemed most of New Yorkers were always working someplace they didn't want to while they waited for their dreams to come true. Maybe that was the way it was in other places too, but at least the people in New York had bigger dreams, although ones with longer odds.

It was early one summer evening, and Dan was searching for a bar on Fifth Avenue which supposedly sometimes hired struggling comedians and gave them a chance. As frequently happened when Dan got outside his area of comfort in New York, about a two-mile square in the east Village, he got lost. He spotted one of those too-cool coffeehouses where pseudo intellectuals congregated to make fun of the rest of the world. He walked in, and before he could even ask about the bar he was looking for, this pretty dark-haired, Hispanic-looking girl came running up to him as if she had known him all her life.

Well, maybe these coffee places weren't so bad after all, he thought.

"Hi, I'm Simone," said the dark-haired girl. "Do you like to read poetry out loud?"

"Well, yeah, if members of my family are being held hostage and that's the only way they'll be released," Dan said.

Simone was oblivious to the sarcasm and said, "Great, what's your name?"

"Dan," he said, not knowing whether to trust her yet with his last name.

"Hey, everybody," Simone said with a bubbly enthusiasm that Dan had not even had as a child. "This is Dan, he's going to read my poetry for me."

With that, she grabbed his hand and took him over to a table where three women sat. Dan was starting to think he might grow to love these coffeehouses, might even start drinking coffee. And if he had to read a little poetry out loud, well, that would just be good training for being less nervous doing stand-up.

"These are my friends, Sara, Donna, and Lantana," Simone said. "This is Dan. He's going to read my poetry for me."

"Well, I didn't actually agree to that yet. Lantana?" Dan said, not wanting to let that name go by.

"Yes, that's her stage name. She's an actress," Simone said. "You like it?"

"Sure. Have you been in anything I might have seen?"

"No, I'm more of a waitress right now, waiting to be discovered," said the dark-haired Lantana.

"Yeah, I know the feeling," Dan said. "I'm a comedian waiting to be discovered."

"How come you don't want to read Simone's poetry?" asked Sara, eyeing Dan with steely blue eyes.

"I didn't say I didn't want to. I'm just not sure."

"What aren't you sure about?" Sara asked in a way that suggested she might bar the door if Dan tried to leave.

"It might be kind of personal, or you know, told from a woman's perspective or something."

"So?"

"Well, it could be embarrassing."

"Look at that innocent face," Sara said, motioning to Simone. "What could she write that would be embarrassing?"

"I don't know. It could be like the *Vagina Monologues* or something."

"That's not a poem," the one named Donna said.

Apparently, the whole group was on Simone's side.

"That's probably only because nothing rhymes with vagina," Dan said, thinking his cleverness might get him out of this.

"North Carolina," Donna said.

"Okay, forget that. It could be a poem about her lusting after some guy, talking about how big his thing was. And then it would seem like I was the one impressed by the size of his thing."

All the women laughed at this one. Dan looked puzzled.

"Dan," Simone said, smiling, "I didn't mention to you that Sara's not only my friend, she's my girlfriend. My life partner."

"Okay, so she might be available in the afterlife," Dan said. There were no laughs, only a smile from Simone. Tough crowd. "So apparently, she won't be lusting after a guy," Dan quickly added, deciding not to try any more jokes.

What were the odds of wandering into a covey of lesbians at a poetry reading in a coffeehouse? He realized it was going to be easier at this point to read the poetry than to try to leave and be beaten up by a covey of lesbians.

"Okay, I'll do it. Do I at least get to read it to myself before I read it out loud?"

With that, Simone gave him a genuinely warm hug that made him glad he had agreed. Those friendly, life-assuring hugs would become something he would grow to expect and look forward to but never take for granted. It was a simple gesture, totally innocent, but it seemed so warm it made you forget all your troubles for a moment.

"Yes, you can read it," Simone said, handing him a sheet of paper. "And I can assure you, there's no mention of vaginas, uteruses, periods, or guys' things."

Dan took it smiling. He wasn't sure he wanted to hang out with the whole group because lesbians usually didn't have a whole lot of use for men. Not that Dan blamed them. If women didn't need men for sex, there wasn't really a lot of reason to have them around, other than to reach things on the top shelf.

Dan had been around men by themselves, and they needed women to keep them civilized. But women hanging out together seemed to manage just fine. But Simone was definitely a keeper, even if she did drive on the wrong side of the road. She seemed softer to him than the others.

He read the poem quickly.

"What do you think?" Simone said expectantly.

"Well, it's good, I guess, although it doesn't rhyme or anything."

"Poems don't have to rhyme," Sara, apparently a district attorney, said. "Where are you from anyway?"

"Arkansas, but I don't think that's ..."

"Ah, I see," Sara said as if being from Arkansas told her everything she needed to know about Dan.

"Hey, Maya Angelou's from Arkansas, and she wrote poems. I'm pretty sure."

"Well, then she could tell you poems don't all have to be in iambic pentameter."

"No, but if they aren't, aren't they just idle, written-out thoughts on a piece of paper?"

"Are you reading the poem or not?" Sara asked demandingly.

"Yes, I already said I would. What's it called?"

"It doesn't have a title, but I think I'll call it 'Idle, Written-Out Thoughts on a Piece of Paper,'" Simone said smiling.

Warm, and a sense of humor, Dan thought, *definitely a keeper.*

The poetry reading went just fine that night, although Dan didn't think he did that good a job with it. Over the next few months, Dan ran into Simone by chance a couple of times. It turned out she lived in the same neighborhood. She was always friendly and always gave him a hug. She called him her poetry-reading knight in shining armor, although she had only asked him to read for her one more time.

But when his marriage had broken up, he had deliberately gone to look for her. She had told him she worked in a bookstore about two blocks from where he lived. He knew she would still be off-limits to him from a romantic angle, but he just really needed a friend at that point anyway.

After several attempts, he had found her at the bookstore, and without meaning to, he had just told her everything about his marriage's failure and how he felt like a failure in general. She hadn't said anything wise, anything profound, mostly just listened. But it was the way she listened and showed genuine concern that made Dan realize he had come to the right person.

Ever since, they had become best of friends. He had come to love her in a way he didn't think was possible for a man to love a woman. He guessed it was like loving a sister, but somehow it seemed more than that to him. With the sex thing out of the equation, it allowed them to be true friends.

He told her everything, and she shared with him too, although never quite as openly. But they could even go to dinner and both be attracted to the same waitress. So not only did her being gay open the door for them to be friends, it even made them seem to have more in common. She could give him advice on how to deal with women, which he found he always needed.

In addition to her warm openness, she had one other quality that Dan had never found in any other person. She didn't get mad. Period. It was so unreal; he constantly made fun of her for being an alien. That and the fact that she seemed to have no recollection of any pop culture before about the year 1985.

It was as if she had been briefed before coming to the planet earth on things like history and geography and government, but they had not deemed pop culture as important. She could recite the sequence of American presidents, but she couldn't tell you one thing about the movie *E.T.* He thought it curious they wouldn't have at least seen that movie on her planet.

*****

And since he had always turned to her when things went bad, that was why he couldn't wait to see her this morning and tell her about Shyanne. She would be so happy for him. Thankfully, Sara had turned out not to be her life partner, since Sara never had liked Dan. Her girlfriend of the past two years, Mattie, liked Dan and never thought anything about Dan calling Simone at all hours or just dropping by. Or if she did, she never complained about it, which was all Dan cared about.

He had thought about calling first, but that broken cell phone reared its ugly head again. Considering he was about the last person in Manhattan to get a cell phone, he sure had grown dependent on it.

He knew Simone would be getting ready for work about right now, and he knew that Mattie was out of town. So unless she was taking a shower or something, she would let him in. And if she was taking a shower, he would just wait in the hall for her.

She only lived twelve blocks from him. It was funny. He was from Little Rock, which population-wise you could wrap up and fit in a little tiny pocket of Manhattan. But parts of this city had more of a small-town feel than his hometown. Pretty much all the people he knew and all the places he went to were in a twenty-block radius. He only ventured out of those areas when he had to.

Chapter 10

Dan found her apartment and rang the bell. Sure enough, she didn't come to the door immediately. Yeah, just his luck, in the shower. He would just sit in the hallway and wait. It would give him time to decide how he wanted to tell her about his night. From the sublime bliss of Shyanne to the absurdity of the clowns. Or get the clowns part out of the way and then tell about Shyanne. Or wait and tell about the clowns another day. Before he figured it out, the door opened a little.

"Dan?" Simone said, peeking out the crack in the door. "What are you doing here so early?" She opened the door a little wider. She just had on a bathrobe.

"Hey, did you just get out of the shower?"

"Yeah, a few minutes ago," she said distractedly. She was talking softly too. "What's up?"

Okay, something was definitely odd. She would have usually invited him in by now, but she was standing in the doorway as if that was the last thing she was going to do.

"I've basically been up all night and just had the most incredible story to tell you, and since I was in the neighborhood … What's up with you though?"

"What do you mean? Nothing."

"You're acting all weird."

"No, I'm not," Simone said, looking behind her again.

"Oh, is Mattie home? I thought she was out of town. Is she still asleep?"

"No. Everything's fine."

An actress Simone was not. Everything was not fine.

"Okay, tell me what's the matter," Dan said, acting as if he was going to come in. But Simone wasn't allowing that.

"If you must know, I've got company, can we talk later? At the place?"

Suddenly it all made sense to Dan. Mattie was out of town, and Simone had hooked up with another woman. It seemed so unlike her though.

"Ah-hah! I get it," Dan said in mock seriousness, but really enjoying catching Simone slipping up. She was always so perfect. "The Mattie's away, and the little mice decided to play. You been doin' a little cheatin' on your woman. I'm shocked, horrified. Who is she? Is she hot? Can I sneak a peek? Let me just wait in the closet."

"Yeah, something like that. But no, you can't come in, and of course, you can't sneak a peek. Please, just leave now and I'll meet you at our place. Please, I'll tell you all about it then."

"Yeah, yeah, okay …" Dan was saying, when from inside came a man's voice, "Simone? Somebody at the door?"

"Just a minute. Don't come out," Simone yelled back.

"My, my, what a deep voice your secret girlfriend has," Dan said, suddenly not so amused.

Just then, the guy came into view, buck naked.

"Stay there," Simone said to the naked guy, pushing Dan back and coming out into the hall with him and closing the door behind her.

"And what a big penis your girlfriend has," Dan said, now disgusted.

"Okay, okay," Simone said. "I know what you're thinking. He's about to leave. I'll come down to the place and explain it to you. But you've got to leave now. Please!"

When she said *please*, he had to go even though he was not feeling too kindly toward her right then. He just stared at her as he started toward the elevator.

"All right, but I hope you've got a good story," he said as he walked away. He turned around. "Which place?"

They had one place they referred to as the place for breakfast, a deli about two blocks away, and another place they referred to as the place for lunch or dinner, a diner over closer to his apartment. But his world had been turned upside down in the last twelve hours so much he wasn't sure even what time of day it was.

"The place where we go for breakfast!" she said, looking at him like he had taken leave of his senses.

"Okay, okay."

With that, he got on the elevator. *Wow*, he thought. *What a shocker.* All these years, she had never even mentioned a guy as anything more than a friend, never acted like any guy was attractive, and now she had a naked guy looking like he was ready for round 2. Man, he hoped they weren't doing it right now. He tried to get that image out of his mind.

He walked toward Casey's Deli on Forty-Ninth Street, thinking what was going to happen to him next. He thought, at this point, even if he walked into the deli and found ET sitting at a table with Elvis and Jesus, he wouldn't have batted an eye, just sat down next to them and said, "Wha's up, guys?" ET was a guy, wasn't he?

When he walked in, there was no ET, no Elvis, no Jesus— just the usual cast of New York characters, which would have been eye-opening enough on the usual day, especially the guy who seemed to be wearing a newspaper as a shirt. In New York that barely elicited a glance from anyone. But this day was far from usual. He had the best and wildest sex of his life with far and away the best-looking woman he had ever had, been threatened by a group of clowns, saw Abe Lincoln get shot, and then found his best friend, a seemingly happy lesbian, hooked up with some goofy-looking young guy.

As he drank some orange juice, he mulled over the events of the past few hours. And all of a sudden it hit him how tired and sleepy he was. He had only gotten a couple of hours sleep, and his mind had basically been on overdrive the whole time he had been awake. If Simone didn't come pretty soon, he was going to have to leave and go home and go to sleep and hear her story later on. And tell her his story.

But just when he was about ready to go, in walked Simone with that irrepressible bounce to her step, just like always.

She smiled when she saw him and said, "Hey, 'migo, you ordered me a bagel yet?"

'Migo was short for amigo, which was what she usually called him. Her mother was from Chile, and she spoke Spanish almost as well as English, or at least it seemed to Dan she did. He called her 'miga in return although his mother was from Little Rock and had the same passing knowledge of Spanish Dan did: uno, dos, tres. Si.

"Don't be 'migoing me like nothing just happened," Dan said, trying to maintain a surly tone.

"Oh, you want to talk about the guy that was in my apartment?" she said, still all sweetness and innocence.

DAN: You mean the naked guy in your apartment. And no, I don't really want to talk about it, but I do want to hear your explanation. And feel free to condense it as much as possible. No gory details.

SIMONE: Mattie was out of town. I went to a party. I got a little drunk. I woke up this morning with a naked guy beside me.

DAN: Boy, you do weave a powerful yarn.

SIMONE: You said you wanted the condensed version. What else do you want to know?

DAN: How? What? Why? How could this happen?

SIMONE: I don't really know, but why does it upset you?

DAN: I don't know. What about Mattie? She's my friend too. What am I gonna say to her? What are you gonna say to her?

SIMONE: First of all, you're not going to say anything to her about it. Ever! I don't know what I'm going to tell her. So that's why you're upset? Mattie?

DAN: Yeah, sure.

SIMONE: When you thought there was another woman in there, you weren't too concerned about Mattie.

DAN: Sure I was.

SIMONE: That's why you wanted to hide in the closet and watch?

DAN: Do you have to remember every single thing I say?

SIMONE: Okay, so why are you upset? Believe me, I'm upset enough for both of us, you don't need to be.

DAN: Yeah, you're just a wreck, I can tell.

SIMONE: No, I am. You know I don't show my emotions that much. I didn't want to cheat on Mattie. I love her.

DAN: So why did you?

SIMONE: I don't know.

DAN: And why with a guy?

SIMONE: That part is really hard to explain. That's what's bothering you? It was a man.

DAN: Well, yeah.

SIMONE: Why?

DAN: I don't know.

SIMONE: Tell me.

DAN: All right, I mean, all this time I've known you, no talk of men, no hint of even being attracted to a guy. It was always men as friends, me as a friend.

SIMONE: So that's what's bothering you. It wasn't you.

DAN: No, well, I don't know, maybe. If it was gonna be a guy, I mean, why not me? I know you care more about me than that doofus you just met.

SIMONE: Sure I do. I didn't plan it. It just happened. I was drinking. He was coming on to me. I told him I was gay, it didn't matter. He kept coming on to me. Finally, he just kind of wore me down. I let him take me home. The details are a little fuzzy to me after that.

DAN: Maybe he slipped one of those date rape pills to you?

SIMONE: Okay, I'd be willing to go with that one.

DAN: So were you attracted to him?

SIMONE: No. I'm not now. Maybe I was for a minute or two.

DAN: Are you bi, now?

SIMONE: No, definitely not. I'm still attracted to women. I still love Mattie. Even as we were doing it, I was thinking, he's not soft and round like Mattie. He was all hard and bumpy or knobby or something.

DAN: Well, I think the hard part is probably a good thing for a guy, but bumpy and knobby, I don't know, sounds like the guy had some sort of problem that needs to be checked out. Did he have some sort of illness?

SIMONE: No. What kind of illness?

DAN: I don't know, the kind that makes you bumpy and knobby.

SIMONE: No, it wasn't that. He was fine-looking. He was just shaped like a guy.

DAN: Okay, beginning to understand why you hadn't been attracted to guys before.

SIMONE: And I'm still not.

DAN: So you can't explain it.

SIMONE: You mean, why I was attracted to Duncan? No.

DAN: Don't need to know his name, don't want to know his name. Don't even remember his name now.

SIMONE: Duncan.

DAN: All right, let me make this clear. Don't want to remember his name. Don't want to talk about it. Dunkin'? As in Dunkin' Donuts?

SIMONE: No, Duncan, D-u-n-c-a-n. Like Duncan …? I can't think of anybody else named Duncan right now.

DAN: Well, there's a reason for that. It's a dumb name.

SIMONE: There's nothing wrong with his name. You just don't like him because you're jealous I guess.

DAN: Well, yeah, okay, so I am. I mean, all this time I've known you, been around you, we've gotten drunk together before.

SIMONE: Listen, you and I are best friends. You know I love you, right?

DAN: Yeah, I guess.

SIMONE: You know I love you, right?

DAN: Yes, okay, I know it.

SIMONE: All right, you see how awkward this is between us now. Imagine, if one night we're hanging together, we both have a little too much to drink, and somehow that had been you and me. Can you just imagine how awkward it would be us waking up in bed together naked the next morning?

DAN, *closing his eyes*: Yeah.

SIMONE: Okay, now stop imagining it. Today I'd still be gay and wouldn't know what to say to you. We might not ever get past it. We might not even be able to be friends again, certainly not as good a friends. Is that what you want?

DAN: No.

SIMONE: Well then, get over yourself. It wasn't about love. It wasn't about you being there or not being there. It was just sex, and it was wrong, and what I did had nothing to do with you. You're not the injured party here.

DAN: All right.

SIMONE: So are we all right?

DAN: Yeah, I guess.

SIMONE: Good, still my 'migo?

DAN: Of course, always.

SIMONE: So you're not going to give me a hard time about this?

DAN: Wait a minute. I never agreed to that. I'll get over it, but that doesn't mean I won't be giving you a hard time. No, you're the one that messed up, not me.

SIMONE: I know that. So you're getting past it, but I'm going to have to hear about it.

DAN: Yeah, that sounds about right.

SIMONE: Okay, I can handle that. But not around Mattie, right?

DAN: Right.

SIMONE: Or Carl. I had a hard enough time convincing him I was gay in the first place.

DAN: Yeah, he's not as hip as me.

SIMONE: True, but you might not want to use the word *hip* anymore.

DAN: Okay. So have you thought of what you're going to tell Mattie?

SIMONE: Still don't know.

DAN: I'm sure it'll be the right thing. Although not as sure as I used to be before last night.

SIMONE: Okay, I see, this is part of the hard time. You sure you can't get it all out of your system today?

DAN: No, no, there'll be a series of editorial comments and snide remarks for some time to come.

SIMONE: Oh good, something to look forward to.

And then they were back to normal. Dan—being his usual cynical, sarcastic self, and Simone—her usual optimistic, unflappable self. Dan knew it was Simone's unsinkable spirit that made her a necessary part of his life. He had often wondered what benefit he offered her. He had asked her one time, and she had simply said, "You make me laugh."

Well, sometimes life was just that simple.

SIMONE: Oh yeah, didn't you have something to tell me?

DAN: Only the best and weirdest night of my life.

SIMONE: Oh good. I love your stories.

DAN: Well, it's a true story.

SIMONE: Okay, even better. So tell me.

DAN: I'll give you the Simone *Reader's Digest* version first. I met the most beautiful girl in the world. She got drunk. We had sex. After I took her home, I was cornered in an alley by some clowns and I only got away because of Abe Lincoln, who got shot during my escape.

SIMONE: Elaborate, please.

Dan then gave her the long version of the story, throwing in the thoughts which had occurred to him at the time. He even threw in the juicy details of the sex. He hesitated slightly before telling her about the spanking part, knowing that most of the women he had known in his life would have interrupted him and given him some sermon about how men shouldn't force women to be submissive—as if he had had a choice in the matter. But Simone simply smiled and said, "Sounds like fun." That made Dan kind of pause, wondering if Simone had a kinky past or present she had never told him about. No, probably not. But maybe.

Finally, he got to the clown and Abe Lincoln portion of the festivities. And her reaction was just what he had thought it would be. Surprised, yes, maybe more than a little. But she didn't doubt for a minute that he had actually seen it. Just thought it extremely odd that he had seen it.

Dan didn't go into as much detail as he ordinarily might have because he was running on fumes by this point and Simone had to get off to work. The only negative thing she had to say was to ask him about Phyllis, the latest woman Simone had tried to fix him up with.

She was always trying to find a woman for him, but so far she didn't seem to have a clue about the kind of woman he was looking for, or maybe she was right and he didn't have a clue.

Anyway, he had been out with Phyllis a couple of times, but she had never crossed his mind last night or since. Of course, Shyanne was the type of woman who could pretty much make every other woman disappear from your conscious and subconscious.

He did ask Simone if she had ever told anyone about the clown script he had written and shown to her. She remembered it but said she didn't think she had ever told anybody about it. She asked him if he thought his script about clowns was related to clowns being the ones who threatened him. He said maybe, but he was already thinking it had to.

He said goodbye to Simone and made it home without anything else strange happening to him. After he got home, he called Shyanne, got her voice mail, couldn't think of what to say and hung up. He hoped she was okay. He thought briefly about phoning Carl, but instead he fell into bed and slept like a big cat after eating a school of tuna.

Chapter 11

While Dan was falling asleep, Hilton J. Jamieson was just getting into his office and hearing a report on the previous night's activities. Unlike most second-generation wealthy people, Jamieson had never had a lazy streak in him. And he still showed up at work every day, even though he didn't really need to.

His father, Shelby J. Jamieson, had made a small fortune running a bunch of car dealerships throughout New York, New Jersey, and Connecticut. He started with one small Ford place in New Jersey, and he just kept expanding until he had more than he could handle. When his only son, Hilton, had begun to get into the family business, he obviously had an even better head for business than his dad.

And it didn't take the younger Jamieson long to realize there was more to be made out of financing the buying of cars than in the selling of the cars themselves. The banks weren't usually the tallest buildings in any town because financing loans was such a risky business. You simply made sure one way or another you always made a profit on each deal.

After ten years or so of running the car business, Hilton began diversifying. He had always been interested in watching movies and in the entertainment business in general as a kid. He knew the movie business was pretty firmly implanted in California, but there was plenty of entertainment dollars being spent in the biggest city in the country.

So he got into the financing of plays, bought some bars and clubs, and in general got ahold of as much real estate as possible in Manhattan. He knew, whatever happened, real estate would always be worth more next year than the year before in NYC. Theaters, both off and on Broadway, comedy clubs, bars with live music, even strip clubs—if there was an entertainment venue—Hilton J. Jamieson was in on it in the New York area. And at fifty-seven, he was still young enough to enjoy the tremendous wealth and live like the king he thought he was.

At the moment he was getting a briefing from his head of security, Anthony Gibraldi. Gibraldi wasn't Jamieson's sharpest tool in the kit, but then he didn't need to be. He was hired to do the muscle work and to make sure nobody harmed Jamieson. And he pretty much took any other assignment Jamieson threw his way. It had been Gibraldi who had cleaned up the mess after that unfortunate incident with the woman. And what he lacked in intellect, he made up in loyalty. He cleaned it up, got rid of the body, and no questions asked. He had been the lead clown in last night's play.

JAMIESON: So everything went smoothly last night?

GIBRALDI: Yes, sir. Smooth as silk. The girl delivered him to the building at exactly the right time. And then she pretended to distract us so he could get away.

JAMIESON: Pretty easy for her to do that, I guess?

GIBRALDI: Yeah, even from a distance, she's got some nice tits.

JAMIESON: And how did he react to the clowns?

GIBRALDI: Oh, he was scared shitless, especially when big Bevo picked him up. Oddly enough, though, when he ran away, he actually threw Micky aside. Didn't think he had that in him.

JAMIESON: Did you guys rough him up much?

GIBRALDI: Nah, not much. Big Bevo tossed him into a pile of snow and ice and crap. Just a few cuts and bruises, I imagine.

(Big Bevo was Benny Bevoniti, Gibraldi's largest enforcer on the security detail. He was so large often the sight of him made people think twice about messing with Jamieson. He was called Big Bevo because he was about the size of a large steer.)

JAMIESON: And Abe Lincoln did his part good? Acted like he got shot and all?

GIBRALDI: Yeah, very realistic. Darwin really ran when the blanks went off.

JAMIESON: I bet he did.

GIBRALDI: There was one hitch, though, nothin' major.

JAMIESON: All right, there always is when you're involved.

GIBRALDI: No, sir, it wasn't my fault. It was the girl.

JAMIESON: What did she do?

GIBRALDI: Well, it seems she got a little more involved with him than we wanted.

JAMIESON: Did she fuck him?

GIBRALDI: Yes, sir, we believe so.

JAMIESON: Jesus Christ! I didn't want her to fuck him. Now the sonuvabitch will be searching the city for her. Jees, a guy like that doesn't get a piece of ass that good-looking and just walk away.

GIBRALDI: Yeah, I'm afraid she might have kind of liked him. I'm afraid she might try to get in touch with him some time.

JAMIESON: Damn, I thought this girl was a pro. Why can't women just fuck somebody without thinking it's some sort of lifelong deal? (*Sighing.*) All right, we got to make her disappear.

GIBRALDI: You mean whack her, sir?

JAMIESON: No, hell no. Just get her out of town for a while, at least until the trial's over. Whack her? Why did I ever let you watch the Sopranos?

GIBRALDI: I didn't know. You say make her disappear, I thought it was like a code or somethin'. It would be easy enough to do.

JAMIESON: Let me make this clear once and for all. This ain't the mob. I don't kill people.

(*Gibraldi looked at him quizzically.*)

JAMIESON: Hey, that wasn't on purpose. The bitch just made me mad. I lost my temper. I hit her. She wasn't supposed to die.

GIBRALDI: Okay, okay, so "make her disappear" means tell her to go to another city. Where do you wanna send her?

JAMIESON: I don't care. I've got clubs all over. Hell, let her pick. She can go work at one of the places for a while and won't lose any money. Or just give her an extra thousand bucks and tell her to take a vacation. I don't care. She can work or not until this trial's over. After that, I don't care what she does. Just get her out of New York.

GIBRALDI: Yes, sir, okay.

JAMIESON: By the way, the idea of the clowns for last night—a brilliant stroke.

GIBRALDI: Actually, that was your idea, sir.

JAMIESON: Ah, yes, so it was. So it was.

GIBRALDI: You told me about him being scared of clowns and all, and you were right. But I don't understand the Abe Lincoln part.

JAMIESON: That's okay. I do. That's all that's important.

Jamieson then dismissed Gibraldi and called one of his other assistants on the phone. This one was considerably brighter, so Jamieson had put him in charge of the other portion of his two-part plan to make sure he would never go to jail. As it turned out, everything was going fine with that part of the plan as well.

Chapter 12

Detective Sam Barker had been at work for a while before the word filtered to him about Dan's story about the clowns. Barker had been on the force for twenty-four years and knew with Jamieson's trial coming up, this wasn't good news. He had been the lead detective assigned to the case and, in fact, was the one who had first taken Darwin's statement about Jamieson. He had tried to develop other evidence in the case, but the plain fact was, without Darwin's testimony, they didn't have a case.

When Barker had made detective, it had been in the days when some people seemed to still be surprised that a black man could actually be in charge of solving a case. And since he had never worried about what he wore and was so persistent once he got on the case, some had taken to calling him the black Columbo when he started out. At 5'11" and 235 solid pounds, he could have bench-pressed Columbo, but Barker didn't mind the comparison too much. After all, Columbo was smart and always got his man—or woman. These days, the younger cops only knew Columbo in reruns, if at all. He looked forward to the day when some young white detective became known as the white Barker.

As soon as he got the news about the clowns, Barker went in to talk to his boss, Lieutenant Raymond Johnson. They had both started on the force about the same time, and since they had been two of the few blacks on the force at the time, they had been friends almost out of necessity. Many perceived they were not friends anymore since Johnson had made lieutenant and had his own squad in homicide and Barker was still doing the legwork solving the crimes.

But the truth was, Barker didn't want to be anything more than what he was. He liked the grunt work, the drudgery, and he liked being the one solving the case, not the one waiting for someone else to do it. And the fact that Johnson was better than him at kissing ass and getting promoted didn't bother him. Somebody had to pave the way.

"Hey, boss," Barker said as he walked into Johnson's office. "Did you see the report that came in last night?"

"Which one?" Johnson asked, looking up from a stack of papers. "And I've told you not to call me boss, Sam."

"Okay, boss. I'm talking about the reporting of clowns shooting Abe Lincoln, and who reported it."

"Yeah, I saw. That's your boy, Darwin, isn't it? Poor guy. You think maybe the pressure's gotten to him? Maybe went off on the deep end."

"I don't know. Last time I talked to him, he seemed okay. What are we gonna do about it?"

"What are we gonna do about it? Well, I think the chances we can tie those clowns to Jamieson are slim to none. And as you know, there was no Abe Lincoln body found in that alley last night. You think he's too scared to testify now?"

"I don't know. I'll call him here in a little bit and ask him. So you don't want me to investigate last night?"

"Six clowns threatening him and shooting Abe Lincoln? I don't see much point in it."

"Okay, but would you mind if I checked it out, just for the helluva it?"

"No, but why do you want to? Just make sure he's not spooked too much to testify."

"I'll do it unofficially, on my off hours."

"But again, why?"

"Here's the thing, boss. You know how many times we can't make a case 'cause we can't get people to get involved, can't get 'em to testify. And usually it's not 'cause they're scared, they just don't want to take the time, they don't want to miss work, they don't see why they have to be involved, why we can't make the case without them. They watch all those damn CSI shows and think all we need is a damn piece of somebody's fingernail or something and we can put somebody behind bars with it."

"Yeah, I know. So?"

"So here we have a guy that not only took the time to report it when he saw Jamieson kill that girl in the first place, he's taken the heat and is still there for us. I mean, this guy's lost jobs 'cause of this, his career's in the shitter, but he's still standing there, doing the right thing 'cause he knows it's right. You know my momma had to put up with a lot of racist shit growin' up, a lot more than you and me. And she told me there was gonna be racists always, there was always gonna be people that didn't like somebody 'cause they were a different color or religion or whatever."

"All right, is there a point here, somewhere?"

"Yeah, she said it wasn't the racists that made it impossible to change things. It was the people who weren't racist and stood by and let the racists get away with it. They were the ones who kept things from changing. Well, this guy's not standing by and letting it happen. He's trying to help. And I think we should have his back."

"Okay, you can do it. On your own time, no more sermons."

"Thanks, boss."

"Just one more thing, Barker. What the hell does racism have to do with it? All these people are white."

"Nothing, boss, the point I was trying to make … never mind. I'll check out his story and keep you posted."

"No, don't keep me posted. I don't know what you're doing."

"Yes, sir, boss."

"And don't call me boss."

Chapter 13

Dan was sleeping the sleep of the dead when the phone started ringing. At first the ringing became part of his dream, then he slowly came to. He had no idea what time it was or where he was, but he knew he had to stop the ringing. As soon as he was sort of awake, he hoped it was Shyanne. It was Carl.

"Hey, baby brother. So how'd did it go last night? You got company there with you, heh-heh-heh?"

"No, she's long gone," Dan said groggily.

"Ah, too bad. No, wait a minute. You got her to come back to your place?"

"Yeah, she was here. She only left after we had wild and crazy sex."

"Yeah, baby. Way to go, bro. So how was she? Was she as hot as she seemed like?"

"Yeah, even better, if that's imaginable. Incredible. Mind-blowing. I never knew it could be that good."

"So now you know what all the fuss is about. Okay, well, I want all the details, but later on, in person. Was there any particular reason she left? Did you not do it right? Did she want more and you weren't quite up to it?"

"No, no, you would have been proud of me. She wanted to go back to her place so she could get ready for work. About four o'clock or so."

"Okay, well, that sounds okay. Did she just leave, or did she kiss you goodbye?"

"Actually, she asked me to take her home, so I did."

"That sounds good. Anything else?"

"Well, yeah, after she went inside her apartment building, six clowns cornered me in an alley."

There was a long pause. "You know I'm usually pretty quick on my feet, but I just don't have a response for that one. So what's the punch line? Oh, I know. Does it have something to do with elephants?"

"No, there's no punch line. It's not a joke. Six clowns, obviously sent by Jamieson, threatened me. And one of them picked me up and threw me into the snow and ice."

Another long pause. "Okay, now you're starting to scare me 'cause it sounds like you're actually serious."

"I am."

"And how did you get away?"

"Okay, you're really gonna like this part. Shyanne distracted them from her apartment above by throwing her bra and panties down in the alley, and then Abe Lincoln opened the door to her building, and I ran in and got away from them."

"Sure, why not? Anything else?"

"Oh yeah, they shot Abe Lincoln."

"Man, Abe just can't catch a break. He goes to a play, gets shot, comes back to life 150 years later and gets shot again. Did this girl literally fuck your brains out last night?"

"No."

"Did you fall out of bed or hit your head while you were doing it?"

"No, I kind of hit my face when the clown threw me, but nothing before then."

"And she didn't slip something into your drink?"

"What, like LSD?"

"Yeah, that could explain it."

"Do they even make LSD anymore?"

"Yeah, sure, but maybe it was something else. Some drug that helps you perform better sexually but leaves you with weird hallucinations."

"No, she didn't put anything in my drink. I saw the clowns. And one of them was really big."

"The one that picked you up and threw you?"

"Yeah."

"Sure, I mean, if you're going to get thrown by a clown, it might as well be a big one."

"Listen, I knew you would have fun with this, and that's okay. But I'm not making it up, and I'm not changing my story."

"All right, but don't tell anybody else. You hadn't, have you?"

"I told Simone."

"That's okay."

"And the police."

"Aw, man, I bet they had a field day with it."

"Yeah, I think I made their day."

Carl paused again. "All right, bro, I can still fix this. Don't tell Mom and Dad, all right?"

"All right. What are you going to do to fix it?"

"I hadn't figured that part out yet. But I'll be working on it. Trust me. I'm going to figure something out."

"Oh good. I feel better already."

"Hey, now, don't go anywhere till I call you back. By the way, did you know your cell's not working?"

"Yeah, it broke when I landed on it."

"When the big clown picked you up and threw you?"

"Yeah."

"Of course it did. If a big clown picks you up and throws you down, of course it's going to break your cell. All right, now stay there till you hear back from me."

"Sure. Hey, Carl, remember that TV pilot deal I wrote about the clowns? Did you ever let anybody else read it?"

"No, can't say I did. It wasn't your best work. Hey, you're still scared of clowns, aren't you? Is that what this is about? I thought I was over feeling guilty about that."

"Yeah, I bet it's been keeping you up nights. No, you don't have to feel guilty anymore. But I just wonder how Jamieson could have known about the clowns. It can't be a coincidence."

"No, you're scared of clowns, you get threatened by clowns, it adds up. Hey, you weren't ever scared of Abe Lincoln as a kid, were you?"

"Not as a kid, not as an adult, not ever. Nobody's ever been scared of Abe Lincoln. I don't get that part."

"Yeah, me neither. But I'll figure it out. Talk to you in a few minutes."

"Okay."

Dan didn't get to go back to sleep before the phone rang again. *Is it Shyanne?* he thought. He wondered if he was going to think that every time the phone rang. He still didn't have caller ID on his home phone, so sometimes he just had to find out who was calling the old-fashioned way—by answering it.

"Mr. Darwin?" a male voice said on the other end.

Dan usually told anybody that asked for Mr. Darwin that Mr. Darwin had died, since it was almost always somebody trying to sell something and it was fun to hear their reaction. But this was a voice he had heard before, so he just said "Yes."

"Hey, this is Detective Barker. I understand you had kind of a wild night last night."

Oh, great, first the cops at the station, then his brother, now Barker. *Okay, fine go ahead and have your fun, world. I saw what I saw.* At least Simone believed him.

"Uh, yes, sir, you saw the report?"

"Yes, I did," Barker said.

Dan could almost hear the chuckle in his voice.

"Listen, Detective, before you say anything else, let me just say, I know it sounds incredible, and if you don't want to believe it, that's all right. But I really don't feel like being made fun of anymore right now. If you want to call me back tomorrow and make some jokes, maybe I'll be in the mood then."

"The boys down at the Eighty-First gave you a hard time, huh?"

"Yeah, 'bout like you'd expect, I guess."

"Actually, Mr. Darwin, I was wondering if you'd like to meet someplace for lunch and talk a little more seriously about it."

"Serious as in you might actually believe me?"

"Well, it is a fairly incredible story, but since you were right about Jamieson, I figure I got to give you the benefit of the doubt on this one. And what the hell, this is New York, there could be a pack of marauding clowns out there on a crime spree for all I know."

"Thank you! So have they struck again?"

"No."

"Have you ever seen or heard of anything like that before?"

"No."

"And did they find the body of that Abe Lincoln guy?"

"No."

"So you're pretty much just humoring me."

"Pretty much, but without the jokes."

"Okay, fair enough. Where do you want to meet?"

"Your call."

"How 'bout Ontario's? You know it?"

"Yeah, that's fine. When can you make it?"

"Let's see, an hour?"

"See you then."

Dan figured an hour would be long enough to take a shower and get there, although he kind of hated to wash away the Shyanne smell that still lingered with him.

After a refreshing shower that poured some life back into him, Dan started getting dressed. Carl had told him not to leave, but knowing Carl, it was probably a good idea if he did. He was probably putting together some kind of intervention group right now. They would all be dressed in clown costumes and tell him to fight his inner demons. Not that he didn't have some inner demons, but clowns were not the major ones—at least he hadn't thought so before. The phone rang again.

"Hey, bro, you still there?"

Still not Shyanne. "Yeah, what did you work out? Are the men in white jackets on the way over?"

"No, I thought it over, and I've decided to believe you."

"Really?"

"Yeah, I believe you thought you saw some clowns."

"Thought I saw?"

"Yeah."

"Okay, I guess that's a start. Carl, I need to get going. I'm going to meet with Detective Barker here in just a minute."

"The guy from the other case? Are you going to tell him about it?"

"He already knows."

"Oh, sure he does. I bet you're the toast of New York's finest this morning."

"Everybody's got to be something."

"All right, you want me to go with you?"

"No, I'm fine. And by the way, bro. He believes me."

"Yeah, me too."

"Uh-huh. See ya later."

Dan found the subway stop closest to his place and got on the line going west. As he was on the subway, he saw the Fifth Avenue station stop and thought about Saks Fifth Avenue. Just before the doors closed, he impulsively jumped out (not literally "jumped out," more like quickly walked and stepped downward, but "jumped out" is a shorter way of saying it, unless you include this explanation).

He wandered along Fifth Avenue not knowing exactly where Saks was. Believe it or not, he had never been there. He had seen an Oprah show one time where she was in New York and went shopping at Saks. She showed up in front of the studio audience wearing some shoes she had bought there, and the crowd went wild.

Dan thought whatever gene that was that made someone get excited about shopping in general and shoes in particular, he was missing. To him, shoes had always seemed like things to keep your feet dry and warm and protected from all the weird stuff you had to walk on top of. How they looked, he never really cared. And the only time he noticed a woman's shoes was if she had on stiletto heels or some kind of sexy boots.

During the wandering of his mind and the thesis he was apparently considering writing on the value of shoes, he noticed a woman carrying a bag that said Saks Fifth Avenue. He looked to see which direction she had come from, and there it was, the Holy Grail of stores for those people who do have that shopping gene. Man, with detective work like that, Detective Barker had nothing on him.

He got inside to discover that not even half his sleuthing work had been done. The place was bigger than some towns in Arkansas, and they had whole floors dedicated to one particle of clothing or another. He finally gave up trying to figure it out and asked somebody. They told him what floor cosmetics was on, and he went there.

Even after he got to the right floor, it was still not apparent where a cosmetologist might be stationed. He was starting to feel like an alien who had landed on earth and was trying to orient itself to totally new surroundings. And the kicker was, there was a whole group of people roaming around who seemed right at home there. After wandering around and asking several more people, he seemed to be in the right area. There were women helping other women pick out and try on makeup. None of them were Shyanne. He picked out the snootiest, most impersonal woman in the area, figuring she would be in charge and asked if there was a Shyanne working there.

"We have no one by that name working here," the snooty woman said, casting a disparaging look down at his shoes. Apparently, she thought shoes should do a lot more than protect your feet, and whatever it was Dan had on his feet was something less than ideal. He wanted to ask her if she was sure about Shyanne not working there, but she seemed pretty sure the first time. He looked around again, hoping he would see her and he could escape this woman's icy stare.

"Maybe she goes by another name here," Dan said. "She's about five four or so, late twenties, blond hair, really good-looking, kind of hot, if you know what I mean."

"Yes, I'm aware of what you have in mind," Snooty said, although Dan thought she wouldn't know hot if she caught on fire. "We have no one here that fits that description. Perhaps you are in the wrong place."

No perhaps *about that*, Dan thought. He started to leave with some sort of parting shot to the woman, but decided she might summon some security guys to toss him out in the snow and ice. Once a day for that kind of thing was enough. So he simply turned and walked out, wondering why Shyanne wasn't there. He hoped she was okay, but he was starting to get an uneasy feeling about her.

Chapter 14

Dan decided to walk the remaining six blocks to Ontario's, thinking that would be quicker than getting back on and off the subway. He was already a little late, although he figured Barker would wait for him.

He got there and noticed Barker seated over at a table next to the window. Barker saw him about the same time and waved.

"Hi, Detective, good to see you again. You ordered yet?"

"No, Mr. Darwin, waiting on you."

"Sorry about that, got sidetracked. I thought we had decided last time you should call me Dan."

"Yeah, but only if you call me Sam."

"Yeah, but Detective's not a name, it's a title, and a cool one. Nobody ever calls me Comedian Darwin."

"I can call you Comedian if you want."

"No, Dan's okay. I'll call you Sam. This doesn't mean we're going to date or something, though, does it?"

"God, I hope not. Now, Dan, I've seen the report. But why don't you tell me what happened. You might have left something out."

Dan recounted the story, pretty much as he had with the other police, although he was a little more relaxed with Barker. He also told him the how the clowns knew his name and called him Comedian, which he thought indicated they had been sent by Jamieson.

"So these clowns never directly said they were sent by Jamieson?" Sam said after Dan finished.

"No, that's not surprising, is it?"

"No, Jamieson's been pretty careful up to now to make sure we couldn't implicate him in anything."

"Except for the murder."

"Yeah, he wasn't so careful there," Sam said. "These clowns, how many of them were armed?"

"I didn't actually notice any of them were when they had me surrounded. But obviously one of them was. Maybe some of the others were packing heat too. Is that what you call it?"

"No, never."

"What do you say when someone's carrying a gun?"

"Carrying a gun. Armed."

"Okay, not too cool, but okay."

"And did you get a look at the limo's license plates?"

"No, I never really saw the back of the limo. It pulled in sideways."

"So you think these clowns were following you? Waiting for the right chance to get you alone?"

"I guess. I mean, how else would they know I was going to be there, in that alley, late at night?"

Sam sat silently, letting Dan think about it. "Can you think of any other way?"

Dan thought for several seconds then realized what Sam was getting at and was disappointed at what he realized.

"Ah, man, you're not thinking that, are you?"

"What am I thinking?"

"I can't say it. You're going to have to be the one. Go ahead and say it."

"The girl set you up?"

"Damn, don't say that."

"You told me to."

"I know. But I'm just not ready for that yet."

Sam paused. "So am I wrong?"

"No, probably not."

"I could be wrong. Maybe they did just follow you at four in the morning."

"Okay, tell me this. If she did set me up, why did she help me get away?"

"I don't know. What do you think?"

"What are you—my shrink? You come up with the answers. You're the detective."

"All right. Maybe she helped you get away because they didn't really want to hurt you—just scare you."

Dan thought that one over. "Yeah, you're probably right again. And it worked. But what about the shots? Not really shooting at me?"

"Or maybe just blanks. I went by there. There's not only no body there, there's no blood, no shells from a gun."

"Oh, you didn't tell me that."

"I wanted to break it to you gently."

"Thanks," Dan said sarcastically. "I guess I should have known. I mean, I was running fast, but it seems like they never even got close to me. And as long as we're going down this road, there's one other thing you should know."

"What's that?"

"I went by Saks Fifth Avenue, where she said she worked, this morning."

"They don't know her."

"No. Dammit, Sam, I mean, it seemed so real. It was the best night of my life. Although at the time, I was thinking, man, what's a babe like this doing with me?"

Sam laughed. "Yeah, I know the feeling. I can't figure out why my wife is still with me."

"You know, though, Sam. She was really good at it. I mean, it really seemed like she liked me."

"Don't be so hard on yourself. Just 'cause she might have been paid to set you up, it doesn't mean she didn't like you."

"So Jamieson pays her to pick me up, get me to that alley at a particular time. How do they know no one else will be there then?"

"Well, at that time of day, in an alley, it was unlikely, but I guess they just took a chance that no one else would be around. Or if they were, they wouldn't report it. Like Abe Lincoln."

"Yeah, just so you know. I don't think it actually was Abe Lincoln, just a guy made up to look like him."

"And what about him?" Sam asked, again letting Dan come to the same conclusion he already had.

"He was part of the setup?"

"I think he had to be."

"But why Abe Lincoln?"

"I hadn't figured that part out yet."

"Good, 'cause it seemed like you had it all worked out."

"I'm not even sure why the clowns. Other than it makes it harder for you to identify them."

"Well, I think I can help you with that part."

"Oh?"

"Yeah, I don't know how Jamieson knew about this exactly, but, Sam, when I was a little kid, four or five years old, something happened to me with a clown. I was so little my memory of it is only a few seconds. But I was with my brother at the state fair and I fell from the front row of the stands. I was probably only ten feet up or so, but this clown came over and caught me.

"So I was scared about falling, and then I look and see the person who caught me was a clown. And I look at his face, that unreal, smiling, scary as hell face, and instead of feeling relief, I was even more scared. And then he held me up to show the cheering crowd I was all right. And he told me in this deep voice, "Shut up, you little brat," all the while still smiling and pretending he was this nice guy. But something in my four-year-old mind knew he wasn't a good guy. And all I wanted was to get away from him. I know it doesn't make much sense, but after that I was petrified of clowns."

"No, I can understand that," Sam said. "When you're a kid, almost anything can frighten you. When I was a kid, I used to be scared of movies where animals could talk. That just didn't seem right to me."

"Yeah, I didn't much like that either. I was worried our family dog was going to start talking to me."

"Exactly. So back to the clowns. You still have a fear of them?"

"I guess so. It's not like a conscious thing or something I think about a lot. It's more like Pavlov's dogs, I see a clown, I have a natural reaction to not want to be around them."

"And certainly not be picked up by one."

"Which is what they did."

"Yes, they did. So how could Jamieson know about this fear of clowns, whatever that's called?"

"Bozophobia?"

"You just came up with that, that fast?"

"It's what I can do. As Rocky said, I can't sing or dance."

"Rocky and Bullwinkle?"

"No, Rocky Balboa."

"Oh, I don't remember that line. So any ideas on how he might know about this?"

"Yeah, I wrote this draft script for a TV pilot where a character has a fear of clowns. But I only showed it to my brother and my best friend. I asked both of them, and they didn't show it to anybody else. So I don't know how he would have seen it. I can't figure that out."

"Okay, that's it then. He's seen it. It doesn't really matter how he saw it. Somehow he did. I don't know, maybe he had somebody break into your apartment and they found a copy, or maybe it's still on a computer disc. That part isn't important. He's seen it, and he was smart enough to figure the character's fear was also your fear.

"And even if he was wrong about that part, almost anybody would still be scared of a great big clown that shoots at you. So he had nothing to lose by dressing his guys as clowns. And you couldn't identify them afterward.

"Any scripts about a fear of Abe Lincoln floating around?

"Abeaphobia? No, I have no idea on that one. I mean, Abe's just not a scary figure to anyone, I don't think."

"No, I wouldn't think so. I don't understand that part."

"Yeah, it could have just as well been a normal guy opening that door at exactly the right time and letting me in and then getting shot."

"Yeah, but it wasn't. I have a feeling if we can figure out why it was Abe Lincoln, that might be the key to this whole thing. Why Abe Lincoln?"

"Okay, well, I'll think on that."

"Yeah, me too."

"So what's the next step?"

"I go back to the building and try to find somebody who saw or heard something."

"And could you look for Shyanne too?"

"I'll look for her first. In fact, when we're through here, if you've got time, we can go over there together and you can show me which apartment she leaned out of naked. Can you remember that?"

"Oh yeah."

"Let me rephrase that. I know you can remember her doing it. Can you remember which apartment she leaned out of?"

"That I'm not so sure, but I'll give it a shot."

The lunch they ordered came, some kind of salad and healthy sandwich for Sam and a big, greasy cheeseburger for Dan. They stopped talking about the case and switched to small talk. Dan discovered that Sam wasn't your stereotypical cop, or at least the kind of cop he thought was stereotypical. He did a little painting for relaxation, liked the opera and Broadway, and was writing a book about a police detective.

"Can I ask you about the book, since you're a creative sort?" Sam asked. "Just to see if it sounds like it would be good?"

"Sure."

"It starts with a murder."

"That's a good start. Is it by a rich, arrogant jerk?"

"No, no rich jerks, no comedians. The two main characters are a detective and a psychiatrist."

"Both based on you, I guess."

"No," Sam said, then laughed. "Okay, I get it. Anyway, at the beginning of the book, one shrink is murdered, and the detective is sure it was one of his patients that killed him. So this other psychiatrist comes in to take over the dead one's patients. The detective wants the new psychiatrist to help him on the case, after he talks with each of the patients. The doctor says he can't really help because he can't reveal what the patients say."

"'Cause of client-doctor privilege."

"Yeah. So the detective, who's sort of like me, only not as smart ..."

"Who is?"

"Anyway, the detective says maybe he could bring up the names one by one and when he comes to the name that might be the murderer, instead of saying anything, the doctor could start whistling some tune, maybe like the theme song from the Lone Ranger. And the doctor says, 'You mean "The William Tell Overture?"' And the detective says, 'Yeah, that sounds right.'"

"So in this story, the doctor is smarter than the detective?"

"At least more knowledgeable about classical music and stuff like that."

"Unlike you, who already knew it was called 'The William Tell Overture.'"

"Yeah, I even know it was written by Giovanni Rossini."

"That's good. I had no idea. I would have said Beethoven."

"Really?"

"I always guess Beethoven. I'm more like your fictional detective, I guess. So by whistling, he could reveal the killer without breaking the doctor-client privilege."

"That's what the detective is hoping for."

"So does the psychiatrist whistle the tune when he hears the killer's name?"

"No, not then. He says he can't do that either. But in the climax of the book, somehow I'm gonna work it in where the psychiatrist is in trouble and lets the detective know the killer is with him by whistling it. But I don't have that scene worked out yet."

"Sounds like a good premise. You don't really have to know exactly how it ends yet, right? Is there going to be any humor in it?"

"Hopefully. Why?"

"I just thought I might could give you some help on that part," Dan said.

"That would be great. Would there be a charge for that?"

"Nah, it would be fun. I've thought about writing a book myself."

"Why hadn't you?"

"Too long. I keep getting stuck after the first chapter. That's why I stick with the comedy routines. I can know how each joke ends pretty quickly."

"I saw you guys onstage one time."

"Really? At the Hyena House?"

"No, at that comedy place in New Jersey, Donatelli's."

"Oh yeah, that was about a year ago, was the last time we were there."

"Yeah, it was before I knew you."

"Were we good?"

Sam hesitated a second. "Yeah, my wife thought you were great. Me too."

"But?"

"No buts. I was just wondering about something you said about writing the jokes. It seemed to me most of your stuff wasn't really written out. Just spontaneous. Ad-libs."

"Yeah, that's how my brother likes to work. He calls it working without a net."

"And you?"

"It's okay. I'd rather have a little more structure to it. So we compromise. A lot of the stuff that seems like ad-libs, we kind of work that out a little bit, and then make it seem like ad-libs."

"But when you talk to the audience, how do you know what they're gonna say?"

"You don't really, it's hard to understand, but when they say a certain thing, I know where my brother's going with it and try to anticipate it."

"Yeah, you're right. I don't understand it."

"That's all right. Comedy's one of those things that shouldn't be explained. It's either funny or it's not. By the way, did we pick on you that night?"

"No, we got lucky."

They had finished their lunch, and the waiter brought them the check. Sam insisted on picking it up. Dan let him, figuring there were worse ways to see the taxpayers' money spent.

"Before we head over there, why don't you give her a call? Did she give you her phone number?"

"Yeah, she's probably not there. She said she was going to be at work."

"At Saks?"

"Oh yeah, sometimes I'm a little slow."

"Try calling it now."

"What do you want me to say?"

"I don't know. Whatever you want to say to her. Whisper sweet nothings in her ear. Just see what her reaction is, see if she'll meet you someplace. See if it's her phone number."

Dan reached for his cell phone and once again remembered it was broken. He asked to borrow Sam's. He dialed the number, which he had already memorized. He got her voice mail. He kind of turned away from Sam as he left the message.

"Hey, Shyanne. Just hoping you were okay. You may have tried to call me, but my cell's broken. Anyway, I'm okay. Just need to hear you are too. Call me back on my home phone. Please. And I'll be coming by your place in a few minutes. Just to see if you're okay. I'm not stalking you or anything."

Then he turned back to Sam. "Casual enough?"

"Oh, I wasn't paying attention."

"Sure you weren't. Casual enough?"

"Maybe could have left the 'please' part out. And the 'stalker' part too."

"Yeah."

"So was it her voice on the voice mail?"

"Yes. You thought maybe she gave me a fake number?"

"I don't know. Did you think she might have?"

"Oh, we're back to the psychiatrist thing again, huh?"

"Sorry. Didn't mean to. What's her last name?"

"She never gave it to me."

"Okay."

"Not looking good, is it?"

"I could still be wrong. She might not have had anything to do with it. She might be calling you back right now."

"You think?"

"Not really."

"Just humoring me again?"

"Yeah."

Chapter 15

They got in Barker's unmarked police car, some sort of Buick sedan, with Dan feeling pretty grown up riding in the front seat of a detective's car. He was kind of hoping Barker would have to put the blue light on top of his car.

"Before we get there, let me ask you about this girl," Sam said.

"Okay."

"Did she seem like she might have done this kind of thing before?"

"Led guys to a dark alley so they could be cornered by a group of clowns, who then shoot Abe Lincoln?"

"No, not that exactly. I mean, did she seem like she knew what she was doing? Was she a pro?"

"She was a pro at making me feel good, but I'm not sure what kind of pro. What kind you thinking of?"

"A hooker?"

"I don't think so. But I don't know. I only know hookers from the movies, and the ones that yell stuff at you when you wander into the wrong area of town."

"Or the right one, if that's what you're looking for."

"Yeah. She didn't seem like them."

"More like the Julia Roberts character in Pretty Woman?"

"Yeah, more like that."

"Not too many of them in real life."

"I wouldn't think so," Dan said. "So when we get there, you gonna go up to the apartment by yourself, or am I going up too as kind of your partner?"

"You watch too many movies. Actually, neither. I want you to go up with me, but not as my partner."

"Okay," Dan said, feeling like a child being scolded.

"I need you to go up with me, so if someone answers the door, you can tell me if it's her. You can identify her, can't you?"

"Oh yeah."

"So the clowns and Abe Lincoln guy, you can't identify, but Shyanne, no problem."

"Yeah, I could pick her out of a darkened movie theater filled with nothing but naked beautiful women."

When Sam didn't respond, Dan looked at his face to see he was smiling.

"Sam, you all right?"

"Yeah, just thinking."

"About a theater full of naked women?"

"Yeah."

"Need me to drive?"

"No, I'm good."

Dan let Sam drive in silence for a minute, apparently still enjoying his theater fantasy. Finally, they got to the building at Eighty-First and Columbus. Dan pointed toward the alley, and Sam wheeled his car into the entrance of the alley. They got out, and Dan headed directly toward the door, not wanting to linger too long in Clown Alley.

"Wait a minute," Sam said to him. "Let's try to figure out which window she was at before we go in. It's my experience these things can be hard to figure out once you're inside."

Dan stopped and looked up, hoping maybe Shyanne might just happen to be looking at them. No such luck. Barker told him to try to remember where he had been last night in relation to the door when the raining of underwear had occurred. Dan tried to retrace his movements, particularly where he was when he landed in the snow and ice.

"Okay, I was about here, not too far from the door," he said after thinking about it. "First the bra comes down, then the panties. We're all looking up. It was definitely the third floor because you

97

could see her pretty well, but not as well as if she had been on the second floor."

"All right, and which window do you think it was?"

"I think it was that one right there," Dan said, pointing to the window which seemed to be three apartments over from the door.

"Are you sure?"

"I'm sure she was topless. The rest I wouldn't swear to."

Sam went to the door and peered in. "Okay, we're in luck. The elevator is straight down the hall from this door, so I think if we go up and get off the elevator, we just have to go three doors down."

Sam had already gotten the code to enter the building, so they wouldn't have to wait for Abe Lincoln to open the door for them to get in. They took the elevator to the third floor. They made their way to the third apartment to the right of the elevator. Sam went to the door and motioned Dan to stand a little ways back, but still close enough to where he could see who answered. Dan's heart began pounding as Sam banged on the door. If Shyanne actually answered, he didn't know what he would say, but he knew how he would feel—relieved and happy.

"This is Detective Barker with NYPD," Sam said as he knocked. "I need to ask you a few questions."

They both waited. Dan didn't hear any noise coming from inside. Finally, after what seemed an eternity to Dan, they heard some rustling from inside.

"Just a minute," a female voice from inside said.

Dan couldn't tell if it was Shyanne's voice or not. The door slowly opened, and Dan felt himself growing more nervous with each inch the door opened. A cute, but not beautiful, dark-haired girl's face emerged. Not Shyanne. Sam looked back at Dan, who shook his head no.

"Yes, sir, what can I do for you?" the girl said.

"Ma'am, as I said before, my name's Detective Barker, and I need to ask you a few questions."

"Okay," she said meekly, with the tone of voice someone usually has that hasn't had any brushes with the law.

"First, what's your name?"

"Rachel Murphy."

"Do you have a roommate?"

"No, I live here alone."

"And did you see or hear anything about four this morning?"

"I was asleep then."

"Nothing happened to wake you up?"

She paused, as if thinking what to say. "Well, I think I remember waking up 'cause of something that might have been gunshots."

"You didn't get up to see?"

"No, I listened for a minute, didn't hear anything else, so I went back to sleep. I mean, this is New York."

"And gunshots, you hear them a lot?"

"No, not really, but more than I did back in Nebraska."

"A little different here, huh?"

"Yes, sir."

"Ma'am, I don't mean to get too personal here, but did you have any company last night, perhaps another woman here?"

Rachel looked down at her feet, reddened a little, then raised her eyes back to look directly at Sam. "No, sir, no one here but me."

"Do you mind if I come in for a second? I don't have a warrant, but if you don't have anything to hide …"

Barker knew from experience that most people who had not been in trouble before, but were feeling guilty about something, would cooperate with the police to avoid looking guilty. It worked with Rachel.

"Well, the place is kind of a mess, but come on in."

Dan waited then Sam motioned him to follow. He wondered if Sam was going to say anything to Rachel about who he was, but he didn't. So he just followed him into the apartment silently.

The place didn't look that messy to Dan, but everything, even messiness, is relative. Dan stopped as soon as he was inside, but Sam went immediately over to the window looking over the alley. He unlatched it and opened it.

He turned around to Dan but said to Rachel, "Ma'am, this gentleman was accosted in the alley last night and saw someone looking out a window. I just want to see if this was the window."

Then he told Dan to go back outside and look up. Dan went back down the elevator, went outside, and immediately looked up. There was Sam, sticking his head out the window with a wry smile on his face. Dan knew Sam was thinking it sure wasn't the same as seeing a topless Shyanne leaning out the window. After seeing him at the window, Dan felt sure it was the same one. Sam yelled to him to wait for him there. Dan did so, but he moved closer to the car, still not feeling comfortable being alone there.

He didn't have to wait long for Sam to reappear. Sam pressed the key remote and opened the doors. As they got in, Dan asked Sam if the girl had said anything else.

"She repeated again she hadn't seen anything last night."

"Yeah, that's not too surprising, is it?"

"No, except I didn't ask her again. Sometimes you can get more from people with silence than to keep asking them questions. She felt compelled to fill the silence by reminding me she was innocent."

"Which you don't think she is."

"No, she may not have been a part of whatever happened here last night, but she knows something. Or knows Shyanne. Are you feeling pretty sure that was the right window?"

"Yeah, I'm pretty damn sure. I was waiting for you to toss some underwear down to recreate the exact crime scene."

"Yeah, well, I don't like to lead guys on like that," Sam said smiling.

Dan laughed. He noticed that Sam still hadn't started the car, and even having a detective in the car with him, Dan didn't want to stick around.

"Is there any reason we hadn't left yet?" Dan asked. "Are we going to do a stakeout or something? Wait for the perp to make a move?"

"You definitely watch too much TV," Sam said. "No, I wanted you to look back up at that window while we're here. Notice anything different about that window from the others?"

"Hmm, not really."

"It's the only one on that floor that doesn't have a screen on it. There's one other one that doesn't, but it's on the fourth floor and way over toward the end."

Dan looked again and saw he was right. "Man, you ought to be a detective or something. So what does that mean?"

"What do you think?"

"It means they had already taken the screen off before I got here last night. And the panty parade was part of the plan. Is that what you think?"

"Damn right that's what I think."

With a satisfied look on his face, Sam started the car, and they backed out of the alley for what Dan hoped would be his last time there.

Chapter 16

The next two days were long ones for Dan as it became more and more clear that Shyanne had set him up. He thought over and over how he didn't even get twenty-four hours of celebrating his night with Shyanne before being brought back to the reality that it was all just a setup.

Nothing had happened, but just the fact he hadn't heard from her made it seem clear that his night of glory was simply a night of chicanery. He briefly thought that maybe something bad had happened to Shyanne and that was why he hadn't heard from her, but he realized that likely wasn't the case. And he didn't like the feeling of almost hoping that something bad had happened to her simply because it would make him feel better.

Barker had not had any luck finding any witnesses thus far. And he didn't have any leads on where Shyanne might actually be, although he found from her phone number that her name was actually Shyanne Sullivan. But Dan knew she was out there somewhere, and even in a city of eight million, he would find her one day. But he wasn't all that sure what he would do when he found her. He was mad at being set up, but somehow that hadn't translated into being mad at Shyanne.

Carl was more determined than Dan to find her. He wasn't that keen on finding the clowns since he hadn't actually seen them and was not all that convinced of their reality. But he knew Shyanne was real, and he knew there was some way to find her. Dan and Carl had gone by the Hyena Club even though they weren't scheduled to work until Sunday night. Louie had called them to say he had a surprise for them.

As they sat outside Louie's office, Carl brought up the Shyanne subject again. He seemed more obsessed than Dan. For Dan, the finding her part would never be as hard as accepting that she had just set him up. In some ways, he kind of dreaded confronting her. After all, if he found her, he would have to face the truth. But Carl had no such qualms. He seemed to know what he was going to do when he found her and had made it his life mission to do so.

"Okay, let's go through what she said again. She had to have given some kind of clue as to what her job was," Carl said.

"You mean, other than the part about working at Saks."

"Yeah, I went by there today. That's definitely out. She doesn't work there."

"What are you looking for?"

"Okay, you said the way she enticed you, lured you on, she knew what she was doing."

"Yeah, she definitely knew how to get a guy's attention and keep it."

"Yeah, I noticed that too. And the way she looked kind of helped."

"Yeah."

"Okay, but you think she wasn't a prostitute?"

"No, maybe she was, but it didn't seem like that. I mean, when we did it, that was the realest part of the night."

"By 'did it,' you mean fucking."

"Yeah."

"By the way, I still don't believe the part about her calling you master and all that. I think you dreamed that part."

"Whatever."

"All right, so when she was leading you on, it seemed like she might be acting?"

"Yeah, sort of."

"But when she was doing it …"

"By that, you mean fucking."

"Yeah, when she was fucking you, no more acting."

"Exactly."

"I got it."

"You do?"

"Yeah. You know who's good at enticing guys, at leading them on, but who never has to follow through?"

"Most of the women I've met in my life?"

"No, well, maybe that too, but no. Strippers."

"Strippers?"

"Yeah, they get you all hot and bothered so you keep giving 'em money. So they know all the moves to lure you on. But then they get to walk away, so they don't have to know how to act when they're actually having sex.

"You saying strippers don't ever have sex?"

"No, I'm just saying that's not part of the gig. When they're having sex, they can just be themselves. They don't have to act."

"Okay, maybe. So the sex was real, you think?"

"Maybe, yeah, I think so."

"I remember now, I did say something about her name being like a stripper's."

"Yeah, what did she say to that?"

"She acted surprised, maybe a little offended."

"But not really, no?"

"No, not at all."

"So she's a stripper. Well, you and I are just going to have to go to every strip joint in this city until we find her."

"Okay, but I'm not really agreeing to go with you because I think she's a stripper."

"But you'll help me with the, um, investigation?"

"Yeah, but not 'cause I want to," he said smiling.

Louie opened the door and called them into his office. He had a shit-eating grin on his face.

Louie: Hey, guys.

Carl: What are you so happy about?

Louie: Tell you in a minute. I got somebody on the speaker phone.
   Say hi, guys.

(*Dan and Carl looked at other, shrugged, and said hi to the unknown person.*)

UNKNOWN PERSON: Hi, fellas. How ya doin'? Louie told you anything yet?

CARL: No, we don't even know who you are.

UNKNOWN PERSON, *laughing*: That fat bastard. He's a riot. You don't recognize my voice.

DAN: No, I'm sorry. You seem to be English, but other than that ...

UNKNOWN PERSON: Welsh, actually.

CARL: Welsh? You don't sound like Catherine Zeta-Jones.

NOT CATHERINE ZETA-JONES: I'm not, but you're warm.

CARL, *to Dan*: You know anybody else from Wales?

DAN: Tom Jones?

TOM JONES: You got it. Not really any relation to Catherine, although I wouldn't mind, if you know what I mean.

CARL: Get out of here. You're Tom Jones? Really?

TOM: In the flesh. Well, not really in the flesh, since I'm not there with you. But I'm out here in Vegas in nothing but my boxers.

CARL: Thanks for sharing that with us, Mr. Jones.

TOM: Call me Tom. And you're Carl and Dan, right?

CARL AND DAN: Yes, sir.

TOM: Can I ask 'em now, Louie?

LOUIE: Let me do it.

TOM: Okay.

LOUIE: Tom's not just out in Vegas in his boxers on vacation. He's working at the MGM Grand. And his opening act had to cancel for the day before Christmas and the day after Christmas. There's no show on Christmas day. Guess who he wants to be his opening act?

CARL: If it's not us, this is like the meanest practical joke ever.

TOM: It is you, guys. Just wondering if you boys would do me a favor on such late notice and be my opening act for a few days?

CARL: Are you kidding me? Would we be the opening act for Tom Jones at the MGM-fuckin Grand?

DAN: What he means to say is, "Yes, sir!"

(*Dan and Carl give each other high fives. Louie is grinning from ear to ear.*)

TOM: So that sounds like a yes, eh, mates?

CARL: You bet, Mr. Jo ... I mean, Tom.

DAN: It would be an honor, sir.

TOM: Louie tells me you boys are funny. Do you think you can put together some really good stuff for Vegas? You ever worked Vegas?

CARL: No, the furthest west we've been is Austin.

TOM: Okay, well, it's not really the same, though, is it?

DAN: No, I imagine not. We've been to Vegas, but just for fun.

TOM: I hope you'll have fun this time too. I'm having a blast. But don't forget it's the work you're here for. And Vegas crowds are different than anywhere else.

CARL: Yes, sir. I'm sure they are. How so?

TOM: There's a lot of drinking out here, which that part's usually good for me, but not always so good for comedians. You got to be tough.

DAN: We will be, sir.

TOM: Okay, we're going to have get rid of that "sir" jazz. You're making me feel old.

CARL: Sorry, Tommy boy.

TOM: Okay, now you went too far. And the other thing with the people here is, about 70 percent of them have lost money, so they need something to take their minds off that.

DAN: We won't disappoint you. Uh, Tom, can I ask you whose place we're taking?

TOM: Yeah, kind of an odd chap named Peter Piper. He's supposed to be the next Carrot Top. You heard of him?

(*Carl and Dan look surprised and somewhat displeased.*)

CARL: No, I was kind of hoping there wouldn't be a next Carrot Top.

DAN: We don't have to do his kind of act, do we? I mean, we will if you want, but we don't really have props and stuff.

CARL: But we'll get some if we need to.

Tom: God, no. I was hoping you boys would actually be funny. I don't get the guy at all. He doesn't do anything for me, but the audiences here seem to like him.

Dan: Yes, well, I'm sure he's great.

Tom: Okay, it's me you got to suck up to, not him.

Carl: Yeah, Tom. You're the best. I was just thinking the other day how it's been forever since I heard "Delilah."

Tom: God, don't get carried away. I was just kidding, you already got the gig, you don't need to suck up. Which one are you?

Carl: I'm Carl.

Tom: Dan, don't you like any of my songs?

Dan: I've always been partial to "What's New, Pussycat?"

Tom: Jesus, I thought you guys were young. I have done some newer stuff than the early '70s.

Louie: I'll let 'em borrow my CDs. They'll know all your songs by the time they get out there.

Tom: Borrow, hell. Make 'em buy the bloody things. I might as well make some money out of the deal.

Carl: Yes, sir, I'll buy 'em all tomorrow.

Tom: You're sucking up again, Carl.

Carl: Yes, sir, I am.

Tom: Well, at least you're open about it. Okay, why don't you mates come out a few days before the twenty-third. Get a feel for the place, have some fun, get loosened up. Sound good?

Carl: Yes, sir, we'll be there.

Dan: Uh, Tom, there is one thing … (*He whispers to Louie to ask if Tom knows about the trial.*)

Tom: Yeah, I know all about you testifying against Jamieson.

Dan: And you're okay with that.

Tom: Hell, yeah. I don't care what that bastard does. He never did anything for me. I hope you testify and they put him away. Louie told me about him trying to ruin your career. You know what I say.

Dan: What?

Tom: Fuck him.

Louie: Fuckin' a, bubba.

TOM: Fat Louie's done more for me than that Jamieson son of a bitch ever did anyway.

DAN: Well, I'm not sure when I'll have to testify, but I'll be out there somehow, someway.

CARL: And I'll get out there tomorrow if Louie will let me.

TOM: Okay, but I understand you're a comedy team, so I'll need the both of you, right?

DAN: Yes, sir. We'll be there. Don't worry about that.

TOM: And you'll be funny too.

DAN: I'll start working on some Vegas stuff right now.

TOM: Good deal. Well, I'll chat with you boys some more later, but I guess that's it for now.

CARL: Okay, Tom, can I ask you one thing before you go?

TOM: Sure.

CARL: Do the women in the audience still go crazy and you know throw their … uh

TOM: Panties onstage? You bet. I can't explain why, but I don't even care why any more. I always say don't look a gift panty in the crotch, if you know what I mean.

CARL: Pretty good one, sir.

TOM: Sucking up again?

CARL: Yes, sir.

TOM: All right, well, save some of that for when you're out here.

CARL: We will.

DAN: See you when we get out there.

TOM: Righto, then. Later.

(*After he hung up, Dan and Carl looked at Louie, who was again grinning from ear to ear. The three of them exchanged high fives like kids at a basketball game. They all knew high fives weren't cool anymore, and they all didn't care.*)

CARL: Vegas, baby!

DAN: Yeah! (*To Louie.*) I never even knew you knew Tom Jones.

LOUIE: Yeah, I ain't a big name-dropper. We met a long time ago. I did him a favor one time.

CARL: Really, what?

LOUIE: There was a girl he was kind of involved with a long time ago. She thought she wanted to be a singer. Her asked me to let her sing here. I did.

DAN: And was she good?

LOUIE: Terrible. But he already knew that. But he couldn't tell her that. He wanted her to see what it was like in front of an audience. She was a looker though.

DAN: So it kind of worked out.

LOUIE: Yeah, for him. Not so much for her. But she quit bugging him about a chance to show what she could do.

DAN: So he really doesn't know anything about us. He's just doing this for you. We owe you, big guy.

LOUIE: Hey, I wouldn't have done it if I didn't believe in you guys. So go out there and make me proud.

CARL: Vegas, baby, here we come.

Chapter 17

While Dan and Carl were getting their good news, Sam Barker was working. He had gone back to the apartment building where Shyanne had supposedly lived. He was already regretting making the little speech to his boss about owing Dan something. This door-to-door detective work was always necessary but rarely productive and never fun. Plus, his wife didn't understand why he had to spend Saturday and Sunday afternoons working on a case he wasn't officially working on.

But Sam was the kind of guy who believed his word was bond, so he would do this because he said he would. It was that simple. There were forty-seven apartments in this building, and he had managed to talk to people in twenty-three of them over the last few days. Not bad, almost half. Of course, he had not found any of those twenty-three who had seen anything. He had found three people who might have heard gunshots, but they had reacted the same as Rachel. Since this was New York, they hadn't done anything to find out why there was shooting. Today he hoped to find another ten to fifteen home and then come back one night and catch the others at home. In any building this size, there were almost always two or three who you just never found. Either they were always gone, had moved without telling anybody, or just wouldn't answer the door.

He got people to answer at eight apartments on the second, third, and fourth floors whom he had not talked to yesterday. Still no luck. Now he went back to the first floor, the floor he thought had the most chance of finding somebody who had seen or heard something. It was just a fact that people who lived on the first floor were more likely to get out of their apartments than those on higher floors.

He went by number 107 for the fourth time. Each time he had heard the TV going when he walked by, but when he would knock, the TV would get turned down and no answer. He was getting annoyed by it. How stupid was the guy in there, or how stupid did he think he was? Once again, he could hear the TV as he knocked, this time even louder. Again, the TV went silent and no answer. Okay, now he was pissed off.

Looking at his printout of the names which went with each apartment, he saw the name Fetters, Frank.

"Mr. Fetters!" he yelled. "This is Detective Barker. I know you're in there. If you're smoking something in there, I don't care. I just need to ask you some questions about something. You're not in any trouble."

He waited. Still no answer. He decided to play his trump card.

"Of course, if you continue to ignore me, you can be charged with hindering an investigation. I don't want to do that, but I will."

It wasn't true, of course, but most people didn't know that. His word was still bond, but there were occasions when stretching the truth was needed for this job. Besides, telling a small lie to get at the larger truth was all right under Barker's moral code. After another thirty seconds or so, the door slowly opened, and he was looking at an odd-looking, short sixty-year-old white man with darting eyes and one of those ridiculous comb-overs which only accentuated the loss of hair. What a troubled life this man named Frank Fetters must have had.

"I ain't doin' no drugs. Who told you anything about drugs? I never done 'em."

"I'm not accusing you of anything, Mr. Fetters. I'm just saying I don't care about that right now. I need to ask you some questions about if you saw or heard anything a couple of nights ago. Thursday night—did you happen to see anything unusual?"

"Maybe—what did you have in mind?"

Sam wasn't going to fall for that one. He knew with guys like this, if he told him what he was looking for, Fetters might agree that he saw it just for attention.

"No, just tell me. Anything odd happen that night?"

"Well, this is New York. Odd is kind of normal, you know?"

"Yeah," Sam said, eyeing Fetters as exhibit A.

"But there was something that did happen that night. I was going outside to walk my dog pretty late …" Sam didn't see any evidence of a dog being close by or hear one barking, but he didn't interrupt. "Now you're gonna think I was drunk or high or somethin', but I looked outside my window to make sure no one was out there in the alley, and there were these clowns that seemed to be harassing this guy. Then one of the clowns threw the guy down, something happened from upstairs to distract the clowns, and the guy ran into the building while they shot at him."

As soon as Sam heard the word "clowns," he was immediately elated and relieved. He thought this Fetters guy is probably crazy, but what were the chances he would make up a story about clowns? That son of a gun Darwin had been telling the truth after all. He had wanted to believe him, but it was one of those stories that was hard to swallow. And it verified his assessment of Darwin that he was just a good guy trying to help. He had a good instinct about people, and he didn't like to be wrong.

"When they were shooting, did they seem to hit the guy?"

"No, but this guy that was coming out of the building seemed to get hit."

"Can you describe what the guy coming out of the building looked like?"

"Well, this is the part where you're gonna really think I was drunk, but he looked like Abe Lincoln."

Bingo, Sam thought to himself. "So this Abe Lincoln guy, you say he seemed to get hit. You not sure?"

"You see, it seemed like he was, he fell over and everything. But as soon as the other guy ran in the building, the Abe Lincoln guy got up and seemed to be just fine. In fact, he was talking and laughing with the clowns."

Wow, Barker thought, *not only confirmation of Dan's story, but additional information.* He now knew Abe Lincoln was part of the setup.

"Did you happen to call the police and tell them about this?"

Fetters looked uneasy. "Nah, I was going to, but when I saw nobody really got hurt, I thought what the hell, the cops ain't gonna believe me anyway. If I'd thought somebody was really hurt, I would have called 'em."

"Of course you would have," Sam said, thinking there was no way he would have called the police unless there were UFOs involved or he wanted to complain about his neighbors. "So did you see anything else? Did the clowns appear to be chasing the guy they were harassing?"

"No, they just talked and laughed some, got in this big limo, and drove away. Didn't appear like they was in no hurry."

"So what did you do after they left?"

"Nothin'. Just went back to bed."

"After you walked the dog."

"Walked the dog? Oh yeah, after that."

Sam still hadn't noticed any signs of a dog, but he decided not to press the point. Fetters probably thought he had a dog.

"Okay, thank you, sir. Here's my card in case you remember anything else."

Fetters took the card but didn't look like he would be calling anytime soon.

"Hey, Detective. What's this all about?"

"I'm not really able to share that information with you right now. But you'll be around if I need to get ahold of you again?"

"As far as I know. No big trips planned."

Sam was pretty sure that last part was true. Fetters was the type that seemed like he hadn't ever been west of the Hudson. Well, he wasn't the most credible person he had ever interviewed, and he definitely wouldn't make the best witness at a trial, but at least this hadn't been a wasted day of work. He had found somebody else who had seen six clowns and Abe Lincoln. And how often did that happen? He looked forward to calling Dan and telling him he could sleep a little easier now. And he looked forward to telling his wife that sometimes these Sunday afternoon hours paid off.

Chapter 18

It was Monday morning, December 6, the day the trial of Hilton J. Jamieson really got started. The selection of the jurors had already taken place, which was a crucial part of the trial, but only interesting if you're reading a John Grisham novel, which this isn't.

Jamieson had a whole pack of lawyers on his payroll, but for this important life-and-death assignment, he had gone outside his legal family to find someone to defend him. He had selected Rita Dawes, a prominent defense attorney, who had handled other celebrity defendants. And the fact she was a woman hadn't been a minor factor for Jamieson. After all, he was accused of killing a woman he had been having an affair with, so it would look better to the jury to have a woman defending him. And he didn't mind at all that Rita was easy on the eyes. Maybe after this was over, a little roll in the hay might be possible.

The district attorney's office chose Lana Stevens, not because she was a woman, but because she was the best person for this job, kind of a novel approach for a governmental entity. Stevens was still young and aggressive, but no rookie. She had already been involved in a couple of high-profile cases and won.

The judge in the case was the Honorable Henry Davenport, although it had been a number of years since he had been concerned about being honorable. Not that he had done anything dishonorable; he just didn't worry about anything anymore. He had always been a kind of no-nonsense kind of judge, but after thirty-four years on the bench and in his last year before retirement, he just didn't give a damn. He was going to run his courtroom the way he wanted to, and if somebody didn't like it, let them appeal. That's what the appeals courts were for. Many people thought a high-profile case like this would last months, but Davenport knew that wasn't happening in his courtroom. He was going to push this case through, and the lawyers would have to deal with it at his pace, not theirs.

Dan would have liked to have been there for the opening statements, but as a witness in the case, he was prohibited from being in court until he testified. The case was getting enough media coverage he would be able to follow it well enough without being there. But he would like to be there just to see if the actual trial would knock some of that cockiness out of Jamieson.

He would have been disappointed to see Jamieson saunter into the courtroom like he was about to announce the acquisition of a new business or the opening of a new movie. Dawes had warned him to be somber, but men like Jamieson had long since quit listening to others. Stevens was glad to see him looking arrogant and somewhat amused by the legal process. It was that arrogance she was counting on.

After Davenport ruled on a couple of preliminary motions, the jury was brought in, and Stevens began her opening statement.

"Ladies and gentlemen of the jury, I'm Lana Stevens, and I'm representing the people in this case. It is my job to present the state's evidence to you and let you make the decision on the guilt or innocence of the accused. Now, you come into this case with an open mind as you are supposed to, but I've got a bit of a head start on you. You see, I've already seen all the evidence, so I know that Hilton Jamieson is guilty of murder, and it's my job to present to you what I know and convince you I'm right.

"I know you are somewhat familiar with Mr. Jamieson. He's wealthy, he's been on TV, he's a celebrity. Now, does that mean anything in this case? No, not a thing. In here, Mr. Jamieson is just another man, standing trial in front of his peers. It probably galls him to think of you people as his peers, but like it or not, he's in America, and in this country, even the rich and the powerful have to be held accountable for their actions.

"And that is your job. Hold him accountable, just like a common crook. But I intend to show his actions were much worse than a common thief and deserve much greater punishment.

"Now let me outline the facts in this case, the ones I will be proving during the trial. Mr. Jamieson is a rich man, a powerful man, and a smart man. But on one summer night, he was not as smart as he would like to think of himself. He had a problem with a young woman he was having an affair with.

"It seems he had tired of her, much like he must have tired of his first three wives and his current wife. But this young woman did not want to go quietly into the night. She wanted some money, some kind of compensation for the time and effort she put into what she believed to be a relationship and what Mr. Jamieson undoubtedly thought was just a good time for himself. Her name was Vickie Smithers, and I hope you will honor her memory by convicting her murderer.

"Because that is exactly what Hilton Jamieson did. He argued with her, fought with her, and when she fought back, he hit her. Why, because he is a man who always gets his way and thinks the normal rules and laws do not apply to him. With one hard blow by Mr. Jamieson, Vickie Smithers fell back and hit her head against a very expensive, very hard table. She died sometime that night, although when exactly, we do not know.

"And why is that? Because Jamieson realized he may have solved one problem, but created another with the body of a dead woman in his office. And if there was any doubt about it being an accident he didn't mean to happen, his actions right after he killed her answered that question. He had his henchmen, his yes-men, his minions, take the body of Vickie Smithers and dispose of it in a trash bin like some old shoes he had worn for a while but tired of.

"And his toadies also got rid of the table, cleaned the room with a fine-tooth comb, and got rid of all the evidence and blood. They even replaced the carpet. You see, the plan was, the police would find Ms. Smithers and no one would ever know how or why she was killed.

"But here's where Mr. Jamieson's plan went awry, where he wasn't quite as smart as he thought. He forgot he had an appointment with one Dan Darwin that fateful night of Vickie's death. And while Mr. Darwin waited for his appointment in an office nearby, he heard some yelling, then some fighting. He didn't know what was happening, so he went to find the source of the fighting.

"And that was when he saw Hilton J. Jamieson murder Vickie Smithers. And Mr. Jamieson made another mistake that night. So involved was he in his bloodthirsty ways he never even saw Mr. Darwin. Now, Mr. Darwin, deciding discretion was the better part of valor, decided to leave at that point. Only as he left, one of Mr. Jamieson's henchman—a Mr. Gibraldi—was coming from the other direction. So Mr. Darwin ducked into a hallway and hid, not knowing what would happen to someone who witnessed a murder.

"And while he was hiding, he heard the whole ensuing conversation that took place between Jamieson and his cohorts. He heard Jamieson direct his employees to take the body and get rid of it, he heard where they were going to take the body, he heard Jamieson direct the whole cover-up of the crime scene. And he will repeat the details of that whole chilling conversation for you when he testifies.

"Now, eventually the Jamieson gang scattered, and Mr. Darwin was able to make his escape. And being a good citizen, the first thing he did was go to the police. And sure enough, when the police got to the location where Mr. Darwin told them the body would be, there it was. Mr. Jamieson's arrest followed shortly thereafter. Ever since, he has refused to talk to the police, except to say he had no idea how Ms. Smithers wound up in a trash dumpster. But the police knew, and I know, and now you people know. And after you hear and see the evidence, it will be up to you to let the whole world know—Hilton J. Jamieson is not only rich, not only powerful, but also a cold-blooded murderer."

Dawes did not wait long to begin her opening defense statement because it was not good to let those last words linger with the jury.

"Hi, ladies and gentlemen, my name is Rita Dawes, and I'm representing Mr. Jamieson in this case. I want to go back to something Ms. Stevens referred to, the facts in this case. Now, she did relay a few facts to you. Yes, Mr. Jamieson is rich and powerful. Yes, he has been married several times, and yes, he was having an inappropriate relationship with the late Ms. Smithers. But that's where the facts end and the conjecture begins.

"Has Mr. Jamieson had a checkered past when it comes to relationships with women? Yes, we will concede that. But that's not a crime. Many of us have had problems from time to time in relationships. But there's a big difference between that and killing someone. And I intend to prove to you that Mr. Jamieson did not kill Ms. Smithers, although it is not up to me to prove anything. It is up to the DA's office to offer proof, and let's talk about facts again.

"The fact is all they have is one person who may or may not have seen something, may or may not have heard something the night Ms. Smithers died. Physical evidence, they have none. The reason Ms. Stevens made a point of talking about the cleaning of the room where the alleged murder took place is because they could find no blood at the so-called scene of the crime. They found some of Ms. Smithers's hair there, but since it was no secret she had been at Mr. Jamieson's office several times, this proves nothing. No blood, no signs of an altercation.

"So as this case progresses, keep asking yourself, where's the proof? What are the facts? And in the end, ask yourself, do you believe beyond a reasonable doubt that Hilton Jamieson had anything to do with this crime? And the answer will be no."

Chapter 19

That was the end of the opening statements, but the beginning of a whole new life for Dan. While the police had been unable to keep Jamieson from finding out who the star witness was, they had done a good job of keeping it out of the press. But as soon as his name was mentioned in court, TV stations and newspapers began searching for him. And it didn't take long for them to track him down.

Dan was at home working on their Vegas routine when the phone started to ring. The first two were newspaper reporters, but he let the machine pick up. The police had asked him to keep a low profile, so that was what he would try to do.

But when an enterprising TV crew found out his address and knocked on his door, he answered the door without thinking. There were the bright lights of the camera in his face, and a very attractive TV reporter with a microphone. She skipped the subtleties of "hello" and "my name is" and went right for a question.

"Mr. Darwin, how does it feel to be the lone witness in the murder trial of Hilton J. Jamieson?" she said, resorting to a trite question right out of the box.

Dan had been a newspaper reporter for seven years while in Little Rock, so he had some sympathy for the media, but he had never particularly liked TV reporters. Most of them not only couldn't scratch the surface of a story with a sledgehammer, they didn't even usually try. Dan shielded his eyes to block the lights and realized he looked like one of those celebrities on trial who tried to cover their faces.

"Hey, time-out! Turn off that damn camera. Introduce yourself, turn off the camera for a minute, ask me if I'll do an interview in a civil manner, and I promise I'll answer any question you want to ask."

The reporter made a motion to the cameraman to cut the camera, then introduced herself as if she was somebody important, shook Dan's hand, and asked him if he would consent to doing an interview. Dan shook her hand back, told her his name even though she obviously already knew him, and motioned to the cameraman to turn the camera back on.

"Okay, what did you want to ask me?"

"Will you consent to an interview? Perhaps inside your apartment? Can we come in?"

"Okay, that's actually three questions. But I'm going to give you a break. The answers are no, no, no," Dan said as he backed up. As he closed the door in their faces, he added, "I said I would answer any question. That was it. Sorry you didn't make your first question a better one."

The reporter knocked on the door several times, yelling something through the door, but Dan had already walked away and turned on some music to drown her out. Then the phone rang again. He hated not answering because of the slim chance it might be Shyanne, but he let the machine pick up. Probably just another reporter.

But when he heard Sam's voice, he picked up.

"Ah, so you are there," Sam's deep voice boomed. He chuckled. "How does it feel to be a star?"

"Not so good. I just closed the door on some good-looking woman who said she worked for channel 11. I don't think I'm prepared for this."

"But you want to be a star."

"As a comedian, not as a stool pigeon."

"Well, maybe this will be good practice for you. Maybe you can even get some comedy club gigs out of this."

"Yeah, that's a thought. Anyway, did you just call to rub it in, or did you have something to tell me about the case?"

"Well, both. I've actually got a couple of things to tell you. I found a guy beside you who saw the clowns and Abe Lincoln too."

"Really? Great. Who is he?"

"Well, that's kind of the bad news part. His name is Frank Fetters and ..."

"Frank Fetters?"

"Yeah, that's his name. He lives on the first floor of the apartment building. Unfortunately, his name fits him. He's kind of a nutcase."

"Oh great, just what I need. One nutcase backing up the story of another. So was he just agreeing he saw it 'cause he's crazy?"

"No, that's the good part. I just asked him if he saw anything, and he provided all the details. The guy actually saw what you did, or at least enough to corroborate your story. The only drawback is ..."

"He's a nut."

"Yeah, there is that. He won't be a good witness, but I thought it might make you feel better just knowing someone else saw it."

"I guess so, but I feel like one of those guys who sees a UFO and then sees some hillbilly living by a swamp in Louisiana who swears he saw a UFO. You don't know whether to feel better or worse."

"And one other thing. He said he saw the Abe Lincoln guy get up after you were inside the building. He was talking and laughing with the clowns. And the clowns seemed in no hurry to chase you."

"So they just wanted to scare me, not kill me?" Dan said.

"That's what I figure. I know you were scared, and I can't tell you what to do. But are you still going to testify?"

"Well, I told the clowns I wasn't at the time. But I'm kinda feeling now more like testifying than ever. I mean, anybody that would go to that much trouble to get to me, well, he should go to jail."

"Good for you. Just wanted to make sure that I wasn't wasting my time out there."

"No, sir. What's our next move?"

"Your next move is to watch your ass. My next move is to try to find this Shyanne girl. The best lead is probably through this Rachel. If I can tie her to Shyanne and then get her to testify, we can add a witness intimidation charge on Jamieson."

"Yeah, on that front, Sam, my brother is pretty convinced she's a stripper."

"Really, based on what?"

"Her ability to lure me on, reel me in …"

"You're sounding like a fish in this scenario."

"Funny, I'm feeling more like a pigeon."

"So he figures a stripper would be good at that sort of thing?"

"Yeah. What do you think?"

"Could be. I'll look into it."

"Carl wants us to search all the strip clubs in the New York area for her."

"Well, I certainly can't stop you from such an admirable pursuit as that. But you probably should leave that to a professional."

"Someone like, say, you?"

"Exactly."

"Okay, have fun."

"Yeah, I may need your brother to explain this logic to my wife. It's not going to be easy making her understand being out every night watching strippers."

"Still, a better gig than talking to Frank Fetters."

"Yeah."

"Good luck with your wife. And let me know if you need me to come to any of the strip joints to identify Shyanne. I'll be happy to help."

"Knew I could count on you. Talk to you later."

Chapter 20

Dan had gone by a cell phone place and gotten a new one, but before he could call Carl to tell him Sam didn't want them playing detective in strip joints, he got a call from Simone, asking him to come by. She didn't say why, but he was always glad when she did. And he hadn't had a chance to even tell her about the Vegas gig yet. He hoped there wasn't anything wrong.

When he got to Simone's, he found Mattie was there, which no longer disappointed him like it once did. He still liked the one-on-one talks with Simone, but he enjoyed his little verbal jousts with Mattie. Simone had decided not to tell Mattie about her one-night stand, so he had to make sure not to kid her about the goofy-looking guy while Mattie was around.

SIMONE: Hey, 'migo, come on in, we've been reading and hearing about you. Can I still call you 'migo when you're famous?

DAN, *feigning a British accent*: But of course, my dear, I might not answer, but you can still call.

SIMONE: And you're gonna talk with what sounds something like an English accent when you're famous?

DAN: Quite.

SIMONE: Okay, can you stop now, since you're not actually famous yet?

DAN: Ah, you didn't like my accent.

SIMONE: No, it was great, but I'll like it better later.

DAN: When I'm actually famous.

SIMONE: Yeah, something to look forward to.

DAN: You got some news for me?

SIMONE: Yeah.

DAN: Good. I've got some news too.

MATTIE: Ours first.

DAN: Oh, is it an ours? You two kids getting married or something?

MATTIE: No, it's really Simone's news. I'm just saying ours 'cause I love her so, and what happens to her happens to me.

DAN: Well, I love her too.

SIMONE: It's not a contest.

MATTIE: Not a close one anyway.

DAN: Hey …

SIMONE: Guys, can I tell it now?

MATTIE: Okay, go ahead.

SIMONE, *to Dan*: Remember when we first met?

DAN: Of course.

SIMONE: And you remember how you helped me out, reading that first poem for me?

DAN: Sure.

SIMONE: And how you encouraged me to keep writing poems, even though I'm not sure you really understood or liked them all the time.

DAN: Yeah, I'm sounding kind of like a loyal dog at this point, but I was a fish and a pigeon earlier, so maybe that's a step up. Where are we going with this?

SIMONE: And you remember how when I wanted to give up you said something about when you quit living your dream, you have trouble sleeping.

DAN: Wow, for a person who writes, you really butchered that one up.

SIMONE: All right, what was it you said?

DAN: What I said was, "When your dreams start to fade away, you no longer even think about them, and then when you go to sleep, all you have left is sleep without dreams."

SIMONE: Okay, well, I didn't understand the last part, but I think I got the gist of it.

DAN: No, the last part was the gist. You missed the gist of it. The point was …

MATTIE, *interrupting*: Her poems are getting published in a book!

SIMONE: Mattie!

MATTIE: Well, you guys were taking too long.

DAN, *getting up to hug Simone*: Really? (*She nodded, smiling.*) That's great, 'miga. I'm so proud of you. Who's publishing it?

SIMONE: Oh, it's just a small company. They're publishing a book of poems by unknown female poets. And I qualify.

DAN: Well, at least until you're published. Can I still call you 'miga when you're famous.

SIMONE, *in a British accent*: But of course. Tell me why we have to talk with English accents when we're famous.

DAN: Not really sure.

SIMONE: Anyway, the company's having a big party next week with all the poetesses there.

DAN: I'm not sure that's a word, but great. Is it like a book-signing party? No, they couldn't already have it in print.

SIMONE: No, no. Just kind of a little celebration for all of us by the publishers. And we can invite a few friends.

DAN: If I'm not one of them, this is kind of a mean way to tell me.

SIMONE: 'Migo, of course you're invited. You're a best amigo.

DAN: I don't think you can be *a* best, I think it would have to be *the* best.

SIMONE: Why do you always have to correct me?

MATTIE: Yeah, who's the published author here?

DAN: That would be Ms. Simone Carlino, I believe, published poetess. (*He and Mattie applauded.*)

SIMONE, *bowing*: Thank you very much.

DAN: That's the best news I've heard, maybe ever. I'm so happy for you, 'miga (*they hugged again*).

MATTIE: Okay, that's enough hugging, you two. (*Simone went to hug her and gave her a kiss.*)

DAN: Okay, that's enough kissing, you two.

MATTIE: Oh, you'd love us to keep going.

DAN: That's true. I should correct what I said before though. It's the best news I've heard concerning somebody else.

SIMONE: Oh yeah, what about your news? You found Shyanne?

DAN: No.

MATTIE: Jamieson killed himself?

DAN: No, but nice thought.

SIMONE: You're going to be on Colbert?

DAN: No. Quit guessing.

SIMONE: Okay.

DAN: At least I don't have to worry about Mattie interrupting me to tell you. (*Mattie stuck her tongue out at him.*) Carl and I got called in by Louie, who had some news for us. He had somebody on his speaker phone who wanted to offer us a job. You'll never guess who ...

MATTIE, *smiling devilishly*: Tom Jones!

DAN, *looking astonished*: How could you guess that? Nobody would guess Tom Jones.

MATTIE: I ran into Carl. He told me.

DAN: That bastard. So you both already know.

SIMONE: Not me.

MATTIE: He told me not to tell Simone or you'd be mad. So I didn't.

DAN, *sheepishly*: Okay, thanks.

SIMONE: I thought we didn't keep secrets from each other.

MATTIE: Well, sometimes it's okay, isn't it?

SIMONE: Yeah, I guess. All right. (*Dan looked at Simone, wondering if she was thinking about the same secret he was. Probably so.*) All right, that's great news. And who is Tom Jones?

DAN: Man, they just didn't brief you on anything before you came here. He was a really hot singer in his day. Women went crazy over him. And he's apparently still drawing 'em in at Vegas. He wants us to be his opening act at the MGM Grand.

SIMONE: That's great. How does he know about you?

DAN: 'Cause of Louie. In the old days, Louie apparently did Tom a favor.

MATTIE: That is great, Dan. I didn't know Tom Jones was still working, or even still alive, for that matter, but that's great.

DAN: Of course he's still working. And not only that, it's in Las Vegas, Nevada—the city of lights.

MATTIE: I think that's actually Paris, but anyway ...

DAN: Why are you here again?

MATTIE: I'm Simone's red-hot lover girl, and we live here together in sin.

(*That was one of the things Dan liked about Mattie. She could give as good as she got. He never had to take it easy with her.*)

DAN: You must be good in bed for her to put up with that mouth of yours.

MATTIE: The two are not mutually exclusive.

SIMONE: Okay, guys, enough. When is this happening? Is the money good?

DAN: Yeah, it is, a couple of days before Christmas. And I want both of you to fly out there—on me. Well, not literally on me. But on a plane—my treat.

MATTIE: I don't know, Christmas in Vegas?

DAN: Or you know, if Mattie can't make it, you can come out without her, 'miga.

MATTIE: Hey, don't cut me out so quick.

SIMONE: I'd like to, 'migo, but what about our families and Christmas and all?

DAN: Ah, see 'em before or after. You got to be there, 'miga. This could be it.

SIMONE: The big break?

DAN: Yeah.

SIMONE: All right, we'll see what we can work out.

DAN: And Mattie?

MATTIE: Yeah, my family doesn't like me all that much anyway.

DAN: I didn't know that, Mattie. Why?

MATTIE: Something about being gay or something. My mom's gotten to where she almost accepts it. But my dad, never.

DAN: Really? In this day and age? Man, if I was a dad, I think I'd prefer my daughter to be gay, so I wouldn't have to deal with all those loser guys who just want to go out with my daughter to have sex.

SIMONE: That might be all her girlfriends wanted too.

DAN: Yeah, maybe. But somehow you expect more out of women. It's more about the romance than just the sex.

SIMONE: Yeah, that's true. We are better.

DAN: Hey, can I ask y'all a question about lesbians and sex?

MATTIE: As we've told you before, no, you can't watch, and no, we're not videotaping it for you to watch.

DAN: No, not about y'all—bout lesbians in general, and not about sex so much as sexual attraction.

MATTIE: Well, we're not really spokeswomen for lesbians, but yeah, go ahead.

DAN: Okay, now don't take this the wrong way …

SIMONE: Oh lord, this isn't going to be good.

DAN: No, I just noticed that when you see a lot of the women who are out and proud to be lesbians, the ones who marched and picketed at the Supreme Court and like that … well, they look for the most part, kind of, uh, butch.

MATTIE: Here comes the stereotypes.

DAN: No, no, I'm saying that's not all gay women, but the prominent ones that you see, they seem to go out of their way to, well, not look feminine.

MATTIE: So some lesbians don't look the way you'd like them to. What's your point?

DAN: No, it's not that it's not the way I'd like them to look. And that's my point. If a woman is gay, she's not attracted to men, right?

MATTIE: No, duh.

DAN: So why would a woman who wants to appeal to other women try to look like a man, whom they're not attracted to?

MATTIE: You see the same thing with gay guys. A lot of them, and I mean a lot, do their best to look like women.

SIMONE: Some of them look pretty damn good as women.

DAN: Yeah, it's the same thing. The same question. Why do they do that?

SIMONE: Do you think we do that? Try to look like guys?

DAN: No, y'all don't. You're not lipstick lesbians or anything, but y'all just look like fairly normal women.

MATTIE, *sarcastically*: Thanks.

DAN: I meant that as a compliment.

MATTIE: Good one. Surprising you're single.

DAN: So what's the answer?

MATTIE: I don't know. I'll ask around at our next meeting.

DAN: What meeting?

MATTIE: Our next lesbian meeting. You have to go once a month, or they don't let you stay in the club.

DAN: Okay, that's good. Have fun at the straight guy's expense.

MATTIE: You should hear us at the meetings.

SIMONE: I have an idea, maybe an answer.

DAN: Okay, what?

SIMONE: It's not so much about appealing to other women, as being proud of who they are, or at least not ashamed, and by looking a certain way, they say to the world, "I'm gay, deal with it."

MATTIE: Ooh, good answer. My girlfriend, I think I'll keep her. (*Simone smiles.*)

DAN: Okay, that was a pretty good answer. Last lesbian question of the evening, I promise.

MATTIE: Good.

DAN: Okay, one more. What time is the next meeting?

Chapter 21

Dan had called Carl when he got home to tell him that Barker didn't really want their help in The Case of the Missing Stripper, but Carl was unfazed. He had simply asked Dan what their next move would be.

"I guess our next move is to get ready for Vegas and hope Barker comes up with something," Dan said.

"Yeah, yeah, sure," Carl said, as if dismissing a small child's idea. "I figure the best way to find Shyanne is to follow this Rachel chick wherever she goes."

"That was what Barker said, except for the stalking part."

"See, I could have been a detective."

"Well, maybe. But you don't even play one on TV right now."

"So are you gonna help me or not?"

"Help you stalk her? That would be a no."

Carl had hung up at that point, acting a little mad. But Dan knew that Carl wouldn't stay mad. It just wasn't in his DNA to stay mad. By five thirty the next afternoon, he called Dan again.

"Hey, bro. I followed that Rachel girl from her apartment, and she's at this little café called Juneau's. You know it?"

"No, you calling me so I can come bail you out when she calls the cops?"

"Call the cops? Nah, I need you to come down here to make sure it's her."

"So right now, you're just following some girl that looks like somebody named Rachel, who you've never seen before. It may just be a random girl wandering around the streets of New York unaware she's being stalked."

130

Again, Carl ignored the sarcasm. "No, I think it's her from your description. But I need you to come down here. It's about two blocks uptown from the apartment building. On Eighty-Third. She's ordered something to eat, but I don't know how long she'll be here. Can you hurry?"

"Yeah, okay. It'll seem less like you're a stalker if there's two of us there."

"Yeah, stalkers usually work alone."

"I'd ask you how you know that, but I don't want to know. I'll be down there as soon as I can."

It took Dan a few minutes to catch a cab at that time of day, but he made it to Juneau's before the girl had left. Dan couldn't say for sure it was her, because she had her hair pulled back and he had only seen her for a few minutes. But he thought it probably was.

They went ahead and ordered something, even though it looked like the girl that was probably Rachel was about through. It turned out Juneau's was not an Alaskan food place, as Dan and Carl had thought. They had speculated that maybe fried walrus and seal cutlets might be on the menu, as well as the obvious—baked Alaska. But it seemed to be just another of those high-priced fu-fu health-food sandwich places that served all its food on weird bread.

"So let's pretend that's her, for the sake of your budding criminal career. What are you gonna do now—follow her some more until she makes a break for it?"

"No, not right now at least. I had another idea while I was waiting for you."

"Oh lord, what?"

"Just stay here and watch me. And be ready if I need you."

"I'll just be here girding my loins."

"You're going to have to explain that one to me sometime."

Dan sat and watched as Carl got up and walked over to the girl that was probably Rachel's table. Fortunately, she was alone. Sometimes watching Carl in action was like watching a car wreck. You just couldn't look away. Juneau's was small enough Dan could hear what was said if Carl started up a conversation with Rachel, which he did.

When he passed by her, he stopped and came back to her table.

"Hey, you look familiar. You work at that place with Shyanne, don't you? It's Rachel, isn't it?"

She looked unsure, but he had definitely caught her off guard.

"Yes, it is. I'm sorry, I don't remember you. You a friend of Shyanne's?"

"Not really. I just know her from the club, more of a client, I guess you could call it. I forgot, what's that place called?"

At that point, Rachel grew wary. And then she looked around the restaurant and saw Dan staring right at her. He tried to look away, but it was too late. Busted. And she definitely seemed to remember Dan.

"I don't know what you're talking about," she said, somewhat angrily. "I don't know you, and I don't know anybody named Shyanne. Do I need to call the manager over here?"

"No, that won't be necessary," Carl said with the coolness of a con man. "My apologies. I thought you were somebody else. My mistake."

With that, Carl went back over to Dan and said in a low voice, "Let's get out of here."

Their weird-bread sandwiches hadn't arrived yet, but Dan didn't care. He and Carl left as quickly as possible without running.

When they got outside, Carl couldn't stop smiling.

"Did you hear that? She fell for it, hook, line, and sinker," Carl said.

"Yeah, I heard. So you established that was Rachel, and she does know Shyanne, probably works with her."

"So what's our next move?"

"Tell Detective Barker and let him handle it."

"Okay, we'll call that our backup plan."

"What's your idea?"

"We follow her, see where she works, see if Shyanne is there."

"Okay, but she knows what we look like now. So we're gonna need some disguises, a long-range infrared camera, and maybe some of those night-vision goggles."

"Really?"

"No! Of course not. We're comedians, not detectives. And definitely not stalkers."

"So you're not going to help?"

"I think the police call it aiding and abetting."

"All right then," Carl said, getting a determined look on his face. "You do what you gotta do, I'll do what I gotta do."

"I don't know what that means. But why do you care so much anyway? She was my once-in-a-lifetime, not yours."

"Because she set you up and you're my little brother. You don't hurt a Darwin and get away with it."

"You don't hurt a Darwin and get away with it? What kind of line is that?"

"Not a very good one, but it's all I could come up with."

"So I may not want to know this, but what are you gonna do if you do find Shyanne?"

"I don't know that. I'll figure that out when the time comes. But I do know that revenge is a dish best served cold."

"You've been watching some bad movies lately."

"I guess so."

Dan smiled at the intensity of his brother. *How could you not like this guy*, he thought. Then he turned mockingly serious himself. "You know what I think, big brother?"

"What?"

"I think if you do find Shyanne, she should be afraid."

"Very afraid."

Chapter 22

The trial was not going well for the good guys (in this case, the prosecution). But it was going extremely well for Jamieson. Thanks to his attorney, Rita Dawes, every piece of supposed evidence against Jamieson was challenged, and most of it was thrown out. The reason might have been technicalities, but it was evidence the jury never got to see or hear. As a result of Ms. Dawes's good work, it was looking more and more like it was coming down to Dan's testimony. It would be a matter of how well he held up in court under what promised to be a grueling cross-examination by Ms. Dawes. She had already made minced meat out of several prosecution witnesses, like the coroner and police officers, people who were used to testifying in court. What chance would a comedian have?

Dan was dreading his day or days in court even more than before. At the same time, he was anxious to get it over with. He was not wavering on testifying, however.

As he and Carl prepared to go onstage one week before their Las Vegas gig, Dan's mind was not as focused as it usually was. He had been working on their Las Vegas routine, even though Carl was ready to go out to Vegas and wing it. Imagine, Dan thought, having that much confidence. So as they entered that night at Hyena's, Dan had done no prepared stuff for the night. And if Carl was ready to wing it in Vegas, he had no hesitancy about doing the same at Hyena's, which was basically their home court. After Dan did a quick intro, Carl headed to the audience.

DAN: Wait a minute. Where are you going?
CARL: I'm going to talk to the audience. Aren't you coming?

DAN: No, you go ahead. I'll just stay here.

CARL: You're not still scared, are you?

DAN: Not scared. I just don't want to run into my ex-wife again.

CARL: Hey, one time she shows up to watch you work. It wasn't that bad, was it?

DAN: It wasn't good.

CARL: So you stuttered a little bit. It was kind of funny.

DAN: Yeah, like you were working with Mel Tillis.

CARL: Good reference, bro. You had to go back to the '80s for that one.

DAN: Well, anyway, I'm not taking any chances. You go ahead.

CARL: I'm already here. (*He stopped at a table where a couple was seated.*) (*Talking to the man.*) Hello, sir. Either of you ever been married to my brother there?

MAN: I'm pretty sure I hadn't been. Honey, what about you? (*She shook her head no.*)

CARL: See, no ex-wives here. What's your name?

MAN: Ed … Ed Franklin.

CARL: Okay, Ed-Ed Franklin (*saying the Ed-Ed as one name*). Kind of an unusual first name.

ED-ED: Actually, it's just Ed.

CARL: That's not funny though. Mind if I call you Ed-Ed?

ED-ED: Kinda.

CARL: Okay, Ed-Ed. What do you do?

ED-ED: For a living?

CARL: No, what do you do when you're riding in an elevator? Of course, what do you do for a living? Isn't that what that question always means?

ED-ED: I own a bait shop in New Jersey.

CARL: Well, this ought to be fun. (*To Dan.*) Feel free to jump in at some point.

DAN: This sounds about like the right time.

CARL: Yeah, just sit back and wait for the bait shop line.

DAN: Okay, I'll bite. What kind of bait do you sell, Ed-Ed?

CARL: Lured you into that one, didn't he?

ED-ED: Just your usual—worms, lures, any fishing-related items. And beer and cigarettes.

DAN: Yeah, those fish love cigarettes.

CARL: Yeah, the tobacco companies love to get 'em started young.

DAN: When they're still in schools?

CARL, *feigns rim shot*: Yeah.

CARL: So beer and cigarettes are fishing-related items?

ED-ED: You must never go fishing.

CARL: No, I live in New York. Not exactly a fisherman's paradise.

DAN: It's no Jersey.

ED-ED: Man, that's the truth.

CARL: You really have places to fish in Jersey?

ED-ED: Yeah, we got some great lakes.

CARL: I thought those were somewhere else. Like up in … uh, Dan?

DAN: Oh yeah, to the West and North, someplace else.

CARL: Thanks.

ED-ED: No, not *The* Great Lakes. Just some great fishing lakes.

CARL: And you have some beer-drinking, smoking fish in these lakes?

ED-ED: Yeah, don't ever order the trout at a New Jersey restaurant. (*The crowd laughed.*)

CARL: Don't try to be funnier than us, Ed-Ed.

ED-ED: I'm not trying. (*Another laugh from the crowd.*)

CARL: That's two, Ed-Ed.

ED-ED: What happens if I get to three?

CARL: Well, let me tell you a story. There's a farmer guy and a woman who get married.

ED-ED: Is she a farm woman?

CARL: No, just a regular woman. Maybe a farm woman. It doesn't matter, Ed-Ed. Anyway, they're riding in this wagon led by a mule.

DAN: Is it a farm mule?

CARL: Will y'all let me finish my joke?

DAN AND ED-ED: Sorry.

CARL: So after a little bit, the mule stops moving, and the woman wonders what her new husband is going to do. He just says, "That's one," and sits there patiently for several minutes until the mule decides to move on his own. The wife is thinking, "What a patient man I've married. I'm so lucky." Then after a while, the mule stops again. This time the man says, "That's two," and again just sits there patiently until the mule decides to start moving. Now the wife thinks she's married a saint or something because he's so calm and patient. Then the mule stops a third time, the man gets down off the wagon, takes his gun, and shoots the mule right between the eyes. The wife gets hysterical. She starts crying and yelling, "You idiot. How could you do that? How could you kill a poor, defenseless animal like that?" The man just looks at her and says, "That's one." (*Carl pauses.*) You get my point, Ed-Ed?

Ed-Ed was not nearly as funny after that, and it wasn't a particularly great night for the Darwin brothers. There were some laughs, but nothing ever clicked just right. Dan thought the farmer joke might have had a chilling effect on the audience. It was okay to be a little mean to the audience, but you didn't necessarily want to scare them. During their time onstage, Dan couldn't help but glance occasionally over at the place where Shyanne had been that night that seemed already like a couple of lifetimes ago. He saw a flash of blond hair at one point, but it was no Shyanne. Who was? He wondered how long it would be until that would leave his mind. Maybe never.

Then as they walked offstage and went back to the dressing room, his cell was ringing.

"Hey, Danny boy."

Oh my god, it was her. He started signaling to Carl that it was Shyanne and looking out at the audience to see if she was out there somewhere.

"Hey, is it really you?"

"Yeah, it's me. I understand you been looking for me."

"You surprised?"

"No."

"Listen, I don't know what happened or why, but I'm just glad to hear your voice."

Carl tried to take the phone from Dan so he could talk to her, but Dan kept moving away from him until he finally got to the dressing room and closed and locked the door.

"Sorry, had to keep the phone away from Carl. He wanted to talk to you. You all right?"

"Yeah, I'm fine. I just called to say don't bother looking for me. And don't bother Rachel anymore. Leave her out of this."

"Yeah, that was more Carl's work than mine. But I do know she knows you, now."

"Yeah, okay, tell Carl good work, Detective. But she doesn't know where I am. And I'm not going to tell you. I will tell you I'm not someplace where you're going to find me. So don't look for me. I have my reasons for being where I am."

"Shyanne, I think I know what they are."

"I doubt it, but even if you do, it doesn't matter. You have to just forget about me, for both our sakes. We had the night, that was it, it's over. Just forget about it. And me."

"That's the one thing you can't ask me to do."

"Why?"

"'Cause that was the greatest night of my life. And I will never forget you. Never want to."

"Oh, dammit, Danny boy. You do make this hard."

"I'm not trying to."

"Well, if you won't stop looking for me, at least be careful. There are some bad people out there. It might be dangerous for both of us if you find me."

"Okay."

"I thought you'd be mad at me."

"I was. I am. I don't know."

"But you're going to look for me anyway."

"Yeah."

"Well, you won't find me. So when I say this, I hope you know I mean it. Goodbye."

"See you later."

"No. Goodbye. I'm serious."

"Me too. See you later."

"One other thing, Danny, boy."

"Yeah?"

"They didn't hurt you, did they? Are you all right?"

"Yeah, I'm fine."

"Good, I'm glad of that. Goodbye."

"See you later."

With that, she hung up, and Dan had a brief sense he had won that little war of words, but then he realized if she never wanted to see him, there wasn't much chance he'd ever find her. New York was a pretty easy place to hide in, even if she was still there at all. But at least he knew she still cared something about him.

After hearing what had been said, Carl was mad at first that Dan had not been mean to her, but then his mood changed to one of anticipation. He was all eager to continue the hunt for Shyanne, saying they had "smoked her out" and they could do it again. He wanted to follow Rachel again, now that they knew she was a friend of Shyanne's. But Dan didn't know whether he wanted to search for her. Fate, or something or someone, had led the two of them together once. If it was meant to be, it would happen again.

Chapter 23

The next night was the poetry book gala. Dan was glad to go for Simone's sake, but he didn't really think a bunch of poetry-writing women was going to take his mind off Shyanne. He wondered if going to the old Playboy Mansion would. But if anything could, it would be seeing Simone happy at finally succeeding. Dan wanted to go even less. But he liked Simone because, well, everybody did.

Since Carl didn't think there was much chance of picking up any women there, he was taking his girlfriend, Andrea, with him. He had been dating her for about six months, a long time for him without proposing. She was a good deal younger than him, but a very good match for him. Dan wondered why Carl couldn't seem to be happy with one woman. He knew if he had Shyanne, he wouldn't be looking for anyone else. Hell, he didn't have her and he still wasn't looking for anyone else. He knew he should be mad at her after the phone call since it proved she was avoiding him of her own free will, but hearing her voice just brought back all the good feelings about her.

While Dan was getting ready, Carl called him to ask him what he was wearing.

"I was thinking my gray pants with the blue-striped shirt."

"Really?"

"I don't know. I don't care. What are we—women? I'm wearing whatever I'm wearing, and you wear whatever you're wearing."

"Yeah, you're right. Andrea's just gonna meet me there, so I couldn't ask her."

"Well, wing it."

140

"Gotcha. See you there, bro."

Simone and Mattie were already there when Dan arrived, along with a fairly sizable crowd, although the gala was at one of those New York City restaurant/bars that were so small any crowd looked big. The restaurant—Cassie's—had been rented out for the evening by the publishers of the poetry book. It seems the publishing of the book was being fronted by an investor, although Simone told Dan she didn't know who it was.

And the party was as much for the investor as it was for the poetry writers. Dan figured the investor was probably a woman because he couldn't really see a guy investing in a book of poetry by women. But this was New York, and stranger things had happened here. Since Carl wasn't there yet, Simone and Mattie were the only faces he knew, and he went over to them.

"Hey, girls," Dan said, knowing Mattie didn't really like it when he called them girls. He hugged Simone and smiled at Mattie, who stuck her tongue out at him. "Congratulations, author."

"Hey, 'migo," Simone said. "Glad to see you here, I was beginning to wonder."

"Wouldn't miss it for the world," Dan said. "Is the investor woman here yet?"

"No, but we heard it was a man," Simone said.

"Really?"

"Why so surprised?" Mattie said. "Can't believe any man would want to further the careers of women just for the benefit of doing something good?"

"Not unless his name is Jesus, no."

"My night, guys," Simone said. "Be nice."

Both Dan and Mattie said "Okay" like two children being scolded. At that moment, a woman from the publishing company knocked on a table or something to get everybody's attention.

"It is my pleasure at this time to introduce the man who is going to make this book possible, someone who everybody already knows as a benefactor of the arts, but who will now be known as a benefactor of women in general and of our ten poets as well. Please give a warm welcome to Hilton J. Jamieson."

As Jamieson strutted in, impeccably dressed as always to a warm round of applause, Dan's heart fell to his knees. No, it couldn't possibly be what he was thinking. Maybe this was just the worst coincidence in the world. But no, life didn't work that way. Jamieson had tried everything else to intimidate him into not testifying. Now he was going to hit him in his most vulnerable place—his love for Simone, a person he would never allow anyone or anything to hurt.

Simone looked as surprised as Dan did, but by the look on her face, he knew the fear that had occurred to him had not hit her yet. How could it? She didn't have a manipulative bone in her body. She looked at Dan, though, and knew something was terribly wrong. Something besides the fact that his archenemy was there and being welcomed as a hero by a group of people who didn't know Dan or his involvement with Jamieson. Dan's face and name had been in the news, but he was hardly a household name. And the way the trial had been going, it didn't look like Jamieson was going to be convicted.

"I'm sorry," Simone said quickly and quietly to Dan. "You want to slip out back before he sees you."

"No, I'm fine," Dan said, although he was anything but.

He had never actually wanted to kill somebody before, but at that moment he knew he could have. But no, he wasn't about to leave. Not until he found out for sure what he knew was the truth. This bastard had crossed the line of human decency now. In a matter of seconds, Dan had already decided he wasn't going to testify if it meant Simone's poetry wouldn't get published, but he wasn't going to leave there without at least telling Jamieson what he thought. Now that he wasn't going to testify, it took the handcuffs off.

Mattie also saw the look of hatred in Dan's eyes. Not as naive as Simone in the ways of the dark side of man, she knew what Dan was thinking. She still hoped he was wrong, but she realized the possibility was there, and she was afraid her girlfriend was going to get hurt out of this.

"Dan," Mattie said, whispering, "maybe it's not what you think. Don't say anything."

"I'm not saying anything. Not yet."

Jamieson had begun to talk about how he had always supported the arts and creative people and he could think of no better group of people to support than this fine group of women poets. Dan's focus on the words wasn't there, but he heard enough to know it was all BS. Jamieson had about as much concern for women poets as a logger had for trees. Okay, there was a better analogy there, but Dan's mind was thinking about what he was going to say and do to Jamieson. He noticed lurking right behind Jamieson was a really large guy who appeared to be armed as well. Obviously some sort of bodyguard or personal security guard or something.

Wait a minute, Dan thought, there was something about the big guy which looked vaguely familiar. Something about the way he just hulked over everybody. Then it hit him. It was the big clown who had picked him up and threw him into the snow. Of course, he couldn't prove it in court, but that was proof enough to him that Jamieson had arranged the whole thing with Shyanne.

After Jamieson got through with his load of crock, he started milling around in the crowd and shaking hands. Simone turned to Dan.

"You still have that look on your face," she said. "I guess I've got to stay, but you sure you don't want to leave?"

"No, I think he and I need to have a little talk first."

"You don't really think that's why he did this?" Mattie asked Dan.

"I don't want to, but I'm afraid that's exactly what I think," he said.

"What are you two talking about?" Simone said. "What did I miss?"

"Dan thinks Jamieson put the money up for this book so Dan would have to choose between you and testifying," Mattie said.

"No, he wouldn't do that," Simone said. "He couldn't, could he?"

"That's exactly what I'm thinking," Dan said. "You think it could just be a coincidence that the man who is financing your book is the same guy as the one who wants me to keep my mouth shut and has shown he will go to great lengths to get that done?"

"But how would he even know about me—know that we're friends?" Simone asked, still incredulous over the possibility that had hit Dan within three seconds of seeing Jamieson here.

"The guy has unlimited money and resources. He probably knows everything about me," Dan said.

"Okay," Mattie said. "The thought occurred to me too, but we don't know it to be a fact. It could be a coincidence. Don't go off half-cocked."

"No, I'm going to be fully cocked before I do anything."

"Is that one of your penis jokes?" Mattie asked. "I don't think this is the time."

"No, that wasn't a penis joke. Well, maybe it was a little bit."

As Dan still tried to determine what he was going to do, he noticed Carl making his entrance. He hadn't heard the intro to Jamieson or his speech. As luck would have it, the first person he saw as he came in was Jamieson. Dan tried to get his attention, but Carl was standing toe to toe with Jamieson, and Carl's surprised look had quickly turned to one of anger. Carl had a worse temper than Dan, so he started making his way quickly toward them, with Mattie and Simone right behind.

Jamieson eyed Carl and noted the look of hate in the man's eyes. Ah yes, this was going to be good.

"Ah, you look familiar, young man," Jamieson said in his most condescending voice. "Aren't you a member of that struggling comedy act—the Dorky Brothers?"

"Listen, jerk-off, my brother can't have anything to do with you 'cause he's going to testify against you, but that doesn't mean I can't tell you what I think of you," a red-faced Carl said.

The big clown guy was already in position to cut in, but Jamieson waved him back. "Well, by all means, tell me what you think."

"I think you can try to intimidate my brother all you want, but he's still gonna put your sorry ass in jail, and you got no right to follow us and show up at a party you're not invited to, just to try to provoke some sort of reaction from my brother."

"Not invited to. Why, I'm the guest of honor here. I guess you didn't hear."

Dan had just gotten to the two of them. He instinctively got between Carl and Jamieson. If anybody was going to hit Jamieson, it was going to be him.

"He's right, Carl," Dan said quickly. "He's the one putting up the money for the book to be published. You know why, don't you?"

Carl took in what he had been told, processed the information, and came to the same conclusion Dan had. He nodded his understanding to Dan and backed away from Jamieson.

"Well, if it isn't dorky brother number 2?" Jamieson smirked. "Come on, you two, tell us some jokes, why don't you? I hear you're good at making stuff up."

Dan slowly turned around from Carl and was now facing Jamieson for the first time. Mattie and Simone were standing right there as well, neither knowing what to do. Dan tried to compose himself before he spoke.

"Listen, Mr. Jamieson," Dan said slowly and carefully. "You and I both know you've kept us from getting jobs, and that's hurt my brother and me, but we've survived, and we will survive. But if you're promising to publish this book because there's a friend of mine involved ..."

"I don't know what you're talking about," Jamieson interrupted.

"Save it. You're not fooling anybody here. Anyway, if what you're planning is to take the book back if I testify, just between you and me, tell me the truth."

"Well, I'm sure I don't know what you're talking about," Jamieson said in his most insincere voice. "I'm planning on financing this book. Of course, if something unlikely were to happen where I had to go to jail or something, well, I guess that could change my plans."

With that last sentence, Jamieson gave a gloating look that made Dan realize he had been right. He was sickened that he was right, but he knew what he had to do.

"Okay, Jamieson, you win," he said. "I knew you were a low-down scumbag, but I didn't know you could sink this low. But I give. You win."

At that point, Simone stepped in with a look of anger Dan had never seen on her face. In fact, he had no idea what her angry look looked like until now.

"'Migo, what are you saying?" Simone asked. "Are you saying you're not going to testify?"

"I'm afraid that's exactly what I'm saying. You've waited too long for this. I can let him hurt me, but I can't let him hurt you."

"Well, I can't let you not testify and let him get away with murder. Not for me. I won't allow it," Simone said in a determined voice unlike Dan had ever heard her use. Then she turned to Jamieson, standing toe to toe with the man who was six inches taller and about 150 pounds heavier.

"Mr. Jamieson, I appreciate your offer to finance this book, but I am not a pawn to be used by you or anyone else. You can finance the book for the other women, but I'm out. I don't want your help. I'm sure you can buy lots of things, even lots of people, but you can't buy me. I'm out of this project. Now go back to the slimy rock you crawled out from beneath, and the next time I see you, I hope you're behind bars where you belong."

The look of surprise on Jamieson's face was nothing compared to the one of utter shock on Dan's. Here was this girl who had never shown anger toward anyone, never had a harsh word about anyone, telling one of the most powerful men in the world to basically go to hell. Dan had never been so proud of anybody in his whole life. He counted his lucky stars for that chance meeting in the coffeehouse those many years ago.

Carl and Mattie were also in as much a state of shock as Dan was. Not surprisingly, it was Jamieson who regained his composure first. He kind of backed a step away from Simone since it looked like she might actually hit him. He shook his head and smiled.

"Well, well, young lady, what a hot-tempered thing you are," Jamieson said in the usual condescending voice he used with women.

Dan had recovered enough to smile at that comment. But then Jamieson did the unexpected; he turned out to be human after all.

"I tell you what, I had no intention of using you as a pawn. And I apologize for upsetting you. Now, what I'm going to do is finance this book just as planned, but only if you're in it. No strings attached, no contingencies. Whatever happens, the book gets published. Feel better now?"

Simone's once-in-a-lifetime flash of anger subsided as quickly as it had risen. "Yes, I do."

"And you'll allow your poetry to be in it?"

"Yes, but that doesn't mean I like you."

"Understood," Jamieson said. Then he turned to Dan. "And this doesn't mean I like you. But I have to envy anybody that has a friend like this. Loyalty like that is rare."

"Yes, sir, she's the best," Dan said, still trying to recover from the double blow of seeing Simone angry and Jamieson human.

At that point, Jamieson extended his hand to Dan and said, "You go ahead and testify. Give me your best shot. I can take it."

Dan shunned the attempt to shake hands. "I will, and I'm sure you can."

With that, the group of Dan, Carl, Simone, and Mattie awkwardly eased away from Jamieson. No sense tempting fate.

Chapter 24

Carl's girlfriend, Andrea, had arrived in time to see the confrontation, and she joined them as they tried to quietly leave. Jamieson had totally recovered from the incident and was milling around in the crowd, assuring everyone things were all right. Since he didn't seem to be leaving anytime soon, the five of them decided to go to a restaurant around the corner. As soon as they got there, Carl excused himself and said he had something he had to do and would be back in a few minutes. Carl being Carl, nobody asked any questions, including Andrea.

As they settled in at the restaurant, the topic of discussion was, of course, Simone's outburst.

MATTIE: Girlfriend, you lit into that bastard. Did you see how he backed down? I thought you were going to hit him.

SIMONE: I can't believe I did that. I'm so embarrassed.

MATTIE: Don't be, honey. You were great. He deserved it.

SIMONE: I know. That's just not like me.

DAN: 'Miga, I've never been so proud to say I know you as I am tonight. The way you took up for me, I'm just so touched.

SIMONE: Well, he was going to use me to get to you. You were willing to not testify just to protect me.

DAN: Yeah, well, nobody's going to hurt you as long as I'm around.

MATTIE: Okay, you two, let's not make this out to be the last scene from *Casablanca*. But I'm proud of you too, honey.

ANDREA: Me too.

DAN, *to Andrea*: Do you even know her that well?

ANDREA: No, but it seemed like such a nice moment, I wanted to be involved.

DAN: Okay.

SIMONE: Thanks. Thanks, everyone. I'm still in kind of a state of shock.

MATTIE: We all are.

(*The waitress—or server, if you like the politically correct nonword of the day—came over, and they ordered. Andrea asked where Carl might be and wondered when he would show up, and then he did.*)

CARL: Hey, did I miss it yet? Has Simone gone off on the waitress because she brought her the wrong tea? I love it when she goes crazy and yells at people.

(*Everyone laughed.*)

ANDREA: Where did you have to go in such a hurry?

CARL: Great news. Hey, bro, remember how we agreed we should follow that Rachel chick some more?

DAN: I remember you said we should follow her and I said no.

CARL: Hmm, weird. I guess I misunderstood. Anyway, I followed her the other night, and sure enough, she works at that strip joint called Bloomers two blocks over on Forty-Third.

DAN: Thanks, I guess. Good work.

ANDREA: What night was this?

CARL: The other night when I was late for our date. Remember, I told you not to worry about it.

ANDREA: Why should I worry, because my boyfriend is stalking a stripper? I feel much better now.

CARL: No, no, not stalking. Following at a discreet distance so as not to be noticed.

MATTIE: Yeah, that makes it better.

CARL: And she's not a stripper, she's a waitress or hostess or something. Anyway, she doesn't take her clothes off.

MATTIE: As I'm sure you spent some considerable time checking out.

CARL: Hey, whose side are you on here?

MATTIE: The woman. Always the woman.

CARL: Oh yeah, I forgot. I am woman, hear me roar, *The Feminine Mystique*, the *Ya-Ya Sisterhood*, *The Story of O*.

DAN: Actually, *The Story of O* is about a woman who likes bondage.

CARL: Yeah, I know, I just threw that one in. That was a hot movie, wasn't it?

DAN: Oh yeah.

SIMONE, *to Dan*: Whose side are you on?

DAN: I don't know. What are the teams? O's side, I guess. She enjoyed being bonded as I recall. And had a nice butt. Why do I have to take a side? I want to be Switzerland. Eat chocolate, look at my nice watch, and stay out of everything.

ANDREA: I think Carl had more to tell us.

CARL: Thanks, sweetie, sometimes me and Dan get off track.

SIMONE, MATTIE, AND ANDREA: No!

DAN: Okay, now I see what the teams are.

CARL: Yeah, anyway, I check out the number of strip joints or places like strip joints in the Manhattan area. There are thirty-eight. So then I go to city hall.

MATTIE: Naturally.

CARL: And of those thirty-eight, there are fourteen that are either owned directly by Jamieson or companies that he has a partnership or interest in or has set up a dummy foundation as the owner for tax purposes.

DAN: My brother, who can't remember what nights we work, suddenly turns into Rainman when it comes to strip joints.

CARL, *doing Rainman*: K-Mart. Definitely K-Mart. She definitely has to buy her underwear at K-Mart.

MATTIE: Wow, you did follow her closely.

DAN: Well, the place is called Bloomers.

ANDREA: Choo-choo. Back on track. Back on track.

CARL: Why is she making train noises? Okay, of those fourteen owned or operated by Jamieson, guess what one of them is?

MATTIE: I want to say Bloomers, but it seems like such an obvious answer.

CARL: Precisely, my dear Watson. (*To Mattie.*) You and I have always been so close.

MATTIE: Close to what?

CARL: Never mind. The point is, she works at Bloomers, owned by Jamieson, and she knows Shyanne, whom Jamieson undoubtedly paid to set up my brother.

DAN: And I'm pretty sure that big bodyguard guy with Jamieson tonight was the big clown who threw me into the ice.

CARL: Okay, that nails it down then. Anyway, back to my plan. So I go over to Bloomers a minute ago to see if Rachel is working tonight. (*To Dan.*) Which sets up our next move. Going over there.

DAN: To what, strong-arm her into telling us where Shyanne is?

CARL: No, no, Rachel's not working tonight. So if we go over there tonight when she's not there, no one will know us or know why we're there.

DAN: Including me.

CARL: Don't you see, we go over there, have a drink, maybe separate from each other, talk to as many of the girls as possible (*to Andrea*) just for the purpose of finding out information.

ANDREA: Of course.

CARL: No, we just casually ask them if they know a girl named Shyanne, have they seen her recently, that kind of thing. Maybe she still works there, although I doubt it, but maybe they know something.

DAN: Gee, I don't know.

ANDREA: I want to go.

CARL: You think my plan will work?

ANDREA: No, not really. But I have always wanted to see what a strip joint is like.

DAN: You've never been?

ANDREA: No.

DAN: Well, this could be interesting.

ANDREA: Oh, goodie.

DAN: All right, but you can't say "Oh, goodie" in there.

ANDREA: Okay.

DAN: Oh, but wait, I don't want to just leave Simone and Mattie here. This is still Simone's night of celebration.

MATTIE: Leave us, hell. We're going too.

SIMONE: Mattie!

MATTIE: Hey, naked good-looking girls shakin' their moneymakers in our faces. Woo-woo!

SIMONE: Mattie!

CARL: Now she's making train noises.

ANDREA: What's their moneymakers?

CARL: It could be different for each girl. But generally, their money-makers are their asses.

ANDREA: Mmm, interesting. I would have thought breasts.

SIMONE: Mattie, do I even know you? You're the one always talking about how these places are degrading to women and force them to act as sex objects for men.

MATTIE: Yeah, but that's when they have to dance for men. It won't be the case if we're there.

SIMONE: They'll be forced to be sex objects for us?

MATTIE: Exactly.

DAN: Well, to hell with finding Shyanne, this is sounding like a party to me.

CARL: Now I'm not sure.

EVERYONE ELSE: What?

CARL: Well, I'm all for all of us going to a strip club and watching some girl-on-girl action up close and personal, but I'm afraid if all of us go in there together, we'll call attention to ourselves. It'll be harder for Dan and me to do our detective work.

MATTIE: Sorry, Hardy Boys, we're going. Besides, why wouldn't the women there be more likely to talk to us than you guys anyway?

CARL: Good point, actually.

MATTIE, *to Simone*: So you in, hon?

SIMONE: If everybody else is going, I guess so.

MATTIE: I do think we should go in separately, though, so as not to draw attention to ourselves. Simone and I can go in, then

Carl and Andrea, and last, but not least, well, maybe not least, Dan.

DAN: Oh, thanks. I get to go as the lone loser guy, so desperate for companionship he has to go to a strip joint alone and pay girls to talk to him.

ANDREA: They talk to you?

DAN: Well, yeah, that's how they hustle you, get you to buy a dance.

CARL: Hey, you can go in with Andrea if it'll make you feel better.

ANDREA: Hey!

CARL: It's almost as good as being with me.

DAN: Hey!

MATTIE: You're doing great, Carl. Want to piss me and Simone off too?

CARL: Not really. But I was wondering why you suddenly took charge of this operation.

MATTIE: I think we all know I'm the brains of this particular outfit.

ANDREA: Okay.

DAN: I don't.

CARL: Me neither.

SIMONE: No, sorry, honey, I don't either.

ANDREA: All right, I don't really think so either.

DAN, *to Andrea*: You don't like to march to the beat of a different drummer, do you?

ANDREA: Not so much, no.

MATTIE: So who is in charge?

SIMONE: Nobody. Nobody's the brains of the outfit. We just all go in there however we want to, and whoever wants to talk to strippers can.

DAN: No, I hate to say it, but Mattie's way was the right way. We'll go in there in three groups, and I'll just have to act like the lonely loser guy.

MATTIE: Good luck with that.

DAN: Thanks.

MATTIE: No, I'm serious. You may be lonely, but you're no loser.

DAN: Thanks, Mattie. You really think so?

MATTIE: Don't push it.

DAN: Okay.

SIMONE: So once we're in there, is it okay to talk to each other? Or do we have to pretend like we don't know each other? Oh, I know, let's use fake names. I can be Raquel ...

CARL: Time out. This is starting to sound like a bad episode of *Three's Company*.

DAN: That's redundant. Raquel?

SIMONE, *pouting*: I just always wanted to be a Raquel, the hot-looking lesbian who frequents strip joints.

MATTIE: Come on, guys, let her be Raquel. I want to see what Raquel's like.

CARL: All right, all right, Simone can be Raquel, but we can still talk to each other after we get in there. I don't think there are going to be video cameras or anything.

ANDREA: Can I be someone else too?

CARL, *disgusted*: Sure, why not. Who?

ANDREA: I don't know. Angie?

CARL: Okay.

DAN: Listen, everybody can be whoever they want to be, but I'm just going as Dan.

CARL: Actually, you're the one person who should use a different name. They might actually be looking for Dan.

DAN: Okay, I'll be Siegfried, or Roy, whichever one didn't get mauled by the tiger. But if we don't go soon, they'll probably be closed.

CARL: No, they're open 'til four. (*Andrea looked at him.*) Research, research.

Chapter 25

With that, they walked over to Bloomers, with Mattie and Simone going in first, followed a few minutes later by Andrea and Carl, and then Dan. The place was far from closing. Despite it being a week before Christmas, the place was hopping. Apparently, Dan thought, nothing put people in the mood to celebrate the birth of Christ like a group of good-looking women prancing around topless in G-strings. He was thinking he shouldn't be thinking sacrilegious thoughts like that, but that thought left his mind when a cute girl dressed in some sort of elfin outfit came over and sat on his lap.

He had positioned himself at a table that was in between where Andrea and Carl were sitting and Mattie and Simone were. He definitely wanted to be able to watch the women if and when they got lap dances. This was reminding him not so much of an episode of *Three's Company* as maybe the *Hardy Boys and Nancy Drew* gone bad.

"Hi, my name's Cricket," said the friendly girl on his lap.

"Well, of course it is," Dan said as Cricket let her hands do the talking, making Dan suddenly forget about detective work and ever so briefly about Shyanne.

"What made you decide to come in here tonight?" Cricket asked perkily. "Feeling kind of lonely during the holidays?"

"I wasn't before, but now I am. No, actually I just came in here to see you."

"Well, good then, you came to the right place."

It was a line Dan always used with strippers. They knew it wasn't true, but they liked it anyway, and it kind of set the tone for the kind of playful back-and-forth lies that strippers deal in every night they work. The really good ones find some physical characteristic they like about the guy and compliment them, even if they wouldn't give them the time of day outside the club. As long as the guy understands the game, everything goes well. She's there to make a buck; he's there to have a good time and give her one (or two or one hundred). End of story.

"So since you came in here to see me, wanna get a dance from me? I'm even friendlier when I dance."

Oops, mistake number 1 from Dan's perspective. A little too greedy, too quickly. Got to go through a little more foreplay before she gets to move on to round 2.

"I'm sure you are," Dan said. "And I promise I'll get a dance or two before I leave. But I just got here, and I like to kind of relax a little before I really get to going."

"You can relax all you want, I'll do all the work. Besides, there's only one part of you I need to be unrelaxed. Is that a word?"

With that, she squeezed the part of him she was talking about in a totally familiar way he didn't even remember his wife ever doing. Certainly not that well.

"Sure, why not?" Dan said, even though he knew it wasn't a word. Best not to expect linguists to be posing in strippers' bodies. Maybe cunnilinguists. Pushing him after he said no was strike 2. "No, I'm going to wait a little while. Besides, I'm not sure I even brought enough money in here to afford you."

"We have an ATM machine," she said, grinning mischievously.

Okay, strike 3. And he couldn't let that last one go.

"Actually, it's just an ATM, since the *M* stands for *machine*."

She looked at him like he was an alien for correcting her. He was sure she was thinking about something mean to say to him but restraining herself because there might still be a dance or two she could squeeze out of him.

"Well, okay, I'll leave, but only if you promise to look me up with those gorgeous blue eyes of yours before you leave," she said.

There was the obligatory compliment. Then it came back to him why they were there. He hoped the others were more focused on the job at hand, although finding out about Shyanne was more Carl's deal than his. He still didn't necessarily want to know the truth, the whole truth and nothing but the truth.

"Hey, wait a minute there, Cricket. Do you know a girl that works here, or maybe used to, named Shyanne? Blond hair, big tits, gorgeous face."

"Yeah, I know the type," Cricket said. "But I've only been working here a week. No one by that name working here now. Besides, you don't need her. I'll be more than you can handle."

"No, no, I was just wondering about her. I think she said she worked here. I'm sure you'll be great."

"All right then, let's go to the back."

"Not just yet."

Why couldn't they just realize *no* means no? Probably because men rarely said no to women like them and never actually meant it. As Cricket slinked away pouting, he looked over to see how the others were doing. It looked like Mattie might have forgotten the task at hand as well, as she had a tall, well-built brunette wriggling around on top of her, with Simone—or Raquel—staring wide-eyed at the action. Must be some sort of new interrogation technique, Dan thought, although maybe the way to a woman's heart was through her breasts. In fact, now that he thought about it, it actually was.

And although it was hard to turn away, he looked to his right to see Carl seemingly dickering with a blond woman over the cost of a lap dance. That was Carl—go to a strip joint and try to negotiate a good deal. Don't go to a strip joint for a bargain, Dan had learned. Just go and pay the piper whatever she asked for. Finally they seemed to strike some sort of deal, and Carl, Andrea, and the petite blond headed to the back—where it was dark and the dancers became friendlier, to use Cricket's term.

He turned his attention back to the Mattie-Simone table. They had apparently opted for the less lascivious but cheaper table dance. Now the well-built woman was dancing for Simone. Simone didn't seem to be getting into it like Mattie had been, but she was enjoying herself, if a little self-consciously. She was kind of giggling and glancing at Mattie as if she needed advice on what to do.

Dan's focus was broken again when a voice from behind said, "Hey, darlin', you want some brown sugar?"

Then he felt some hands reach across his chest and what he imagined were breasts in the back of his head. He turned around to see he had been right. A coffee-with-cream-colored black girl was giving his face a breast-whipping. With difficulty, he pulled back and decided to get the question over with first. He asked about Shyanne and described her.

"No, man, don't remember ever meeting a girl named Shyanne. What's a matter, you only like the white chicks? You know what they say about the sisters, don't you?"

"Once you go black, you never go back?" Dan said.

"And you know why?"

"Some sort of unusual way of performing sexual acts which you've managed to keep a secret from all the white women?"

"Ain't no secret, man. We just like sex more, that's all. And we ain't performin' when we do it. We're just doin' it. No holds, or should I say, no holes, barred."

"Well, all righty, then," Dan said, trying, but not succeeding, in keeping his voice at its natural octave. "That's good to know. But I was really needing to get ahold of this Shyanne girl. Not for sex, just to ask her something."

"Well, like I said, ain't no Shyanne working here since I been here, and I been here two years." Only this time when she said it, she kind of looked around to see if anyone was watching. "She in some sort of trouble? You a cop?"

Dan sensed the girl might know something, and maybe the cop angle might work with her.

"No, no she's not in any trouble," he said. "And this is more of an unofficial investigation."

"So you are a cop?"

"I'd rather not say. This isn't really a job thing anyway. This is more of a personal thing."

"She got to you, did she?"

"You have no idea."

"I got some idea."

"Yeah, you probably do. Guys here always falling in love with you?"

"Yeah, it comes with the job."

"You seem like a really good person. What's your name?"

"Delilah, as in Samson and Delilah. And, honey, I ain't always good. Sometimes I can be very bad."

With that last line, Dan decided he might as well take advantage of being in this place. And he wanted to see how bad she could be. So they went to the back room, where Dan couldn't see more than three feet ahead of himself. A couple of trips to the ATM and a couple of hundred dollars later, Delilah walked him back to his original table, which was now occupied. He tried to adjust his eyes to being in a place with lights again. He told her he would find someplace to sit, and she gave him a quick kiss on the lips and squeezed his butt. He asked her once more about Shyanne, but she was evasive once again. With that, he saw Mattie and Simone still sitting at the same table. Alone, this time. He didn't see Carl and Andrea around. He suddenly felt drained of energy. He didn't know whether Delilah's theory about all black women was true, but she sure knew how to enjoy herself, and make sure her customer did too. He had totally forgotten about Shyanne while he was back there with Delilah.

"Hey, ladies," Dan said as he walked up to Mattie and Simone's table. "See anything you like?"

"Man, how do you guys afford these places?" Mattie asked. "These girls can take your money quick."

"Doesn't seem so much like they're the ones being used now, does it?" Dan said laughing.

"No way, not at all. They're the ones in control."

"And what about Raquel here? Did you have a good time?"

"Yeah, it was fun," Simone said. "But it seemed kind of weird having a woman on top of me with Mattie right next to me."

"Well, I can bring you here sometime without Mattie if you like," Dan said, smirking at Mattie.

"Hey, and after I said something nice about you earlier," Mattie said.

"Oh yeah, I forgot. Sorry," Dan said.

"No, I wouldn't want to be here without her," Simone said. "I'm just saying it was weird. I didn't feel comfortable."

"Yeah, me neither," Mattie said.

Both Dan and Simone gave her questioning looks.

"What? I wasn't comfortable," she said insistently.

"I'd hate to see you when you were," Dan said. "Or maybe I'd like to. But not for Simone's sake."

"Okay, so I enjoyed it. But I wouldn't have if you hadn't been here, honey. It actually kind of turned me on having you watch."

"Oh, really," Simone said, arching an eyebrow. "Ready to go home then and see Raquel give you a lap dance?"

"Yeah, I am," Mattie said.

About that time, Carl and Andrea emerged from the dark back room. They came over to their table.

DAN, *to Simone and Mattie*: Before y'all go back and do things to each other for free that you just paid somebody to do, could you tell me, did you ever think about asking about Shyanne?

MATTIE: Yeah, we asked everybody we could. Even the bartender. No luck.

DAN, *to Carl and Andrea*: And you guys?

CARL: We struck out too. But I did get the sense that some of them were lying. It may have been my imagination, but it seemed like they had been told what to say.

MATTIE: Yeah, now that you mention it, they did almost all say the same thing.

ANDREA: Yeah, I noticed that too.

DAN: Yeah, okay. I think Delilah knew something.

CARL: Which one's Delilah?

(*Dan looked around for her and didn't see her.*)

DAN: This hot girl who took me for a couple of bills.

CARL: Really? I tried to share the wealth, you know, so I could have contact with more girls—more chances for information.

SIMONE: Yeah, we sure didn't spend $200 on anybody. That's what you meant by two bills, isn't it?

DAN: Yeah, well, I was trying the "put all my eggs in one basket" theory, so to speak. Thought the more I spent on her, the more likely she might tell me something.

MATTIE: Sure you did. Can we go now?

DAN: Sure, I think our work here is done. (*As he got up to leave, he took his wallet out to see if he was going to have to borrow cab fare to get home. When he took his wallet out, a piece of paper fell out with it.*) Hey, wait a minute. There's a note here … from Delilah, I guess. (*He read it quickly.*) It says Shyanne did work here but hasn't been here in a while and they were told not to talk about her.

CARL: Quick, put that up. We don't want to get anybody in trouble.

DAN: Yeah.

With that, they all put on their coats and left, this time not bothering to leave separately. Once they got outside and walked away about half a block, Dan took the note back out.

"It says she doesn't know where she is, but she did work here until recently. She's pretty sure she left the city," Dan read out loud. "She says be careful, the people who run this place are not to be fooled with."

"So I was right," Carl said proudly. "She's a stripper."

"Yeah, okay, you were right," Dan said. "Can we let it go now? She's out of the city. She could be anywhere, and my guess is, she will be until after the trial's over."

"Are you s-s-s-scared?" Mattie asked. "'Fraid of the big bad clowns?"

"Scared, yes, but not of them."

"Scared of what you might find out when you find her?" Simone said.

"Yeah," Dan said.

But in his mind, he already knew. He supposed he should thank Jamieson for giving him that one great night. But for taking it away from him just as quickly, well, for that, he hoped there would be a special place in hell for him. Not only that, but he had tried to use Simone against him, and would have succeeded except for Simone's unusual outburst. He couldn't wait to testify now.

Chapter 26

Dan found out the next day he was going to get his chance much sooner than he thought. It had originally looked like they would not get to him until after Christmas. The trial was going to break for a few days before and after Christmas, so Dan was assured of getting to go to Vegas. But because Judge Davenport had been moving the trial along so quickly, Dan's testimony had been moved up to the next day, Tuesday, December 19, five days before their Vegas gig with Tom Jones.

Davenport had cut the lawyers off every time they did anything which hinted at a delay. Even if the opposing side didn't object, he would interrupt them and say something like, "Is there a point to be made sometime in my lifetime?"

At one point, when the prosecution called the coroner to testify and went through its routine preliminaries of what his job duties are, Davenport interrupted and said, "I think everybody and their dog know what a coroner does, don't they? He picks up dead people and takes 'em back to the morgue." The lawyers were constantly looking over their shoulders as they asked the questions. It may not have made for a fair trial, but it was definitely a speedy one.

Partly because of that, Lana Stevens, handling the case for the prosecution, expected Dan's testimony to last no more than two days, one day to lay out his story for their side and one day to be grilled by Jamieson's attorney, Rita Dawes. But she could only guess as to what the other side was going to do. She called and gave Dan the news Monday and asked if he could come in and go over his testimony with them during the lunch recess. He asked if this was like a dress rehearsal, and she said she guessed so. She didn't laugh much, Dan thought.

163

So Dan spent the rest of Monday morning trying not to think too much about the nerves he was going to have when they called his name to testify. He was used to getting up in front of crowds, but this was different, somehow. For one thing, if he messed up doing stand-up, you just moved on to the next joke, or made a joke about messing up. If you messed up testifying, you could go to jail. Of course, he wasn't really nervous about telling the truth. He knew what it was, and he was going to tell it. Which also made him wonder why he had to rehearse. How do you rehearse telling the truth?

What he found out when he got to Stevens's office was they wanted to try to prepare him for what the other side was going to do. Stevens's assistant on this case, Jerry Finley, a thirty-ish good-looking guy with a touch of lawyer arrogance, led Dan through his testimony. As he did, Stevens played the part of Dawes and threw in objections to try to disrupt the testimony. Dan realized the objections, even if overruled, could be distracting and that he wasn't going to get to just tell his story from beginning to end as he had pictured in his mind he would.

Dan thought he held up pretty well with his story of what he saw and heard the night Jamieson killed that woman. Finley constantly reminded him not to digress from the story and to stay focused. But then when Stevens started cross-examining him in the role of Dawes, he knew this was not going to be something to look forward to.

And although she was just guessing as to what the other side was going to do, she was fairly convincing to Dan in her role as the mean attorney. She made fun of him for being a comedian; she tried to get him to admit he had some sort of grudge against Jamieson; she badgered him over what he actually saw and heard. And she and Finley constantly reminded him to answer the questions as succinctly as possible—yes or no if he could—and not elaborate on anything, because that was what the defense wanted him to do.

The next day was D-Day for Dan, the day he had looked forward to and dreaded at the same time since that day almost a year ago when he saw a man kill a woman and try to get away with it. Now it looked like without a perfect couple of days from Dan, he would get away with it. He tried to remember the last time he had strung a couple of perfect days together. He realized it must have been some time when he was five or six and his biggest worry was what time his favorite TV show would come on. He didn't actually remember those days too well, but there must have been some good ones.

Those thoughts momentarily depressed him, so he took a shower and thought about what he was going to wear (in court, not the shower). Stevens had told him a suit, so a suit it would be. But the only actual suit he had was the one he had gotten married in, and that wasn't happening. In Dan's world of fashion, a coat and tie was the same as a suit. However imperfect his days might have been, at least he had never been forced to work a job in which a suit was a daily necessity. So he picked out his nicest pants and a sports coat that he believed went with it. The tie was a problem since none of his were particularly new. He wasn't quite sure what the latest trend was in ties, but whatever it was it must have changed in the last five years or so. Oh well, dark blue seemed like a good-enough choice. After all, he wasn't on trial; Jamieson was.

With that crucial decision made, Dan was off to the races. Gentlemen, start your engines.

Chapter 27

When Dan arrived at the courthouse, he met somebody from the prosecutor's office named Carol and was escorted past several TV cameras and news people. He wasn't surprised to see Simone there waiting for him; she was always there when he needed her, but he was a little surprised to see Mattie with her. Carl had, of course, already flown off to Vegas to "get the lay of the land," whatever that meant. Dan stopped briefly to talk to Simone, who told him he looked great and assured him he would do great.

"Just tell the truth and knock 'em dead," she said.

"I don't know, it's been a while, I don't remember it all that well," Dan said.

Carol looked a little worried by that comment.

"Don't worry," Mattie told Carol. "He tends to make jokes at inappropriate times. But he probably won't make any while he's testifying. Will you?"

"Not unless there's a good straight line by the judge or something," Dan said, looking at Carol. "See, I did it again. Hey, Mattie, I didn't expect to see you here, but thanks, it means a lot to me."

"Sure," Mattie said.

"Hey, what about me?" Simone said.

"It would have even more impact on me if you weren't here," he said.

"Thanks, I guess."

With that, the Carol woman became concerned some of the news people might be able to hear them, so she whisked Dan off to the witness room. He sat down in the rather plain room—not big, not small, not bright, not dull, just plain. After Carol left, he was there by himself, which made sense since he was the only witness left. Stevens and Finley stopped by briefly to make sure he was ready to go. He assured them he was and didn't make any jokes. Since he had already figured out Stevens didn't like to laugh much during normal times, this probably wouldn't have been the time to get his first laugh from her. That was how the comedian's mind measured success, the first laugh he got from somebody.

Dan sat in the nondescript room alone for what was about an hour and a half, but it seemed like two or three days. He couldn't hear what was going on in the courtroom. There were no computers to play games on, not even a TV set. Hell, even at the doctor's office, they had TVs for you to watch.

Finally, through a little speaker he hadn't even noticed being there, he heard his name called. He went to the door, where a bailiff was waiting to escort him into the courtroom. He could almost hear his heart beating as he entered the courtroom and neared the witness stand.

He placed his hand on the Bible and took the oath, wondering briefly if he would get a laugh if he paused for a while when answering the "Do you swear to tell the truth, the whole truth" question, as if he was considering. *Focus, Dan, focus. Not the time. Don't be funny. Don't be funny.* Humor had always been the way he had avoided taking anything too seriously, and now on the most serious occasion of his life, he couldn't use that mechanism.

"Would you state your full name for the record?" Stevens started out the questioning.

"Daniel Paul Darwin," he said, thinking once again about using Banter as his middle name, as a kind of inside joke only Shyanne would get, who wasn't even there. *Or was she?* he wondered as he looked around the packed courtroom for a flash of platinum-blond hair. Not there.

STEVENS: And your occupation?
DAN: I'm a comedian.

(*Stevens had decided to get that out of the way early, because she knew the defense would try to make an issue of it.*)

167

STEVENS: So you tell jokes for a living?

DAN: Yes, ma'am.

STEVENS: But you're not here to tell jokes today, are you?

DAN: Absolutely not.

DAWES: Your Honor, if she's going to lead the witness like this, wouldn't it be easier if she just testified?

DAVENPORT: Is that an objection?

DAWES: Yes, Your Honor.

DAVENPORT: Then state it as such.

DAWES: I object.

DAVENPORT: On what grounds?

DAWES: Leading the witness.

DAVENPORT: Overruled. When she gets to the important stuff, I won't let her lead him.

DAWES: Thank you, Your Honor.

STEVENS: Now, Mr. Darwin, let's get to the important stuff, the reason you're here today, the events of January 17. Can you take us through that day?

DAN: The whole day, or just the important stuff?

(The judge didn't laugh, and Stevens glared a hole through him, but he did hear a couple of laughs in the audience, or galley.)

DAN, *in his mind: Okay, kind of a tough crowd. Focus, focus.*

STEVENS: Let's start with your trip to Mr. Jamieson's building.

DAN: Okay, I had scheduled an appointment through one of Mr. Jamieson's employees, a Mr. Franklin, to meet with Mr. Jamieson about an idea I had for an off-Broadway play. I had run it by Mr. Franklin, and he thought his boss might be interested.

STEVENS: At this time, Your Honor, we would like to enter as people's exhibit 42 Mr. Jamieson's appointment book for that day.

DAVENPORT: You want to show there was an appointment? Is there some dispute over that?

STEVENS: Actually, the appointment book shows no such appointment.

DAWES: Objection, Your Honor. Relevance? What next? Would she like to enter my appointments book, since I had no meeting scheduled with Mr. Darwin that day either?

DAVENPORT: You want to enter something that shows there was no such appointment, Ms. Stevens? Why?

STEVENS: We believe the fact that no such appointment was logged— it enters into why Mr. Jamieson did not realize Mr. Darwin was there.

DAVENPORT: And you're not going to ask for Ms. Dawes's appointment book?

STEVENS: No, Your Honor.

DAVENPORT: Objection overruled. I'll allow it. Go ahead.

STEVENS: About what time of day was this?

DAN: At 7:00 p.m., although I got there a few minutes before that.

STEVENS: Kind of late for an appointment, wasn't it?

DAN: I thought so too, but Mr. Franklin said Mr. Jamieson took late meetings, especially in the entertainment field.

STEVENS: So you didn't ask any questions?

DAN: No, ma'am.

STEVENS: Because you were just there to sell your idea?

(*Dawes started to object, but Davenport motioned her to sit down.*)

DAVENPORT: Borderline, Ms. Stevens, but I'll let it go. Let him tell the story.

DAN: Yes, I was just there to sell my idea.

STEVENS: Okay, what happened next?

DAN: I got to Jamieson's office building—The Jamieson Palace, I believe it's called. The security guard called up to Mr. Franklin, and Mr. Franklin told him to let me go to the top floor, the fifty-fifth story, the penthouse suites. The guard told me to go to my right when I got off the elevator and go to the first door on my right.

STEVENS: And what happened when you got there?

DAN: I knocked on the first door on the right. Nobody answered, so I went on in, not sure whether I was supposed to or not. When I went in, nobody was there.

STEVENS: What did you do then?

DAN: It was not a big office, there was a desk there, so I went over to it. Behind the desk, there was a door with Mr. Jamieson's name on it. The door was open, leading into a much bigger room. I looked around, waited for a minute, called out to ask if anybody was there. Nobody answered.

STEVENS: At this point, what was your state of mind, surprised no one was there, upset?

DAN: No, no, I wasn't upset, and not surprised Mr. Jamieson wasn't there waiting for me. I knew he was an important man and I'd probably have to wait. But I was curious as to why Mr. Franklin or a secretary or somebody wasn't there.

STEVENS: Okay, continue on, please.

DAN: After waiting a few more minutes, I started to wonder what kind of office a rich man like Mr. Jamieson would have. So I kind of peeked inside to get a look. The lights were on in there, so I could see pretty well. And that was when I heard some voices talking loudly.

STEVENS: Where were the voices coming from?

DAN: Well, I thought at first they were coming from his office, but they weren't clear enough, I thought, so it seemed like they were coming from another room.

STEVENS: So what did you do?

DAN: I went on into Mr. Jamieson's office, and then I could hear the voices a lot more clearly. There was obviously some sort of serious disagreement going on.

DAWES: Objection, Your Honor. Speculation.

DAVENPORT: Sustained. Mr. Darwin, just tell us what you heard and saw, not your conclusions.

DAN: Yes, sir, I'm sorry.

(Actually, during the rehearsal, Stevens had told him they would object to that, but he should go ahead and put it that way anyway.)

STEVENS: So, Mr. Darwin, you heard voices talking loudly. Did you determine where the voices were coming from, how many people were involved?

DAN: There were two voices, one male, one female, and they were coming from another room on the other side of the office. There was a door open at that end, and that seemed to be where the voices were coming from.

STEVENS: Besides the loudness, was there anything that indicated that this was anything other than a casual conversation?

DAN: Yes, the tone of voices was strained, and either because I was getting closer or they were getting louder, I started to hear what they were actually saying.

STEVENS: What were the first words you heard, that you actually could distinguish what they were saying?

DAN: I heard the woman saying "I won't let you do that, you son of a bitch." (*To the judge.*) I'm sorry, is that okay to say that in here?

DAVENPORT: Sure, why not?

STEVENS: At this point, were you still at the front of the office you had entered?

DAN: No, my curiosity had gotten the best of me and I was moving toward the back, where the voices were coming from.

STEVENS: Did you recognize either of the voices?

DAN: No, ma'am.

STEVENS: Okay, please continue.

DAN: I heard the man say in a voice not as loud as the woman, but still loud enough for me to hear, "Don't make this hard on yourself. You've been paid well for your services. And nobody calls me a son of a bitch." Then she said, "Oh yeah, well, how do you feel about being called a cock-sucking son of a bitch?" (*Dan looked at the judge again.*)

DAVENPORT: I wished you'd asked me about that one.

DAN: I'm sorry.

DAVENPORT: That's all right. If that's what she said, that's what she said.

DAN: That's what she said.

STEVENS: What did you hear next?

DAN: I heard him hit her.

DAWES: Objection! Your Honor!

DAVENPORT: Mr. Darwin, now I told you before, no conclusions, just what you actually heard. The jury will disregard that last comment. Now don't make me tell you again.

DAN: Yes, sir. I heard what sounded like a slap and the woman's voice responding rather loudly.

STEVENS: What did you hear her say?

DAN: She said, "Oh, what a big man, hitting a woman. That's gonna cost you big-time." Then the man said, "I'm not paying you a dime, and if you tell anybody about this, it'll be the last thing you say." Then she said, "So now you're threatening me?" And he said, "Take it however you want. Now get out of here, you little whore." By this time, I was at the door. It sounded to me like whatever was going on in there needed to be interrupted. I looked in and saw the woman raise her hand as if to hit the man, and then he grabbed her hand and swung his fist. He hit her flush in the face, hard, and she fell backward.

STEVENS: Did you say anything at this point?

DAN: No, I may have gasped or something, but whatever noise I made didn't seem to be noticed. Anyway, when the woman fell, she hit her head on a table really hard.

STEVENS: And what did you do?

DAN: I'm not proud of this, but I ducked behind the door.

STEVENS: Did you see the man long enough to recognize him?

DAN: Yes, I did.

STEVENS: Is that man in the courtroom today?

DAN: Yes, that's him over there—Mr. Jamieson.

(Dan had seen this move in enough movies to make his pointing out of Jamieson an appropriately dramatic gesture, he thought.)

STEVENS: For the record, it was Mr. Jamieson?

DAN: Yes.

STEVENS: And did you realize at the time that was who it was?

DAN: Yes.

STEVENS: And how did you know that?

DAN: I had seen him on TV enough to know it was him.

STEVENS: Okay, please continue. What happened next?

DAN: As I said, I ducked behind the door, but I looked through the crack and saw Mr. Jamieson standing over the woman, looking down at her. He leaned down to see if she was still alive, I guess—oh, sorry, that's a conclusion. He leaned over for some reason. After he did, he got back up and started to turn back toward me. I was about to back my way out of his office and leave when I heard some other people coming in from the front office.

STEVENS: So what did you do?

DAN: I hid behind the door again. The two guys whom I had heard walked right past me and into the bedroom.

STEVENS: Could you still hear them talking from there?

DAN: Oh yes.

STEVENS: And what was said, then?

DAN: One of the guys said, "What happened?" and Mr. Jamieson said, "She tried to hit me, and when I tried to stop her, she fell and must have hit her head on this table or something. Anyway, she's dead now." Then one of the guys asked if he was sure, and Mr. Jamieson said he was sure.

STEVENS: And from what you witnessed, was Mr. Jamieson's account of what happened accurate?

DAN: No, ma'am. He left out the part about him hitting her, which is what caused her to fall.

STEVENS: Okay, please continue.

DAN: Next they talked about what they were going to do. One of the men suggested calling the police since it was an accident and self-defense, and Mr. Jamieson and the other guy said no.

STEVENS: Was that the last mention made of calling the police?

DAN: Yes, Mr. Jamieson said the police would try to make it look like a murder, and there was no more talk about calling the police.

STEVENS: What did they decide to do, or what did they say, which indicated their intentions?

DAN: They started talking about getting rid of the body and cleaning up the place so there would be no evidence of a crime. Mr. Jamieson said, "We've got to go over this place with a fine-tooth comb so that there will be nothing left."

DAWES: Objection, Your Honor.

DAVENPORT: What grounds?

DAWES: Your Honor, I've been letting this go, but it's gone too far. The witness is reciting dialogue like he had a tape recorder or was making notes while he was hiding behind the door.

DAVENPORT: Maybe he just has a really good memory.

DAWES: Better than any witness I've ever heard.

DAVENPORT: Could be, but you'll get your chance on cross to ask him how he remembers everything so well.

DAWES: Yes, sir.

(*Stevens was silently gloating over the last exchange, since the jury got to hear the judge saying her witness might just have a good memory. She was sure that was not what Dawes had in mind when she objected.*)

STEVENS: Now, Mr. Darwin, can you call on your excellent memory again to tell us what they said next?

DAN: Yes, one of the guys suggested taking the body to a trash dumpster in an alley behind a fish place in Chinatown. He gave the address. He said it was a perfect place.

STEVENS: And are you aware that is where the body was found?

DAN: Yes, ma'am.

DAWES: Objection, Your Honor, unless this witness is going to testify he followed them to the location or was somehow involved in the disposal of the body himself, he has no direct knowledge of where the body was found.

DAVENPORT, *to Dan*: Do you have any direct knowledge of where the body was found?

DAN: I'm sorry, sir, what do you mean by that?

DAVENPORT: How did you find out where the body was found?

DAN: I was told by somebody from the prosecutor's office.

DAWES: What, no direct quote as to what they said?

DAVENPORT: That's out of line, Counselor. I'm going to sustain your objection, but leave the personal comments to yourself.

DAWES: Yes, Your Honor.

STEVENS: Mr. Darwin, was there anything else you heard before you left?

DAN: They talked some more about cleaning the place up, getting rid of the table because it had blood on it, maybe even replacing the carpet.

STEVENS: Any more direct quotes you remember?

DAN: Yes, Mr. Jamieson saying, "Whatever it takes, get it done. I want it so clean that the entire cast of all the CSI shows couldn't find anything."

STEVENS: And at what point did you leave?

DAN: When it looked like they were about ready to move the body and start cleaning, I quietly started making my way back into the front office and then the hallway. Finally, I got to the elevator and went to the first floor.

STEVENS: Did anybody ever see you?

DAN: On the first floor, the security guy saw me and asked if the meeting was over. I said, "Yeah," and left as quickly as I could without running.

STEVENS: As far as you know, did anyone beside the security guard ever see you during the entire time you were there?

DAN: As far as I know, no.

STEVENS: And no one followed you?

DAN: No, or if they did, they didn't catch me.

STEVENS: Thank you, Mr. Darwin. And what did you do when you got safely away?

DAN: I went by a police station and told them what I had seen and heard.

STEVENS: And about how long did that process take?

DAN: Maybe a couple of hours. I tried to get them to hurry to the trash dumpster so they could be there to see them dump the body in there.

STEVENS: But they didn't seem in a hurry to you?

DAN: No, I think they were a little reluctant to believe me, what with it being Mr. Jamieson and all.

STEVENS: But they finally did believe you?

DAN: Yes, well, at least to the extent that they indicated they would investigate.

STEVENS: Did they give any indication to you while you were there how they were going to investigate?

DAN: They said they would go to Mr. Jamieson's place first and ask him about it.

STEVENS: Instead of going to the trash dumpster first?

DAN: Yes, they talked like they would do that later.

STEVENS: And it was later that you heard from someone on my staff that was where the body was found?

DAN: Yes.

STEVENS: And after the body was found, did you talk to the police again?

DAN: Yes, ma'am.

STEVENS: And did you notice any change in their attitude when they questioned you this time?

DAN: Yes, they seemed far more interested in every detail I had to tell them.

STEVENS: And to the best of your knowledge, did you recount the story to them the same way as you did here in court today?

DAN: To the best of my memory, yes.

STEVENS: Thank you, Mr. Darwin. The prosecution has no further questions of this witness, Your Honor.

DAVENPORT: Ms. Dawes, would you like a brief recess before you begin your cross-examination of the witness?

DAWES: Actually, Your Honor, the defense asks for a recess until tomorrow?

DAVENPORT: For what reason?

DAWES: We have received some last-minute information that is pertinent to the questioning of this witness, and we have not had time to review it properly. We can be ready to go first thing in the morning.

DAVENPORT: And you consider this information important enough that you can't proceed without it?

DAWES: Very much so, Your Honor.

DAVENPORT, *looking disgusted*: Okay, I'll allow it, but I hope, for your sake, this is not a delaying tactic.

DAWES: No, sir, Your Honor.

DAVENPORT: All right, court is adjourned until eight o'clock tomorrow morning. See everybody bright and early tomorrow.

Chapter 28

With that, Davenport left the courtroom first, and everyone followed suit. Dan breathed a little sigh of relief and realized he had been tense the entire time of his testimony. His shoulders felt as tight as a drum. And that had been the easy part. He was sure the worst was yet to come, especially with Dawes's surprise announcement that they had some new information.

Dan left the courthouse with the prosecutor's staff out a side door into a hallway which was not accessible to the media. The judge had warned him before he left not to discuss his testimony with anyone, so he figured that probably included the press.

The group of them managed to get to a waiting car with only a few seconds out in the open where the cameras were rolling. Dan thought briefly about covering his face like the mob bosses always did, but he decided the humor would be lost on most. In the car, Stevens complimented him on his testimony. She was on the phone trying to find out what new information the defense had.

"I wouldn't worry about it," she said to Dan after hanging up. "They probably just did that to make you nervous. Make you think about it overnight. But I don't want you to think about it at all."

"Sure," Dan said, thinking that was like telling somebody not to think about a pink elephant. That image was then ingrained in your mind. Now, though, he was thinking about a pink elephant testifying in court and not being able to fit in the witness chair, placing his trunk on the Bible, having the lawyer talk about his excellent memory.

The movie scene rolling in his mind was interrupted when the car arrived at Stevens's office, and they briefed him again on what to expect the next day and repeated their instructions not to volunteer anything that wasn't asked for.

"Dan, you were great today," Stevens said to him as he was leaving. "You had the judge totally on your side. He was even talking about what a great memory you have. Just be the same tomorrow, but don't get too cocky. It can all turn around in a heartbeat."

Thanks, Dan thought. Something else not to think about that night.

After that, he called Simone and asked if he could come by there instead of going home, since he was sure the press would be waiting for him at his apartment building. Simone and Mattie told him he did a good job, and the three of them had a quiet, peaceful dinner. Dan even slept on their couch, not wanting to be alone with his thoughts all night.

Carl called at one point and said he had seen him on TV out in Vegas. Dan told him how the testimony went. Carl told him he had met Tom Jones and really liked the guy. Dan asked him if he was working on material or just living it up. Carl assured him he could do both at the same time.

Carl left Dan with a cryptic comment that he had "found out something very interesting that he was going to check out," but he couldn't reveal what it was at this point. With Carl, Dan knew that could mean either something important or something so meaningless that he wouldn't even remember to tell Dan about it later.

Chapter 29

The next day, when Dan got to the courthouse bright and early, he was escorted directly into the courtroom. No waiting in the plain little room this time. He was reminded by the judge that he was still under oath.

DAVENPORT: Ms. Dawes, did you have time to review the information which caused us to delay this trial yesterday?
DAWES: Yes, sir, Your Honor, we appreciate the court's indulgence.
DAVENPORT: All right, are you ready to proceed then?
DAWES: Yes, sir, Your Honor.
DAVENPORT: Your witness, Ms. Dawes.

(Dan didn't like the sound of that last comment, but he was ready for battle.)

DAWES: Now, Mr. Darwin, you told us your occupation yesterday was a comedian, correct?
DAN: Yes, ma'am.
DAWES: And could you tell us please what you consider that job to be?
STEVENS: Objection, Your Honor. To paraphrase you, I believe everybody and their dog knows what a comedian does.
Davenport, *to Dan*: You make people laugh, right?
DAN: Yes, sir, I try to, at least, although not so much here. (*Stevens frowned at that last one.*)
DAVENPORT: Here you just want to tell the truth, right?

DAN: Yes, sir. (*Stevens smiled at that one. She liked the help she was getting from the judge.*)

DAWES: Okay, Your Honor, I'll accept your definition, but I would like to explore this occupation just a little bit.

DAVENPORT: Okay, but be quick.

DAWES: Mr. Darwin, tell me how do you come up with the jokes you tell.

DAN: Well, a lot of our stuff is impromptu, spur-of-the-moment reaction jokes to what the audience members say.

DAWES: But you do have some jokes that are planned in advance?

DAN: Yes, ma'am.

DAWES: And how do you come up with them?

DAN: I don't know, just from current events, things that are going on, put a little twist on real life, is that what you're looking for?

DAWES: Not exactly. I assume you don't steal other people's jokes, or copy them.

DAN: No, ma'am, never.

DAWES: Then where do they come from?

DAN: Inside my head, I guess.

DAWES: You make them up?

DAN: Yes.

DAWES: So your job is basically to make things up, come up with new ideas from your creative mind?

DAN: Yes, ma'am.

DAWES: So basically you make up things for a living?

(*Stevens started to object, but Davenport motioned her to sit down.*)

DAVENPORT: Okay, I'm going to stop this here. You made your point, Ms. Dawes, now move on.

DAWES: Okay, Mr. Darwin, now you said yesterday you were at Mr. Jamieson's to try to sell him an idea for a play.

DAN: Yes, ma'am.

DAWES: Could you tell us what the play was about?

(Dan hadn't anticipated this question, but he knew what the play was about, so it seemed harmless enough.)

DAN: It was kind of a comedy love story about an average kind of guy who falls for a girl who turns out to be the girlfriend of a mob boss.

DAWES: And then what happens?

STEVENS: Objection, Your Honor. Relevance.

DAVENPORT: Is this going to be quick, Ms. Dawes?

DAWES: Yes, Your Honor.

DAVENPORT: Go ahead.

DAWES: You were saying, Mr. Darwin? How does it end up?

DAN: It ends up with him having to convince the girl to testify against the mob boss and go into the witness relocation program, where hopefully they live happily ever after.

DAWES: And you thought of this idea yourself?

DAN: Yes, ma'am.

DAWES: Very creative. Have you thought of other story ideas, either for plays or movies or TV?

(Dan was getting an uneasy feeling all of a sudden, and for some reason, Barker's words, "Why Abe Lincoln?" came to him.)

DAN: A few.

STEVENS: Again, Your Honor, what is the relevance?

DAVENPORT: Wrap it up, Ms. Dawes.

DAWES: That's fine, Your Honor. We'll come back to it. Okay, Mr. Darwin, let's go back to your testimony of yesterday. Now, when you were telling your story yesterday, you seemed to have a very vivid recollection of everything?

DAN: Yes, ma'am. It was a very memorable night.

DAWES: Yes, I'm sure. But when you were giving exact quotes, it seemed more like you were reciting dialogue from a play?

DAN: That's just the way my mind works, I guess.

DAWES: Yes, part of being creative, I suppose. You're used to taking what people say and expanding on it.

DAN: That's not what I was doing.

DAWES: Is that not what you meant by saying that's how your mind works?

DAN: No, ma'am. I just meant that I remember conversations in their entirety, not on purpose, I just do.

DAWES: I see. Even conversations that took place almost a year ago.

DAN: Yes, ma'am.

DAWES: So you shouldn't have any trouble remembering what you said yesterday.

DAN: Well, I was kinda nervous, but I guess so.

DAWES: So what did you testify were the first words you heard the deceased woman say that night?

DAN, *thinking for a few seconds*: I said, "She said I won't let you do that, you son of a bitch," then I asked the judge if that was okay to say, and he said, "Sure, why not?"

DAWES, *hesitating, not sure to go on at this point, but deciding she was already committed to it*: And what was the last thing you said you heard Mr. Jamieson saying?

DAN: He said, "Whatever it takes, get it done. I want it so clean in here even the entire casts of all the CSI shows couldn't find anything."

(*Dawes obviously had the transcript from the day before in front of her. Too late, she realized she had made a mistake. Stevens also had a transcript and saw how close Dan had come to exactly quoting what he had said before. She decided to make a point of it.*)

STEVENS: Your Honor, I was wondering if Ms. Dawes would like to read to the jury the transcript of what was said, to see how good Mr. Darwin's memory is.

DAWES: Or at least how well rehearsed he is.

STEVENS: Your Honor!

DAVENPORT: That's out of line, Ms. Dawes. You started this fishing expedition. You can't object when you catch something you didn't want. You want to end it now?

DAWES: Yes, I'll move on. Now, Mr. Darwin, you said you didn't recognize the two people's voices before you saw who they were?

DAN: Yes, ma'am.

DAWES: But you were quite certain it was Mr. Jamieson when you saw him?

DAN: Yes, ma'am. I am certain it was him.

DAWES: So you knew what he looked like, but not what he sounded like?

DAN: Yes, ma'am.

DAWES: And how is that?

DAN: Well, I had seen him on TV and pictures of him in newspapers?

DAWES: Is that what you said yesterday?

DAN: No, yesterday I just said I had seen him on TV.

DAWES: You added the pictures in the newspaper part today?

DAN: Yes, ma'am.

DAWES: Why did you add that part?

DAN: I realized when you asked your question, that must be why I knew more what he looked like than what he sounded like.

DAWES: That quick, you deduced that?

DAN: Yes, ma'am.

DAWES: Is that the truth, or is that just how quick you can come up with an answer?

DAN: I think it was quick because it was the truth.

(*Stevens was ready to come over and give Dan a hug at this point. Dawes was glaring at him and looking forward to seeing how smug Dan would be later.*)

DAWES: Now, Mr. Darwin, you had never met Mr. Jamieson before that night?

DAN: No, ma'am, and I didn't really meet him that night.

DAWES: But you know what an influential man he is in the entertainment business?

DAN: Very much so.

DAWES: Are you sure you didn't meet with him that night, and he rejected your idea, and you made up this story to get even with him?

DAN: Yes, ma'am, I'm sure that didn't happen.

DAWES: But it is a fact you don't like Mr. Jamieson?

DAN: I don't know. I didn't have a good or bad opinion of him before.

DAWES: And why do you dislike him now?

DAN: Besides seeing him kill that woman and all?

DAWES: Yes, some personal reason.

DAN: Well, he has been putting pressure on people not to hire us since then. (*Dan realized too late he shouldn't have added that part.*)

DAWES: Oh, really? Do you have any proof of this?

DAN: Just what people have told me.

DAWES: And are these people going to testify to this?

DAN: No, they don't really want to go against Mr. Jamieson.

DAWES: So all this alleged interference has made you more determined to testify against him? Kind of holding a grudge?

DAN: No grudge. I just want to do what's right, tell the truth.

DAWES: Of course. When did you actually first meet Mr. Jamieson?

DAN: A few nights ago. We wound up at the same place, a party to celebrate the publishing of a poetry book, financed in large part by Mr. Jamieson.

DAWES: How did you wind up being at the party?

DAN: A friend of mine is one of the poets being published.

DAWES: And did you and Mr. Jamieson have a confrontation at this party?

DAN: Yes, ma'am.

DAWES: What prompted it?

DAN: I realized he was going to use my friendship with this woman as a way of getting me not to testify.

DAWES: Did he say that?

DAN: It was more implied than stated. He implied he might not finance the book if I testified.

DAWES: Yes, I see. So when you confronted him with this accusation, what did you say?

DAN: I told him I wasn't going to let him hurt my friend and that I wouldn't testify.

DAWES: So what happened to change your mind?

DAN: My friend told him he couldn't use her to get to me, and she didn't want his help in getting published if it meant I didn't testify.

DAWES: And what did Mr. Jamieson say?

DAN: He said he was going ahead with his plans to finance the book.

DAWES: So you were wrong about his motivations to publish the book?

DAN: No, I don't think so. I think Mr. Jamieson changed his mind.

DAWES: But you don't know that?

DAN: No, ma'am, that's just what I believe.

DAWES: Just as you believe Mr. Jamieson's trying to hold back your career?

DAN: Yes, ma'am.

DAWES: Sounds like you're becoming quite paranoid about Mr. Jamieson?

STEVENS: Objection, Your Honor.

DAVENPORT: Sustained. You don't need to answer that, Mr. Darwin. Let's move on, Ms. Dawes.

DAWES: Mr. Darwin, let's go back to the timing of the night in question. How long would you say the entire conversation and alleged fight between the two people take?

DAN: For the part I saw and heard, less than ten minutes. Maybe less than five minutes.

DAWES: So not long?

DAN: No, not at all.

DAWES: Is it safe to say then that if you had gotten there ten minutes later, you would have missed the entire thing?

DAN: Yes, I think that's accurate.

DAWES: And if you had gotten there ten minutes earlier, you wouldn't have heard anything?

DAN: I don't know how long they had been arguing, so I couldn't say for sure.

DAWES: But you would agree that the timing of your arrival was very crucial to you being witness to this argument?

DAN: Yes, I suppose so.

DAWES: And you figure you were just lucky to arrive at the exact moment when you could testify against Mr. Jamieson?

DAN: No, ma'am. I don't think I was lucky at all. I wish I hadn't seen it at all.

DAWES: Oh, really?

DAN: No, ma'am. It was not something I wanted to see, and it certainly hasn't made my life any easier.

DAWES: But if you hadn't seen it, Mr. Jamieson could have just gotten away with it, according to you.

DAN: Well, no, I wouldn't want him to get away with it. I just wish it had been somebody else to see it. Maybe somebody else could have done something to stop it.

DAWES: Yes, since you brought that up, let's talk about what you did. You said you started to enter the room because it looked like the woman needed help?

DAN: Well, I think I said it looked like something needed to be interrupted, but that was what was going through my mind.

DAWES: Yet before you actually went in, you ducked behind the door.

DAN: Yes, ma'am. I'm not proud of it, but that's what I did.

DAWES: So what stopped you? You were going to help her, then you stopped and hid.

DAN: By that time, he had already hit her, and she hit her head, so I was already too late to stop him. But I should have gone in anyway.

DAWES: But you didn't?

DAN: No, ma'am.

DAWES, *pausing to look at her notes*: So, Mr. Darwin, have you witnessed any other crimes since that time?

(*As soon as she asked the question, it suddenly hit Dan "Why Abe Lincoln?" But it was too late.*)

DAN, *trying to stall*: I'm sorry. What crime are you talking about?

187

DAWES: Just any crimes you might have witnessed. I know this is New York, but witnessing a crime is certainly not an everyday experience for you.

DAN: No, ma'am.

DAWES: So just tell me about any other crimes you might have witnessed since the one you alleged occurred with Mr. Jamieson.

STEVENS, *realizing Dan was not ready for this*: Your Honor, if Ms. Dawes could just tell the witness what she is referring to, it might make it easier to answer.

DAVENPORT: Yes, Ms. Dawes, if you have something specific in mind, please tell the witness.

DAWES: Okay, I'm referring to an incident about three weeks ago, December 7, in which you reported to the police a crime.

STEVENS: Your Honor, Ms. Dawes seems to be reading from something. If she has some official police report, could the prosecution have a copy of it?

DAVENPORT: Ms. Dawes?

DAWES, *holding up a yellow legal pad*: Your Honor, I'm just reading from notes I made on my legal pad. We have requested the police report, but we have not received it yet. As far as I know, I don't have to give copies of my notes to the prosecution. We will enter the police report in the record when we get it.

STEVENS: Your Honor, if she doesn't have the police report, how does she know anything took place?

DAWES: Your Honor, there are sources other than the police department. If Mr. Darwin didn't witness anything, I'm sure he can tell me that.

STEVENS: Your Honor, may I have a recess to discuss whatever this incident is with Mr. Darwin?

DAVENPORT: No, no more delays. Let's move on.

STEVENS: I object then, Your Honor, on the grounds of relevance.

DAWES: It goes to the veracity of the witness, Judge. If the jury is to believe his testimony about this alleged crime, they should hear about other potential crimes he may or may not have seen.

DAVENPORT: Yes, I'll allow it.

DAWES: So, Mr. Darwin, did you or did you not go to the police and report a crime on December 7?

DAN, *thinking: Well, here we go. It seemed so obvious now, the whole clown and Abe Lincoln thing had been set up for this very minute. Nothing to do but go ahead and tell the truth. (Speaking aloud.)* Yes, ma'am, I saw something I thought at the time was a crime.

DAWES: And you reported it to the police?

DAN: Yes, ma'am.

DAWES: Can you use your excellent memory to tell us what occurred on that night?

DAN: I walked a woman home around four in the morning. As I was leaving her apartment building, six men cornered me in an alley and threatened me.

DAWES: How did they threaten you?

DAN: Well, they surrounded me, and then one of them picked me up and threw me into the ice and snow.

DAWES: And what did they say?

DAN: What do you mean? What did they say when he threw me?

DAWES: No, what did they say when they first surrounded you? They weren't silent, were they?

DAN: No, ma'am, one of them started asking me questions.

DAWES: Surely with your excellent memory, you must remember what the questions were?

DAN: Well, yeah, they didn't make any sense.

DAWES: Okay, but what were they?

DAN: He asked me "Was it safe?" then "Did I order the code red?" and then "Did I feel lucky, punk?"

DAWES: So you don't know why they asked those questions?

DAN: Not really. Those are lines from movies, but I didn't know what relevance to me they had.

DAWES: But you said they threatened you? What did they say to indicate that?

DAN: Well, they called me Comedian and then by my name, so I knew they knew who I was.

DAWES: And?

DAN, *knowing he was falling into her trap but not knowing what to do about it*: I told them I knew Jamieson must have hired them, and if they were there to intimidate me into not testifying, then I wouldn't.

DAWES: And what did they say?

DAN: The one who seemed to be in charge said they had no connection to Jamieson.

DAWES: But you still thought they did?

DAN: Yes, ma'am.

DAWES: And I still haven't heard anything that indicated they were threatening you. Was there anything?

DAN: After the big one threw me, the lead one said maybe they wouldn't have to kill me because I seemed to be a smart guy. And maybe they would just rough me up a little bit. And then he added their orders were unclear, so I knew they were working for someone.

DAWES: But they never said who?

DAN: No.

DAWES: And these six men? Anything unusual about them?

DAN, *thinking: Here goes nothing. (Speaking aloud.)* They were dressed as clowns.

DAWES: You say they were dressed as clowns?

DAN: Yes, ma'am.

DAWES, *pausing to enjoy the moment*: So you were cornered in an alley by six clowns who you assumed were employees of Mr. Jamieson?

DAN: Yes, that's right.

DAWES: Did you find that unusual?

DAN: Very much so.

DAWES: So what did you do after the big clown picked you up and threw you down?

DAN: I got up. (*A few laughs from the crowd. Dan thought this sure wasn't the time for laughs. He felt like he was sinking in quicksand.*)

DAWES: And then?

DAN: A bra came floating down from a window above and then a pair of panties.

DAWES: Really?

DAN: Yes, everybody kind of looked up to see where they came from.

DAWES: And where was that?

DAN: It came from a third-floor apartment, and the woman I walked home was leaning out the window.

DAWES: And how was she dressed?

DAN, *realizing Dawes had been briefed on the whole thing and how thorough the setup had been*: She was naked, at least from the waist up.

DAWES: You couldn't see the rest of her?

DAN: No.

DAWES: And did you mention this woman's name, I don't remember?

DAN: It's Shyanne.

DAWES: Any last name?

DAN: I don't know it.

DAWES: And did Shyanne say anything as she leaned out the window topless?

DAN: She said she seemed to have dropped her underwear and could somebody please get it for her.

DAWES: And did anyone?

DAN: All the clowns started to, and that's when I made a break for it.

DAWES: And did anyone notice you?

DAN: One of the smaller clowns tried to stop me, and I pushed him aside.

DAWES: Okay, then what happened?

DAN: The door to the apartment building opened up, and a man came out.

DAWES: Another clown?

DAN: No, ma'am.

DAWES: What did he look like?

DAN: He looked a lot like Abe Lincoln. (*The not-so-muffled laughter from the crowd in the courtroom indicated his story was having the desired effect for Jamieson's side.*)

DAWES: Abe Lincoln! Wow! So far we have six clowns threatening you and Abe Lincoln opening the door for you. Is that right?

DAN: I don't know whether he opened the door for me or just happened to be there at the right time for me.

DAWES: So what happened when Mr. Lincoln opened the door?

DAN: I started to go inside, and then a shot rang out. The guy who looked like Lincoln grabbed his chest and keeled over.

DAWES: Was he dead?

DAN: I don't know. Another shot rang out, and I closed the door behind me and kept running.

DAWES: And did you think to call the police while you were running away from the clowns who had just shot Mr. Lincoln?

DAN: I tried to call the police, but my cell phone had been broken when I was thrown down. And I'm not saying it was Abe Lincoln, just a guy that looked like him.

DAWES: My mistake. So what then? Did you look for a pay phone?

DAN: I'm not sure there are pay phones anymore. I started walking around looking for the nearest police station.

DAWES: And did you find one?

DAN, *deciding to skip the part about the doughnut shop*: Yes, ma'am.

DAWES: Did you consider before you went to the police station how fantastic your story was going to sound?

DAN: Yes, I knew they weren't going to believe me, but I went ahead with it anyway.

DAWES: And what was the reaction of the police when you told them?

DAN: About what I expected. They didn't seem to believe me. They asked if I had been drinking.

DAWES: And had you?

DAN: About five or six hours earlier, but I wasn't drunk.

DAWES: You were as sober that night as the night you witnessed the incident at Mr. Jamieson's office?

DAN: Yes, ma'am.

DAWES: And when the police were skeptical of your story, how did you react? Did you get angry?

DAN: No, I didn't blame them. I probably wouldn't have believed it if I hadn't seen it.

DAWES: So do you expect us to believe your story here today?

DAN: I don't know. It doesn't really matter. I know what it means to swear to tell the truth though.

DAWES: And that's what you've done here, tell the truth as you know it?

DAN: Yes, ma'am.

DAWES: Very admirable. Let's go back to what you said a few minutes ago. You said at the time, you thought it was a crime. Did something happen since then to convince you it may not have been a crime, not an abduction?

DAN: Well, the police told me no body was found in the alley, and so I don't know now whether he was shot or not. (*He decided to hold back what he thought happened.*)

DAWES, *not letting it go*: Well, if he wasn't shot, do you think he was part of this growing conspiracy?

DAN: I don't really know.

DAWES: But what do you think happened?

DAN: I don't have any proof, so I'd rather not say.

DAWES: We just want to know your opinion.

STEVENS: Judge, the witness has said he doesn't know.

DAVENPORT: I'd like to hear it. Go ahead.

DAN, *deciding to not hold back anymore*: I think the whole thing was set up by Mr. Jamieson to make it look like I was not a credible witness.

DAWES: Really? So in addition to murder, you think Mr. Jamieson arranged for six clowns to surround you, Abe Lincoln to open the door for you, and somehow they all knew you would be at that exact location at that exact time?

DAN: Actually, I think he set that part up too.

DAWES: He arranged for you to be at that building at four in the morning? That must have taken some doing.

DAN, *at this point, he figured the case was already blown, so the pressure was off to watch what he said*: Not really. I think he paid Shyanne to make sure I was there at that time.

DAWES: This is quite a conspiracy you've got going on. So far, we have six clowns, Abe Lincoln, and a woman who drops underwear out of a window all paid by Mr. Jamieson to set you up? Why do you think this woman Shyanne was involved?

DAN: Well, she picked me up at the club, we had sex at my place, then she asked me to walk her back home at the time I did to the place where she said she lived.

DAWES: But you don't think she actually lives there?

DAN: No, I don't.

DAWES: Why not? Have you tried to contact her?

DAN: Yes, the place she said she worked at, she doesn't, and a police detective told me he hasn't been able to find any signs she lives at that building.

DAWES: And have you tried calling her?

DAN: Yes, the only time I talked to her, she said not to try to find her.

DAWES: So a woman you had a one-night stand with lied and doesn't want to see you again, and you figure that must be Mr. Jamieson's fault.

DAN: Yes.

DAWES: So the way you figure it, Mr. Jamieson has gone to a lot of trouble to make your life difficult?

DAN: Yes.

DAWES: But you don't have a grudge against him?

DAN: I don't like him, but it's not a grudge.

DAWES: Okay, if you say so. Let's talk about another script you wrote, Mr. Darwin.

STEVENS: Objection. Relevance.

DAWES: I think if the witness is allowed to answer the subject matter of one of his scripts, we will see the relevance.

DAVENPORT: Okay, but ask him specifically about whatever script you have in mind.

DAWES: Mr. Darwin, did you write a screenplay about clowns?

DAN, *as soon as he heard clowns, he just about blew a fuse, knowing it meant Jamieson's people had stolen the script from either himself, Simone, or Carl*: How did you get a copy of that? Whom did you steal it from?

DAWES: Your Honor, would you instruct the witness to answer the question?

DAVENPORT: Mr. Darwin, just answer the question, and be careful with accusations.

DAN: Your Honor, that script was never seen by anyone except me and my brother and best friend. And they wouldn't have given it to her.

DAVENPORT: Be that as it may, Ms. Dawes's knowledge about this script is not at issue here. If you want to make some sort of accusation against her, you can do so through a formal complaint at a later time. This is not the time. Please answer the question.

DAN, *knowing he had blown it but not really caring anymore*: Yes, ma'am, I wrote a pilot script for a TV series that featured clowns solving crimes.

DAWES: And how did the lead character feel about clowns in your script?

DAN: He was scared of them.

DAWES: And did you have a fear of clowns—before this incident occurred?

DAN: Yes, ma'am.

DAWES: Mmm, interesting coincidence, don't you think? You write a script about a person like you who is scared of clowns, and then you are surrounded by clowns who you feel threatened you?

DAN: Maybe not a coincidence at all if Jamieson had somehow obtained a copy of this script without my consent before he set me up to witness what I did.

DAWES: Oh, so this goes right along with your conspiracy theory about Mr. Jamieson. He steals your script, reads it, gets the idea about clowns, pays a woman to seduce you, pays clowns to pretend like they're threatening you, pays Abe Lincoln to set you free and arranges it so that the whole city of New York is not watching—only you. Is that the extent of your conspiracy theory, or are there some aliens involved in this as well?

STEVENS: Objection, Your Honor.

DAVENPORT: Yes, I'm going to stop this right now.

(*Dan didn't take the last statement as a victory for himself as much as the judge sounding like he was the referee in a boxing match stopping the fight because one contestant was bleeding so badly.*)

DAVENPORT: Ms. Dawes, do you have any other questions for Mr. Darwin related to this case?

DAWES, *sensing she didn't need to go any further*: No, Your Honor. I'm finished with this witness.

(*Dan thought that sounded like gloating on her part, but he just wanted to get out of there at this point.*)

DAVENPORT: Ms. Stevens, any redirect?

After a few seconds of looking at her notes, Stevens tried to ask Dan a few questions about the clown incident to make it seem more believable, but she soon realized she should just let it go. Finally, the judge adjourned the trial for the day.

Chapter 30

Shyanne turned off the TV set in her hotel room with disgust. They were making Dan out to be some sort of a loon, and for what, telling the truth. And here she sat, many miles away, doing nothing but letting him twist slowly in the wind. And it was all her fault.

Well, not all her fault, since it was Jamieson who had orchestrated the whole thing. But she had gone along with it, just for the money. They had assured her Dan would not be hurt if she delivered him to that apartment building at four o'clock on that fateful morning. And indeed, he hadn't been physically hurt, at least not much.

But now he was a laughingstock, and that couldn't feel good, even for a comedian. And the worst part was that Jamieson was now going to get away with murder, and knowing him, he would continue to make Dan's life miserable. She wondered if he would ever work again. They had told her it was just some sort of elaborate practical joke, but she should have known by the amount of money they paid her, it was more than that.

Meanwhile, she was living it up at a posh hotel, all expenses paid. In addition, she was making more money as a stripper here than she had ever made in New York. She would have liked to call Dan, at least, but she knew he probably hated her by now. She had picked up the phone a dozen times to call him but never could go through with it. If only she hadn't liked him. If only he had been like so many of the jerks she had met in the strip clubs. If only she hadn't been so desperate to make enough money to get out of the stripping business and follow her one true passion. If only he hadn't made her laugh.

Dan didn't know of Shyanne's regrets, but it probably wouldn't have mattered at this moment. He left the courtroom as quickly as possible, not wanting to look at Jamieson's gloating face. Why couldn't life be more like those movies where some bad guy seems to have gotten away with it on a legal technicality, but by the end of the movie, someone shows up and blows the bad guy away.

No, life had to be more like *Law & Order*, where the bad guy gets off thanks to his weaselly lawyer (possible redundancy) and walks away smirking and shaking hands with his lawyer like they had just won a basketball game. He could still see that Dawes woman standing in front of him, eyeing him like a vulture swooping in on her prey. Maybe in Dan's movie, she would get shot too.

Dan managed to exit through a side door and avoid most of the press. The ones who did catch him and try to get a comment from him didn't even get the obligatory "No comment." He just kept walking away from them, staring straight ahead. Since he was sure he would be branded as some nutcase, he didn't have any image to protect or project.

Fortunately for Dan, he had arranged a flight out of Laguardia for that night to Las Vegas. Their first night onstage as Tom Jones's warm-up act was the next night—Christmas Eve. He had never wanted to leave New York so much, not even those first few weeks when he had moved to New York not knowing a soul, and the Big Apple had almost swallowed him whole. It had been a particularly cold, uncaring city in those days when he first arrived.

Now it didn't seem so cold and uncaring as much as hostile and unrelenting. If he stayed, he would be watching over his shoulder for reporters everywhere he went. Not to mention clowns and dead presidents. Time to leave all this behind for the warm fantasy world of Vegas. And since their comedy act wasn't well-known enough for anybody to notice, none of the press would know where Dan had gone.

And fortunately, Mattie and Simone were flying with him. Andrea had flown out the day before to be with Carl, who he was sure was writing jokes in between gambling and drinking bouts.

Chapter 31

Since the MGM Grand had offered to pay for him and his guests to fly out there, they had opted for first class. It was the first time he had ever been in first class except for that time American had overbooked a flight and they had to put him in first class out of necessity.

He had called Simone and told her they should just meet him at the airport since he didn't want to subject them to any press hounding in case they caught him at his apartment.

When he first saw them, Simone didn't say a word, just gave him one of her hugs. He felt the ugliness of the trial almost instantly leaving his body as she embraced him. Amazing how those hugs were just what he needed when things were at their worst. He could tell they both knew how badly things went because even Mattie hugged him, something she rarely did.

"Ready to go take Vegas by storm, 'migo, and become rich and famous?" Simone asked him with that cheery lilt to her voice that also picked his spirits up.

"I think I've already had my fifteen minutes of fame, but not in the way I wanted," Dan said. "So, yeah, I'm ready to go kick some Vegas ass."

"And maybe tell some jokes in between fights?" Mattie asked in her sarcastic tone that let him know her hug had only been a temporary cease-fire between them. That was reassuring in its own way since he enjoyed their little jousts, and he wouldn't know how to feel if she was nice to him for any extended period of time.

Dan just grinned at her because he had suddenly decided that everything was going to be all right. After all, he hadn't done anything wrong, just told the truth. And he was about to go to the most exciting city in the world and realize what had been a dream of his for longer than he could remember: appear on a Las Vegas stage. The days of the Rat Pack were long since gone, but appearing in Vegas was still the epitome of cool in Dan's mind. In fact, Vegas was cool before there was a cool.

They talked a little as they boarded the plane, with Simone trying to reassure him that the jury could still find Jamieson guilty and Mattie even trying to sound like it was a possibility. He could tell neither one of them believed it any more than he did.

After being seated in the three seats on the second row, with Simone naturally sitting in between him and Mattie, they ordered drinks at Dan's insistence. He was determined to make this a celebratory trip, not a wake.

But after about thirty minutes of sipping on a couple of scotch and cokes, Dan started to think about Shyanne, and his mood turned more melancholy.

"Can I ask you guys something?" he asked.

"Only if you don't call us guys anymore," Mattie said.

"Oh, you know what I mean," Dan said. "I was just thinking about Shyanne.

"Oh, good," Mattie said, rolling her eyes. "So that's what changed your mood."

"No, no, I know y'all aren't like her or anything, but maybe you can answer this, since you are women and all. All right, let's say she set me up just for the money and she never cared about me."

In unison, Simone and Mattie said, "She set you up just for the money, and she never cared about you."

"Okay, that was cute. And don't call me Shirley."

Both of them looked at him questioningly.

"We didn't call you Shirley," Simone said.

"Oh, I thought we were doing a scene from *Airplane*, the movie," Dan said. "The characters would sometimes repeat something in unison for comic effect."

He saw the look of recognition in Mattie's eyes, but still nothing in Simone's.

"Oh yeah, I remember that movie, but no, we weren't doing that, although that would have been good, seeing as how we're on an airplane and all," Mattie said.

"You didn't see the movie, did you?" Dan asked Simone, knowing she hadn't, since *Airplane* had come out before 1985. She shook her head no.

"Before your time, I guess," Dan said. "Anyway, so we're not doing scenes from *Airplane?*"

"I'm not," Simone said.

"So anyway, back to what I was going to say—" Dan started before Simone interrupted.

"Why did you think we called you Shirley?"

"That's from *Airplane* also. You see, one of ... Never mind. I'll explain it some other time, or Mattie can. Or we'll rent the DVD sometime."

"Okay, good," Simone said. "Go ahead with your story."

"All right, well, it's not really a story, but anyway, we all agree she set me up for the money and she didn't care about me. But just for argument's sake, what if we're wrong?"

"Wrong about setting you up?" Mattie said.

"No, she definitely did set me up, but if she had actually cared about me, would her actions have been any different? I mean, she would still have acted like she enjoyed the sex, and as you know, most guys can't tell the difference if a woman is acting like she's having an uh ..." He looked around to see if anyone else was listening.

"Orgasm?" Mattie said. "That's true, from what I hear. What's up with that anyway? Why can't men tell?"

"I don't think most guys care, to be honest with you," Dan said. "They're just glad they did."

"Pigs," Mattie said scowling.

"Hey, I didn't say me, I said most guys. Anyway, can I get to the point now?"

"Oh, is there one?" Simone said. Every once in a while, she would zing him, seeming to take one of Mattie's lines. Dan would feign hurt feelings, but he really enjoyed it.

"Yes, okay, so she acts like she wants to have sex and enjoys it, or she actually does want to and enjoys it, I may not know the difference. Then afterward, either way, she has to disappear so that I wouldn't find her and find out the truth."

"I'm still not with you, 'migo," Simone said. "What are you saying?"

"I'm just saying, from my point of view, her actions would have still been the same. I couldn't have told the difference between a cold, calculating bitch and someone who just agreed to do something for money but actually ended up liking me."

"No difference, I guess, and she probably did end up liking you," Simone said. "You're a likable guy. Nobody's blaming you for falling for it, or for her. It's not your fault."

"No, I'm not saying that. I'm saying, from my viewpoint, there's no way of knowing exactly how she felt."

"No, but what difference does it make now?" Simone asked. "Unless you just prefer to believe she liked you so you can feel better about her."

"Trust me, it's better if you hate her," Mattie said. "You're likely never going to see her again, so it's better to forget her, and that's easier to do if you aren't pining away for her."

"Yeah, you're probably right."

"Let me ask you this though," Mattie said. "I've been wondering, could she have set you up without having sex with you?"

Dan had obviously thought about this a lot. "Yeah, she could have. The sex made it easier, but she could have gotten me to follow her to that building with or without. I mean, when you look like she does, it doesn't take much to get a guy to follow you. Why, you think that says something?"

"Maybe, maybe not," Mattie said. "Here's the thing. I've thought about this. Every day at work, this girl pretends to like men and does everything but have intercourse with them, whether she likes the guy or not. How much money she makes depends in a big way on how well she can fool the guy, right?"

"Yeah, I think that's true."

"So every once in a while, let's say some guy comes in the club that she might actually like, as opposed to all the ones that pretty much disgust her. Does she act any different with him than she does with the ones she doesn't like? Probably not. After a while, she gets so used to it, she doesn't even know she's acting anymore. That's just her work-time persona."

"Okay, I'm with you so far."

"So she agrees to do this gig with you—and gets paid pretty well, I imagine—to make sure you get to that building at a particular time. She takes on her stripper persona to pick you up 'cause she knows that'll work. It always works with guys in her experience. She meets you, maybe she likes you, maybe she doesn't, but it doesn't really matter. Except maybe afterward she feels some regret about it. But chances are, she doesn't even care any more about a real relationship, doesn't know what it's like not to be acting with a man. After a while, the stripper persona melds in with her other personality and she either can't distinguish between the two or doesn't care. She only knows one kind of relationship with men, so it really wasn't a big moral decision for her. This was just life as she knew it."

"Wow," was all Dan could muster.

"My girlfriend, the psychologist," Simone said proudly.

"When did you figure all that out?" Dan asked.

"Oh, I started thinking about it after we went to the club. I saw how the women there made their money, and I figured Shyanne must be somewhat like them. But I hadn't met her. I could be wrong."

"I doubt it," Simone said.

"No, I think you're right too," Dan said. "Can you analyze me now?"

"I already have, but it'll cost you $200 an hour to hear it."

"All right, but I'll have to start charging you for the jokes you get to hear now for free."

"Oh, dear Lord, what will I do?"

"All right, I'm cutting you off then. No more free jokes for you."

"Oh, please, not that. Anything but that," Mattie said in mock desperation.

"No, that's it. You made your bed ... You get $200 an hour?"

"You just now heard that?" Simone said. "Are you on some kind of time delay?"

"I hear all the words, but I don't always process them all at once."

"Oh, I see," Simone said.

"Do you really?"

"No."

"So what are you saying?" Mattie asked. "I'm not worth $200 an hour?"

"Yeah, if you cure everybody in the first hour," Dan said.

"In the first place, you don't really cure mental illness, you treat it …"

"Oh, great, so not only do you charge them $200 an hour, you do so with the expectation they might be paying you for the rest of their lives."

"You got a problem with that?"

"No, no, if you can get 'em to pay it, more power to you. Let the marketplace decide."

"Damn straight they pay it. And I don't hear any complaints from them about it being too high."

"Okay," Dan said. "What was the second place?"

"What?"

"You said 'in the first place.' Usually, there's a second place."

"Oh yeah, in the second place, you can't put a price tag on mental health."

"I can. Two hundred dollars an hour for three sessions."

"So $600 is all you would pay for a healthy mental state?"

"Yeah, $600, maybe $700 if I had something really bad, like split personalities or something like that."

"For split personalities, I charge 'em twice. They never know the difference."

"Really?"

"No, that's an old psychiatrist joke."

"Oh, good one."

"Speaking of jokes, what kind of guarantee do you offer for your comedy act?" Mattie said.

"If you don't like the joke, don't laugh."

"What about the money they pay to see you?"

"You mean, like the $15 cover they charge at The House of Hyenas? Yeah, I guess we could refund that. But you can't really put a price on the gift of laughter."

"As opposed to the price of mental health."

"Well, laughter is the best medicine."

"For what?"

"I don't know. The heartbreak of psoriasis?"

"Okay, I don't know what that is …" Mattie said. Dan started to interrupt, but she stopped him. "And I don't care. What about out in Vegas? They put a pretty stiff price on the gift of laughter. I'm sure the tickets are more than fifteen bucks."

"Yeah, but you also get to see and hear Tom Jones. You're actually paying to see him. You just get us for free."

"When you say 'You're paying to see Tom Jones,' you're not talking about us, are you?" Simone asked. "We get in for free, don't we?"

"Yeah, probably. You don't want to pay to see Carl and me at the MGM Grand?"

"You said you were free, we were paying for Tom Jones."

She might not have meant it, but Dan knew that for a person so generous of spirit, Simone could be something of a penny-pincher sometimes.

"I'll make sure you don't have to pay," Dan said.

"I'm just kidding, 'migo," Simone said. "Of course we'll pay for our tickets."

"Yeah, I guess I'll have to too" Mattie said, adding sarcastically, "since I won't be getting your jokes for free anymore."

With that, the alcohol kicked in a little more, and the conversation started coming to a lull. Dan suddenly realized how tired he was and how late it was. Being tense all day had taken a lot out of him. He had wanted to think about some jokes for the next night, but instead he did something rare for him, drifted off to sleep on an airplane.

Chapter 32

The plane didn't land in Vegas until after 1:00 a.m. Dan woke up when the plane started descending, making his ears pop. He didn't feel refreshed, though, just groggy.

The three of them trudged down to the baggage claim area, and Dan started wondering whether it was going to be hard to find a taxi this late. No, not in Las Vegas, the city without clocks.

As they made their way outside, there were sure plenty of taxis and limos waiting, but there was no need for that. Standing there with a big grin on his face was Carl proudly holding a big sign reading "Dan Darwin—Comedian." That was the great thing about Carl: he would come up with something to boost your spirits when you least expected it, and embarrassment was not in his vocabulary.

Apparently, it was in Andrea's vocabulary. She was kind of halfway holding up a sign with Simone and Mattie's names on it.

"Hey, bro," Carl said, "welcome to Vegas, the city that launched a thousand careers."

"And sank about a million," Dan said.

They hugged. Without saying a word about the trial, Carl had let Dan know everything was going to be all right.

"Hey, why are our names not as big as Dan's, and our sign is smaller too?" Mattie said, looking at the small sign Andrea had.

Carl looked knowingly at Andrea and winked.

"Hey, you two start appearing at a major Las Vegas casino, we'll see what we can do," he said.

"Fair enough," Mattie said. "You got a ride for us, or you just here at one thirty in the morning for kicks?"

"Have I got a ride?" Carl said grinning.

With that, he escorted them across the street toward a parking lot. He hit the keyless entry button, and the lights flashed on a white limo.

"And the best thing about this limo ride, Danny—no clowns inside," Carl said. Seeing Dan's frown, he added, "Okay, too early for the clown jokes apparently."

"Just a tad," Dan said.

"Okay, hop in, I was going to take us by Circus Circus first, see if any clowns were lurking around, but I guess not now," Carl said. "We had a driver earlier, but I gave him the night off. So I'm your chauffeur for the evening. Where to, ladies and gent?"

"I think maybe the MGM Grand," Dan said.

They all hopped into the spacious back seat area except for Carl.

"Andrea, you not riding up front with me?"

"No, I want to ride in the back," she said. "I never have gotten to ride in the back before."

"Except for earlier today."

"Oh yeah, I forgot. I want to see their faces."

"Shh," Carl said to Andrea.

"What's going on?" Mattie asked.

"Never you mind now," Carl said, grinning again. "All aboard for the MGM Grand."

They made their way on the short trip from the airport to the MGM Grand. Dan, Simone, and Mattie had all gotten their second winds from the long day and the long flight. There was nothing like Las Vegas to get the juices going again.

Instead of taking the back way around, which was the way cab and limo drivers usually took passengers to the hotel part of the casinos, Carl went right down the strip. Dan briefly wondered why, but it soon became apparent.

As they neared the MGM Grand, Carl slowed down even though the traffic was not awful at that time of night. He opened the window that separates the front from the back.

"And now if you will cast your eyes upward, I think you will see one of the prettiest sights you've ever seen," Carl said, using the speaker system in the limo.

Dan wasn't sure the sight was one of the prettiest, but it did take his breath away. There in huge letters on the Grand's sign read "Tom Jones," and underneath in much smaller letters, but still several feet high, read "With the comedy team—The Darwin Brothers."

"'Migo, look," Simone said, "it's you!"

"Well, me and the chauffeur, to be exact," Dan said.

Mattie and Simone and Andrea all clapped. Dan looked toward his brother, who had stopped the car and was looking back, beaming from ear to ear. They momentarily just looked at each other and enjoyed this moment, one they were never sure would happen.

"You like?" Carl finally said.

"What's not to like?" Dan said as they all got out of the car to stare up at the sign like a group of tourists looking up at the Eiffel Tower for the first time. Actually, the Eiffel Tower replica was just up the road. Dan and Carl hugged each other, then Dan hugged Simone.

"You did it, 'migo."

"Well, we hadn't actually done it yet, but I'm pretty pumped up," Dan said.

"And next time, it'll say, 'The Darwin Brothers, with Tom Jones,'" Simone said.

"Okay, let's not get carried away. Tom may be too old to sing by the time that happens."

"We got to send a picture of this to the folks," Carl said. "Dad's still mad at us for not following him into the accounting business."

"I think he might not be too mad now," Dan said.

"No, I think he'll be pretty damn proud of his two boys when he sees that. And Mom too."

"She's always been proud of us. She says next time we appear, she's coming out, Christmas or no Christmas."

"I like the sound of that, bro. Next time."

They all took turns taking pictures and posing in front of the sign. To the casual observer, Dan and Carl looked more like the average tourists than the opening act for Tom Jones.

Finally, everyone had had enough, and they went inside the hotel to head off to their rooms. Carl had already picked up everybody's keys, or those card things that pass for hotel keys. They all had adjoining suites on one of the top floors. Simone and Mattie went to theirs, Carl and Andrea went to theirs, and Dan went alone to his huge suite, with Carl yelling at him to check out the view before he went to bed.

At other times, he would have felt a little lonely and a little left out being the fifth wheel, the only one checking into a room alone. But right now at this particular time, he felt anything but lonely.

When he got to his room, he opened the curtains and looked out. There, at almost eye level, was the sign with their name on it. He started to call Carl, but then he just decided to sit there and stare at the sign and enjoy the moment.

He reflected on all the things he had been through in his life and all the events of the past few weeks. Jamieson and Shyanne and the dueling lawyers and the cranky judge seemed so far in the past. They might go out and bomb the next night and never be heard from again. But life at that particular moment seemed as close to right as he could remember. And he supposed it would be nice to share this moment with someone else, but it was kind of nice just the way it was.

He thought about what the audience would be like the next night and tried to anticipate what some of the potential jokes might be. But his mind was totally spent, and he ended up going to sleep with the curtains still open and facing the sign.

Chapter 33

The next day was Christmas Eve, but it didn't feel like Christmas anything to Dan. Vegas was just not a Christmas kind of place. He wondered what kind of people would be spending their Christmas vacation in this unholiest of cities. New Year's Eve, yeah, but Christmas? He started picturing what kind of people they would be, then he stopped when he realized whoever those people were would be his audience that night.

Dan spent most of the day away from the others, trying to get his mind right and his jokes in order. He wished Carl would do the same thing, but he was off on some sort of secret mission. He remembered the vague reference to finding out something he had mentioned on the phone before Dan had gotten here. Oh well, you couldn't hurry Carl on these things. He would tell him what he was up to when he got ready, or if nothing happened, Dan would never hear what it was about.

As it came closer to showtime, Dan became more nervous. And meeting Tom Jones didn't help calm the nerves. The man was at once smaller in real life, and yet larger than life. He was very friendly and engaging, but that only added pressure because Dan didn't want to let the man down.

Ordinarily, Dan would have joined the others and cruised the strip, going from casino to casino and enjoying the sights. But there would be plenty of time for that later. He did get out enough to notice that the people wandering around looked pretty much like the normal Vegas crowd, which was to say not so normal at all. He thought of that brilliant Vegas tourism line: "What happens in Vegas stays in Vegas." It was enticing, but very much untrue. All the people he had ever known who had been here couldn't stop talking about what happened here. That was half the fun, talking about it later.

He called the box office late in the day and was told the show was sold out. He would have liked to have felt proud, but he knew it was Tom that was still packing them in after all these years. Okay, just what he needed, more pressure.

He also called Detective Barker back in New York. Barker told him he had made another last-minute attempt to find Shyanne but had struck out. He couldn't get Rachel to admit she knew her, and he hadn't had any luck getting any of the girls at Bloomers to talk.

As a desperation measure, the prosecution had called Frank Fetters to testify, since he was the only one who could verify Dan's story about the clowns. But that attempt had backfired. Fetters's mind had apparently played tricks on him. He remembered the clowns all being armed with rifles and even recalled one of them riding a horse. And he mistakenly said the guy coming out the door looked like George Washington. When he corrected himself, it just made it look like he had forgotten his lines. By the end of his testimony, Dan looked even worse in the eyes of the jury.

Barker told him the judge had called a recess for Christmas, so they wouldn't know anything for several days. Of course, Dan felt like he already knew the outcome.

The last few hours dragged by like days. As he and Carl got ready in the dressing room, they went over the opening part a little more. The only difference in this and their usual routine was, they were dressed in tuxes this time—a first for Carl onstage and a first for Dan ever. But Tom Jones had thought it was a good idea when Carl suggested it, and Dan saw no reason to go against Tom Jones—the man who could make their careers if he liked them.

As usual, they were going to count on their ad-libbing for the most part. Dan suddenly realized they were going out in front of a Vegas crowd for the first time with basically no material. Oh well, this was what separated the men from the would-be men.

Tom stopped in to wish them luck. Carl, who now acted like he and Tom had known each for years, told him he hoped he liked the show. Tom said he was sure he would, but Dan couldn't tell whether he was even going to watch or not. He kind of hoped he wouldn't at this particular time.

Chapter 34

"And now making their debut appearance in Las Vegas, please welcome the comedy duo from the stages of New York, the Darwin brothers, Carl and Dan."

As the announcer's words lingered in Dan's ears, he thought about the House of Hyenas and whether that could be called the stages of New York. Not exactly Broadway.

They made their way onto stage to a considerable amount of applause. Tom had told them the Vegas audiences started out generous, but could turn on you pretty fast.

DAN: Hi, I'm Dan Darwin, this is my brother, Carl. Well, what do you think? Pretty exciting being here in Las Vegas, huh? Sin City.

CARL: Yeah, I kind of wish the announcer hadn't told everybody this was our first time here. Now they're going to be looking to see how nervous we are.

DAN: I think my chattering teeth might have given me away anyway.

CARL: Yeah, but that nervous tic you have might have gone by unnoticed.

Dan: But not now.

CARL: Oh, sorry, bro.

DAN: That's okay, I think I got it under control now. (*On purpose, he made his face twitch a couple of times.*)

CARL: Yeah, you're the picture of cool now.

DAN: That's not exactly true about the first appearance in Las Vegas though. I was out here in the '80s with Ann-Margret.

CARL: Did she know that?

DAN: Probably not. She was standing here onstage, and I was over there at that table. But still from the right camera angle …

CARL: You appeared together.

DAN: Exactly.

CARL: Well, this is *our* first time appearing here. Think we should start being funny right off the bat?

DAN: No hurry. We're just killing time for Tom Jones anyway. (*Some in the audience applauded.*) Okay, thanks. So Christmas Eve in Las Vegas. You folks must be thrilled. Nothing says Christmas like Vegas. For instance, the hookers we ran into last night on the strip.

CARL: Well, their bustiers were red and their stockings were filled with green.

DAN: And made of fishnet as I recall.

CARL: They seemed kind of Christmasy to me. They were certainly in a rather giving mood.

DAN: But only if we were.

CARL: Well, tit for tat.

DAN: So to speak.

CARL: And what about that guy we ran into after that, the jolly fat man with the long, white beard yelling out "Ho, ho, ho." You didn't think that was Santa?

DAN: No, I think he was just a fat drunk guy looking for the hookers.

CARL: Hey, how come I'm being the straight man and you're getting all the punch lines?

DAN: Yeah, I forgot it's hard for you to be straight, isn't it?

CARL: You did it again.

DAN: Okay, we'll switch.

CARL: I think we should go into the audience and talk to the people. (*He headed into the crowd. Dan didn't.*) You not coming?

DAN: I'd rather not. You go ahead.

CARL: You're not still scared about jealous husbands taking a swing at you, are you? It only happened that once.

DAN: Once is enough.

CARL: You see, one time Dan got a little too friendly with a woman in the audience after the show, and the next night, the woman's husband showed up and took a swing at Dan. Wasn't that what happened?

DAN: Actually, it was you that got a little too friendly with the woman *and* her sister. And both their husbands showed up and confused me with you and wanted to fight with me. Did you forget that part?

CARL: No, it's just more fun to hear someone else say it.

DAN: Glad I could be of service to you.

CARL: Anyway, here's a nice-looking couple, and just to be safe, let me talk to the man. Would you mind standing, sir? (*A fifty-ish distinguished man with graying hair was seated next to a rather stunning-looking, dark-haired woman in her early forties. He stood up, somewhat reluctantly. Carl shook his hand.*) How are you, sir?

DISTINGUISHED MAN: Just fine.

CARL: What's your name?

DISTINGUISHED MAN: Dr. Ben Parrin.

CARL: And are you a doctor? Or did your parents just think that would be a cool first name?

DR. PARRIN: I'm a doctor.

CARL: Of course you are. And this lovely woman is your …

DR. PARRIN: My wife.

CARL: Oh, okay, good, good. I was just going to say if this was your first date, I'd go along with the doctor story if you wanted me to.

DR. PARRIN: I am a doctor.

DAN: Uh-oh. I sense another angry man coming back to see us. Doctor, for the record, that's Carl. I'm Dan.

CARL: No, no, I'm not going to make him angry. I'll smooth things over. Where are you from, and what takes you away from home on the night before Christmas?

DR. PARRIN: We live in Beverly Hills, and my wife just loves Tom Jones and always wanted to see him in person. So we drove over to see him tonight, and we're driving back home tomorrow to enjoy Christmas with our family. I like to make my wife happy.

CARL: And if making her happy means letting her lust after Tom Jones ...

DAN: When does the "smoothing things out" part come in?

CARL: I'm getting to that. And, Doctor, what's your field?

DR. PARRIN: I'm a cosmetic and reconstructive surgeon.

CARL: Is that like a plastic surgeon?

DR. PARRIN: That's what a layman would call it.

CARL: And I fall right into the middle of that category.

DAN: In more ways than one.

CARL: So a plastic surgeon in Beverly Hills. That's kind of like shooting fish in a barrel, isn't it?

DR. PARRIN: There's lots of competition.

CARL: But I bet you're the best, right?

DR. PARRIN: I can hold my own.

CARL: And other people's too, apparently. So what's kind of the hot thing now, cosmetic and reconstructive surgery-wise?

DAN: I guess the big-boob phase has come and gone.

CARL: Bite your tongue.

DAN, *biting his tongue, repeated the same line unintelligibly.*

DR. PARRIN: Actually, breast enhancement is still popular.

CARL AND DAN, *yelling*: Yes!

CARL, *paused and changed his voice back to normal*: I mean, that's interesting. But what's hot besides big boobs?

DR. PARRIN: Actually, buttock enhancement is quite the thing now.

DAN: The J-Lo, Kardashian phenomenon.

CARL: Yes, let's talk about big butts.

DR. PARRIN: And penile implants are um ...

CARL: On the rise?

DR. PARRIN, *finally smiling*: Yes, you could put it that way.

CARL, *to Dan*: See, I finally got him to smile. I think I should move on to someone else while he's happy.

DAN: So big boobs and big butts, you don't mind talking about. But enlarging penises ...?

CARL, *lowering his voice*: Not a topic I need to know anything about.

DAN, lowering his voice: Yeah, me neither. Let's move on.

CARL, *moving to the next table with a big group of people at it*: Wow, is this all one group? (*Several of them said yes.*) Okay, I want to talk to the leader of this group, the decision-maker. (*An older man at the end of the table stood up.*) All right then, no questions asked, you're the man, huh?

OLDER MAN: Well, this is my wife, my four kids, their wives and husbands and three grandkids, and none of them would be here today without me.

CARL: Sounds like your wife might have had something to do with it too, but okay. What's your name, sir?

OLDER MAN: Isaac Samuels.

CARL: And how old are you, if you don't mind me asking?

ISAAC: I'm eighty-two years young.

CARL, *to the crowd*: How about that? Eighty-two. Did you hear that, Dan?

DAN: Yes, I'm still wondering what hand he had in creating the spouses of his kids.

CARL: Well, I don't think we need to get into that. It could be embarrassing to talk about.

DAN: Just wondering.

CARL: So, Isaac, may I call you Isaac?

ISAAC: That's my name.

CARL: Not going to make me call you a doctor?

DAN: Not unless he gets sick. Sorry, I forgot you were tired of being straight man.

CARL: That's okay. Can I ask him a question now and have him answer?

DAN: Yeah, if you want to try something new.

CARL: What brings you and all these people you created from scratch here so close to Christmas?

ISAAC: In the first place, we're Jewish.

CARL: Well, okay then.

DAN: I don't think he needs a second place.

CARL: No, I think that's explanation aplenty. So Christmas not a big celebration then. (*To Dan.*) Where to now?

DAN: Ask him about Hanukkah.

CARL: Okay, what about Hanukkah?

ISAAC: It's over.

CARL: Good one, Dan. Oh, I know. What about Jesus?

DAN: Oh, Lord.

CARL: Well, if you want to use his title.

ISAAC: What about Jesus?

CARL: I mean, he was Jewish, right?

ISAAC: I believe so, yes.

DAN: At least on his mother's side.

CARL: Well, it just seems ironic to me that all the people that believe in Jesus are not Jewish.

DAN: Do we really want to go down this road on the day before Christmas?

CARL: What road is that?

DAN: The Highway to Hell, I think. Talking about Jesus the day before his birthday—I mean, we're already in Sin City for Christmas. It seems like we're kind of tempting fate by making jokes about Jesus.

CARL: No, it'll be all right. So what about it?

ISAAC: Is it my turn now?

CARL: Dan?

DAN: Sure, go ahead.

ISAAC: We believe in Jesus, he was a great man, just not the Messiah.

CARL: That's kind of his claim to fame, though, isn't it? Without that walking-on-water thing, he's just kind of a carpenter who liked helping people a lot.

DAN: Can you wrap this part up before the plague and pestilence hit Vegas?

CARL: It's probably overdue here anyway. All right, I'll move on. Where you from, Isaac?

ISAAC: Saint Paul, Minnesota.

CARL: Ah, Minnesota. The Land of (to Dan) how many lakes?

DAN: A whole bunch.

CARL: Yes, I believe that's the state motto—"the Land of a Whole Bunch of Lakes."

ISAAC: Actually, it's "10,000 Lakes."

CARL: That is a whole bunch. Think anybody ever counted them?

ISAAC: I'm sure somebody must have.

CARL: You think it's exactly 10,000, or maybe the guy that was counting got to 9,972 and just said, "The hell with it, let's say there's 10,000."

ISAAC: I really couldn't say.

CARL: Kind of a state secret, huh? Okay, I understand. So how did you decide on Vegas for this big family reunion? It's kind of a long way from Minnesota.

ISAAC: Actually, only one of our kids still lives in Minnesota. The rest have moved out West.

DAN: They were probably tired of trying to get around all those damn lakes.

CARL: Yeah, you apparently can't walk twenty yards without falling into water.

DAN: That'll shrivel up your Minnesota Twins in a hurry.

ISAAC: Can I get back to why we're here?

CARL: Yeah, if you insist on interrupting.

ISAAC: Well, we have one son who lives in Idaho, another lives in Arizona, and our daughter lives in California …

CARL: Dan, you getting this all down?

DAN: Yeah, Mom and Dad and one of the kids and their spouse live in Minnesota, one son and his wife live in Idaho, one son and his wife live in Arizona, and the daughter and her husband live in California. I don't know yet where the grandkids are located.

ISAAC: Let's see, two of them …

CARL: Okay, we'll log onto the internet after the show and check out your entire family tree, but for now, can we get back to the subject? Why Vegas?

ISAAC: It was actually my wife's idea. It seemed like a good place that everybody could get to fairly easy. And she just loves the slots.

CARL: And since I assume you hadn't heard of us, who's the Tom Jones fan here?

ISAAC: That would be my wife again. She saw him a long time ago, and she probably wouldn't want me to say this ... (*He paused and looked at his wife.*)

CARL: But you're the one in charge here. You don't need her permission.

ISAAC: I guess so ... (*He looked again at his wife, who nodded her approval.*) She threw her underwear onstage at him.

CARL: All right! All this time, I've been talking to the wrong Samuels. She chooses Vegas, she decides to come see Tom Jones, and she likes to throw her underwear onstage. Ma'am, would you mind standing up? (*She did, hesitantly. She appeared to be in her seventies with silver hair, but still quite attractive.*) What's your name, ma'am?

MRS. SAMUELS: Sara.

CARL: So is that true? You really threw your underwear onstage at Tom Jones.

SARA: Not all my underwear. Just my panties. (*She lowered her voice when she said "panties."*)

DAN: I'm sorry, Carl, I couldn't hear that last part.

CARL: She said she only threw her panties onstage. Apparently, she didn't take her bra off.

DAN: Or wasn't wearing one to start with.

CARL: Dan, this is a classy lady, you can tell by looking at her. And still quite hot, I might add. Of course, she was wearing a bra that night. Weren't you?

DAN: Oh no, you're not going to hit on her, are you?

CARL: No, of course not. So, Sara, you keeping all your clothes on tonight, aren't you?

DAN: Sounds like you're hitting on her to me.

CARL: No, I meant during the show.

SARA: Yes, I'm a little beyond the pantie-throwing years. Tom wouldn't be interested in my old lady underwear.

CARL: Who said anything about Tom? I was thinking of during our act. Okay, okay, maybe I am hitting on her. I'm sorry, Isaac.

ISAAC: Quite okay. I know how lucky I am.

CARL: Yes, you are. Maybe I better move on, though, before Dan gets
    beat up by an eighty-two-year-old man.
DAN: Yes, please do.

*(Carl couldn't see it, but Dan saw the signal they only had fifteen minutes
left. He used the code word* penguins *that he and Carl had agreed on.
So Carl went to a few more tables, and then they thanked the crowd and
left to what seemed a very good reaction from the appreciative crowd.)*

Chapter 35

As they made their way backstage, Dan and Carl looked at each other and smiled and hugged each other. It might not have been their best performance ever, but they both knew it had gone well. And the adrenaline was at a level where they were both on a natural high.

It didn't take long for Andrea and Mattie and Simone to make it backstage. They were all smiles as well. And they took turns hugging Dan and Carl.

"Great job, 'migo," Simone said. "You guys hit some home runs out of the park tonight."

"If you hit it out of the park, it has to be a … Okay, never mind. Thanks." Dan stopped himself, knowing sports were not her thing. "Yeah, I thought we did pretty good. Carl was on top of his game."

"You too, bro," Carl said. "You were like inside my head tonight. It was like great sex."

"Okay, I think we might have to go to Mattie on that 'inside your head' thing. And nothing's like great sex," Dan said.

"That's true. But I feel so juiced we have to go celebrate. Where do you guys want to go?"

"I was thinking," Dan said, "I want to go celebrate too, but shouldn't we stick around to hear Tom Jones? I mean, we're only here because of him."

"Yeah, you're right," Carl said. "You guys mind sticking around too?"

"No, but we're not guys," Mattie said.

"Yeah, yeah, whatever."

"Hey, can we watch him somehow from backstage?" Simone asked. "I've never got to see a show from backstage."

"Yeah, I don't see why not," Carl said. "I'll find us a good spot."

Carl did find a good spot, and they found Tom Jones still put on a good show. The audience, which seemed pretty enthused about Carl and Dan, went crazy for Tom. Afterward, they waited around for a few minutes to tell Tom how much they enjoyed his show. He told Carl and Dan they had been great.

Dan couldn't tell whether he had actually watched or not, but then he added that he would like them to open for him all the way through December 30, his last five nights in Vegas on this gig. They tried to act cool when he asked them, but as soon as he was gone, they started celebrating like they had just won the World Series.

"That's right, ladies and gentleman," Carl said. "We just got our stay at the MGM Grand in Las Vegas, Nevada—entertainment capital of the world—extended."

"What did you say, who got their stay at the MGM Grand in Las Vegas, Nevada—the entertainment capital of the world—extended?" Dan asked him.

"That would be us—the Darwin Brothers. I think I'll go catch him and tell him we will if they make the letters a little bigger on the sign."

He started to leave, and all four of them began to stop him.

"Wait a minute, Mr. Darwin, the elder," Mattie said. "Not so fast on the prima donna attitude."

"Yeah, we might find ourselves appearing at the Ramada Inn in Elko, Nevada," Dan said.

"I was just kidding, guys … and Mattie," Carl said grinning.

That was Carl. He probably was kidding, but you didn't really know. And he probably wouldn't have actually gone through with it even if he wasn't kidding, but you really didn't know that either.

"I would say a double celebration is in order tonight … my treat," he said. "Let's go party like it's 1999."

"Okay, but I didn't really do much in 1999," Dan said.

"Yeah, I was kind of young to be partying too late in 1999," Andrea said.

"And Simone and I didn't even know each other in 1999. Can we make it 2005?" Mattie said.

"No Prince fans here?" Carl said. "Party like it's 1999? Come on, folks."

"I remember the artist formerly known as Prince. Is that the same guy?" Dan asked.

"Okay, you guys can play dumb all you want," Carl said. "Nobody's raining on my parade tonight. Not even a purple rain."

With that, he began to do some dance that was unrecognizable to the rest of them.

"Parade or not, don't ever do that dance again, for any reason," Dan said.

That just prompted Carl to start dancing again. Eventually, Dan joined along, then Simone and Mattie, and finally Andrea. It was a spontaneous moment of unadulterated glee that adults rarely allow themselves to enjoy.

The group found plenty of places to party, even though it was Christmas Eve, and then on into Christmas. Apparently, Christmas in Vegas is pretty much like Groundhog's Day or Armistice Day or Tuesday.

Later on, when they had all slept for a while, they got together for breakfast and discussed what to do to celebrate Christmas. None of them were terribly religious as far as organized religion goes, but they wanted to do something besides hang out and gamble.

It was Carl who suggested going in the limo to see the Grand Canyon. Everyone liked the idea, but Simone warned them it might be closed on Christmas.

"The thing's like two hundred miles long," Carl said. "You can't close a two hundred–mile canyon."

They gathered up their presents, a nice picnic lunch, and got in the limo. As it turned out, the Grand Canyon was closed on Christmas Day—all two hundred miles of it. But they found a nice little place out in the middle of nowhere with a nice view of Lake Meade and all the mountains and plains that were so much a part of the western vista.

All in all, it was a pretty nice Christmas after all. The beautiful setting and the general good mood of the whole group moved Dan to say a prayer before they ate. He thanked God for having such good friends and creating such beauty in the world. The prayer surprised everyone but Simone, who knew that deep down Dan was a religious person.

"Thanks, 'migo," she said, "I'm grateful for you too. And especially my Mattie and everyone here."

That broke the ice, and everyone thanked each other and told each other "Merry Christmas." Then Carl said it was getting too mushy, and the conversation went back to its normal irreverent tone.

Chapter 36

The Darwin Brothers appeared the next five nights in Las Vegas and continued to do well. Dan called Detective Barker to find out how things were going at the trial. Both sides had presented their closing arguments, and the case was now in the jury's hands. Dan figured it probably wouldn't take too long for the jury to make its decision. It was December 30, and Jamieson would probably be acquitted in time to celebrate the New Year, Dan figured.

He had made his peace with that, however, and he was still in a celebratory mood after they finished their last show at the MGM Grand. He wanted to stick around and watch Tom Jones for his last show. He thought everyone should stay—as a matter of good manners, if nothing else—but Carl said he and Andrea had something to do. Then a little later, Simone and Mattie said they were tired and ready to retire for the evening.

So Dan stayed there for a while, thinking, this was great—their last night in Vegas and everyone left him all alone. He finally decided to go out and try his hand at the slots for a while. He walked up the street to the New York, New York casino because he had always had good luck on the slots there—meaning, he didn't lose as quickly there as most places.

Before he got there, his cell rang, and it was Carl.

"Hey, bro, you holding on to your hat?" Carl said before he could even say "Hi."

"I don't think I've worn a hat since the late '80s, but okay," Dan said.

"Are you sitting down?" Carl asked in a tone much more serious than he ever was.

"No, actually, I'm crossing the street right now. What's up?"

"Okay, good. No time for jokes. Grab a cab right now. I'll tell you what's going on as you ride. Are you getting a cab?"

"I guess so, but I'm not agreeing to that 'no time for jokes' part. What's up? Tell me."

"She's here."

"Okay, who's she, and where is here?"

"Shyanne. She's in Vegas. She's working at a strip joint called Temptations. Have you got a cab yet?"

"No, you just told me. What the hell do you mean? Shyanne's here—in Vegas. How? Why? What?"

"I'll tell you all that as soon as you get in a cab and start heading here."

"All right already, I'm getting a cab." He made his way to the area outside New York, New York where the cabs lined up. "I'm lined up waiting for a cab now. Can you tell me what's going on?"

"All right. First, when you get a cab, tell the cabdriver you want to come to Sarasota's on Paradise Avenue."

"Not Temptations?"

"No, Sarasota's is a little bar across the street from Temptations. That's where I am. But don't say anything to him about Temptations."

"Oh, are we being detectives again?"

"Kinda. Do you want to hear what's going on or not?"

"Go ahead."

"Okay, before I left from New York, I started thinking about where Shyanne might have gone if she left town. I thought she might have gone to one of Jamieson's clubs in another city. So I did some more research and found that Jamieson has six or seven places in Jersey, but I figured that was too close."

"Of course," Dan said sarcastically. He wanted to make a joke, but he didn't want to interrupt.

"So he also has a couple of places in Miami, three in Los Angeles, one in Chicago, and one right here in Vegas."

"Probably called Temptations."

"Right you are, bro. So I figured as long as we were gonna be out here anyway, I might as well see if she was here too. I've been checking on it since I've been down here. I thought I saw her one night, but she disappeared before I could tell for sure. But tonight I snuck in with Andrea, and we saw her. We got out of there before she could see us, and now Andrea and I and Mattie and Simone have got the place staked out. If she tries to leave, we'll catch her."

"Okay, good job. Did you already call in Clemenza and Tessio's men to help out?" Dan said, making a reference to *The Godfather* that he knew Carl would get.

"All right, this is really not the time. We need you over here. Are you in the cab yet?"

"I'm getting in now," Dan said, telling the cabdriver where to go. "No, I'm not trying to make light of your thorough and border-line-obsessive work, but have you figured out what we're going to do now?"

"No, that's gonna be your call. That's why you need to get over here fast."

"All right, I'm not driving the cab, just riding in it. You want me to tell him it's life-and-death and there's an extra $10 in the tip if he can get me there in five minutes?"

"Well, the life-and-death thing sounds good, but you might want to up the ante a little bit. Ten dollars sounds a little cheap for life-and-death."

"I was just kidding. We'll hurry."

Dan told him he had to hang up so he could hurry the cab-driver, but he really just wanted a few minutes to reflect by himself. He had pretty much made up his mind he was never going to see Shyanne again, and now he was only moments away from possibly seeing her again. He was shaking a little with either excitement or nervousness. What would he say? Did he hate her? Did he love her? He didn't know. Maybe both, if that was possible.

He arrived at Sarasota's in about ten minutes since it was on Paradise Boulevard, not far from the strip. He could see Carl stationed at a table close to the entrance peering out the window. He went inside, and Carl motioned him over to his table.

"Good, you're here. She hasn't left yet," Carl said, still in his detective mode.

"Okay, how do you know she hasn't left, and more importantly, why did you find her? I wasn't expecting to see her. I don't know if I'm ready to see her."

"I thought you were, Danny. I mean, she set you up. She made you look like a fool at the trial."

"Thanks."

"I'm sorry, man. But she helped Jamieson get off."

"I know she did. But I don't know … Okay, okay, presuming I do decide I want to see her, what's your plan?"

"All right, here's what's going on. Simone's inside keeping an eye on her from the inside. She's never seen Simone, so she won't suspect anything. Mattie's keeping an eye on the side entrance over there, and Andrea's got the back door covered. I'm watching the front.

"As far as the plan, I'm open to suggestions, but my idea is to somehow grab her when she leaves there and get her to talk to us. I think she'll want to confess to you if she sees you."

"So you're thinking kidnapping and some sort of torture?"

"No, not kidnaping. We just confront her when she leaves, or follow her when she leaves if they have bodyguards walking her out. Then I figure, you and I together can grab her at some point and force her into the back of the limo."

"Well, good. There for a minute I was afraid you were proposing something drastic. How is that different from kidnaping?"

"We're only going to hold her until she talks. Then she can go free."

"Do you work for the CIA or something?"

"What's with all the negativity? I thought you would be happy I found her."

"Oh, don't get me wrong. I'm grateful you went to all this work and are offering me a chance to aid and abet in a major felony."

"I told you, I was open to suggestions. But at this point, it's either that or go inside and confront her with all the bouncers there to protect her."

"Well, as much as I would like to see how this episode of Carl's Angels turns out, I'm going to have to pass on the kidnaping plan."

Carl had kept his eyes glued to the entrance across the street even as he talked, and despite himself, Dan had been watching also.

"Or we could just wait for Simone to walk out with her and bring her across the street to talk to us," Carl said, because that was exactly what was happening.

Chapter 37

Crossing the street now were Simone in her khaki pants and pullover shirt and Shyanne in her short black dress and high heels. They were a total contrast in styles. Not only did it appear Shyanne was not being forced against her will, she and Simone seemed to be engaged in a rather pleasant conversation.

"That's Simone for you," Carl said, shaking his head admiringly.

"Yeah, if you'd thrown her into Gettysburg during Civil War days, the Yankees and rebels would have ended up having a big picnic," Dan said smiling. "And the Gettysburg Address would have just been an announcement about who won the sack races."

The two women entered the bar and headed over to the table. Carl quickly called Mattie and Andrea on his cell phone and told them the stakeout was over. Shyanne didn't look directly at Dan at first, but when she did, her look of sadness and regret made Dan even more unsure of what he was going to say. And damn it, she still looked as good as she had that fateful night.

"Hi, guys," Simone said. "I introduced myself to Shyanne, and we talked for a little bit. She said she would come over and talk to you. And she's sorry."

"Yeah, yeah, whatever," Carl said. Her look of sadness and regret had had no effect on him. "Are you willing to admit what you did to my brother so we can tell the prosecutor in New York?"

"It's too late for that," Dan said. "The case has already gone to the jury. They won't let any new evidence be introduced."

"Can I sit down?" Shyanne asked, now looking directly at Dan.

Dan motioned her to sit down. Mattie and Andrea showed up and hurried over, not believing their eyes that Shyanne seemed to be willingly talking.

"All right, maybe it's too late to undo what you did," Carl said. "You've already helped Jamieson go free. But I still want to hear you say what you did and tell us why you helped set my brother up."

"Danny, I am sorry," Shyanne said. "And I'll tell you whatever you want to know. But can I just talk to you by yourself?"

"Yeah, Carl, I do appreciate what you did, all of you," Dan said. "But I think this is kind of between me and her. I'd appreciate it if you'd let us talk, just the two of us."

Carl grudgingly said yes, and Simone and Mattie and Andrea were glad to leave them alone, since they felt uncomfortable. Carl said they would be over at another table if Dan needed them.

"I don't think I'm in any danger," Dan said.

"Do you hate me?" were the first words Shyanne said after the others were out of earshot.

Dan looked at her. She seemed genuinely sad at the prospect of him hating her. It made him feel bad for a second, but then he remembered how easily she had fooled him before. And what a fool he had been made of on the stand.

"Yeah. No. Not anymore. I don't know. Can we come back to that question later?" Dan asked. Shyanne nodded. "I need to hear first what exactly happened. Did you set me up? I just need to hear you say it."

"Yes, I set you up. I wish I hadn't, but I did it. I'm sorry, you have no idea how sorry."

"Okay, and it was Jamieson that paid you to do it?"

"Yes. Actually, it was another guy, but he worked for Jamieson."

"And what exactly did he pay you to do?"

"To make sure you were at that building between four and five so you could see the clowns. And the Abe Lincoln guy to come out when he did."

"And Abe wasn't really shot?"

"No, it was all a setup, just like you said on the stand. And I knew they were going to harass you a little bit. I had no idea they were going to toss you around. And there's no reason you should believe me, Danny, but I swear I never knew why they were doing it. This guy came to me at the club I worked at and said Jamieson wanted to play a practical joke on someone. He said they picked me 'cause I'm a stripper and because of the way I look, and they figured I could lure you to that spot."

"Well, they certainly figured that right. You could have gotten me to jump into the Hudson River that night."

"I guess deep down I knew it wasn't a practical joke, 'cause nobody pays $25,000 for a practical joke, not even Jamieson."

"Twenty-five thousand! I didn't dream it was that much. Of course, it paid off for him, he'll be a free man soon, so I guess not a bad investment."

"Yeah, I knew it wasn't something I should have done, but I don't want to be a stripper forever, and I thought it would help me get out of the business a lot sooner. Then when I realized why they did it, I wanted to call you. I picked up the phone fifty times to call and tell you about it."

"But you didn't."

"No, I didn't."

"And why tell me now? Because the trial's already over?"

"Not really. That sweet girl, Simone, came over and introduced herself to me. We started talking, she asked if I would come over and talk to you. It just seemed like maybe I would feel better about myself if I did."

"And do you?"

"Not so far. You seem so cold. It seems like you do hate me."

"Shyanne, how would you feel if you had the single most enjoyable experience of your life, and it all turned out to be a sham, a joke, and you were the patsy being fooled?"

"Okay, I understand. I don't blame you. I would hate me too. But that night, the way I felt about you, it wasn't a joke or a sham to me."

Dan paused for a moment, not wanting to ask the next question.

"All right, now for the $64,000 question—or in this case, the $25,000 question—was having sex with me just part of the act?"

She looked at him with her soft, green eyes, looked down, and back up again.

"Not at all. In fact, they told me not to sleep with you because they didn't want you looking for me afterward."

"Well, thanks for saying that, at least. Of course, I have no idea whether it's true or not, but I can at least think it's true."

"Again, you have no reason to believe me, but it is true. I didn't plan on liking you, much less having sex with you. But I started drinking, and you were …"

"Ah, so you slept with me because you were drunk?"

"No, that's not what I'm saying at all. It's just that I was drinking and I found myself actually liking you, which I didn't intend to do. Most men I meet, I don't like, but you … well, I just wish we could have met under different circumstances."

Dan thought she probably wouldn't have even talked to him under different circumstances, but he didn't say it. He tried to think of what to say, but nothing came to him.

"So what happens now?" Shyanne asked after the silence lingered on. "Where do we go from here?"

"I guess I go back to my world and you go back to your stripper world, or whatever world you can get into for $25,000. I don't hate you, if that's what you want to hear, but I don't know how there could be an Act II after the Act I we had."

Shyanne looked sad again, so Dan turned away from her. He couldn't stand to see that face looking sad. Then she slowly smiled.

"If it would help, I think I still know a way we can get Jamieson."

"How? I'm sure the jury's already come back with its verdict by now. They didn't have much of a case without me."

"Okay, I don't know if what I'm going to tell you is true …"

Dan had to smile at that one; then Shyanne realized what she had said, and she smiled also.

"Let me rephrase that. While I was at the club in New York, the night Jamieson's guy came by to hire me, I heard he was looking for another girl to play a part. It was part of another plan to get Jamieson off in case my deal didn't work out."

"But it did."

"I know, but he wouldn't know that until he saw what happened at the trial. So this other girl from the club told me they were going to wait until the jury was selected, and if the jury wasn't sequestered, they were going to kidnap one of the jurors, or pay them to disappear or something. Then they were going to take her or somebody else and make them up to look like the missing juror. With makeup and prosthetics, they can totally change someone's appearance. That way he would know he couldn't be convicted. I know it sounds crazy …"

"Uh, yeah."

"Any more crazy than having clowns threaten you and shoot Abe Lincoln? Say what you want about Jamieson, but he does have a diabolical mind."

"Okay, you have a point there. But the jury was sequestered, so they would have never had a chance to make the switch."

"Yeah, that's what I thought too, until yesterday. I hadn't talked to the girl I know until yesterday. She said they ended up using another girl as the stand-in, but the jury was selected one day and not sequestered until the trial started the next day. So they had a day to make the switch."

"So did she hear that they actually went through with it?"

"That's what she said."

"So if Jamieson had one juror who he knew would vote not guilty regardless, the worst that could happen would be a hung jury."

"Exactly. Do you think there's anything we can do about it?"

Dan paused, thinking. Carl was better than him at knowing this stuff.

"Can we call Carl over here to help? I wish you had told me this earlier when you first got here. It may be too late now."

"I was more interested in seeing whether you hated me or not. Sure, call him over."

Dan didn't pause to reflect on that last statement. All the peace he had made in his mind about Jamieson getting off had suddenly left, and he didn't want to let this chance get away from him. He waved Carl and the others over. Just as he was doing so, he got a text message. He looked at it, and it was from Detective Barker.

It simply said, "Jury back. Not guilty. Sorry."

"Okay, gang, here's what's happening. I just got a text message from Detective Barker saying the jury found him not guilty. I've got to call him back right now. Shyanne will tell you why while I call him."

As Shyanne told the others what she knew, Dan called Barker. Fortunately, he answered on the first ring.

"Hey, got your message. Is the jury still there?"

"Yeah, I guess so. I just left the courtroom so I could send you the message. Why, you want me to go give them a good talking-to?"

"No. We found the girl, Shyanne, out here, and she heard something interesting about the jury."

"You found her out there. How? What's she doing?"

"I'll tell you that later. You think you can get back in there and get the judge to hold the jury for a few minutes? One of the jurors may be a fake."

"A fake. What do you mean?"

"One of them is a plant put in there by Jamieson. We're too late to change the murder verdict, but I think we could still get him for jury tampering or something. Can you get in there quick?"

"Sure, I'll try. Stay by the phone. I'll call you right back."

They hung up, and Dan told the others what had been said. Shyanne had already told them her story.

"So what do you think about what she told you?" Dan asked them.

"Sorry, bro, but how do we know she's not just saying this to make you look bad again?" asked Carl, the cynic.

"Okay, I'm not going to defend what she did before," Dan said. "But that just doesn't make any sense."

"No, Carl, there's no reason for her to make that up," Simone said. "Besides, she's sorry for what she did."

"Okay, let's focus, people," Mattie said. "Barker's going to call back here in a minute. We need to give him as much information as we can. What do you know about this person, Shyanne? Is it a man, a woman, black, white, do you know?"

"I don't actually know that much, other than it's a woman," Shyanne said. "But my friend might know. Let me call her."

"Okay, let's walk outside or find someplace quieter than here," Dan said. "We need to be able to hear what's being said on the phones."

They walked outside and gathered on the sidewalk outside Sarasota's. It was not library-quiet, but it was about the best they could do at the moment. Shyanne called her friend and started talking to her. Dan could partially hear what she was saying, but he couldn't tell from Shyanne's reaction whether the other woman was telling her anything or not.

"All right, all she knows is, she's a white female, probably younger than forty," Shyanne said after hanging up. "But she's not sure about the age thing."

"What about the rest of it?" Carl asked. "Is she sure she's white?"

"I think so. I didn't cross-examine her."

"Just your impression? Did it sound like she was sure?" Carl continued.

"Yes, it seemed like she was sure."

Carl turned to Dan. "Do you remember how many of the jurors were white females?"

"Not really. I didn't look at them that much. I remember one of them being kinda cute."

"I think there were five white females, and a couple of them were definitely over forty," Mattie said.

"Actually, there were four white females, and two of them were over forty," Simone said.

"Oh yeah, I forgot y'all were there too," Carl said.

"Okay, that's not very many then," Dan said. "I'm gonna text the white female part to Barker. He might still be in the courtroom. I wish I was there now. I'd like to see Jamieson's reaction."

Indeed, Barker was in the courtroom right at that moment, and indeed, Dan would have enjoyed seeing Jamieson's reaction. When Barker entered the courtroom, the jury had just been dismissed, and the judge was going back to his chambers. Barker quickly got one of the bailiff's attention and whispered to him quickly to stop the jurors from leaving. He then yelled across the courtroom.

"Judge Davenport! Please, Your Honor, if I could talk to you. It's very important."

Davenport turned and recognized Barker from testifying in his court on other occasions.

"Yes, Detective, can you tell me back in my chambers?"

Barker headed toward the judge as the courtroom went from a raucous one to one of almost silence as everyone turned to see what was going on. Jamieson had been smiling like the cat that ate the canary and glad-handing everyone around him. His smile suddenly froze.

"Your Honor, it can't wait," Barker said as he approached the judge.

"Okay, Detective, go ahead, tell me then. What's so important?"

Barker got close enough to him to whisper what he had heard about the jury.

Davenport took a moment to take it all in and said, "Is this for sure? Is it a reliable source?"

"The source was not sure, but if it's a possibility, we have to stop the jury from leaving, or we'll never find out. It's your decision, of course, Your Honor, but I believe we have to find out the truth."

"Yes, you're right," Davenport said.

He turned to the waiting crowd with a solemn look on his face. Jury tampering was only slightly more detestable in his mind than child molesting.

"Bailiffs, would you escort the jury members back to my chambers? And, Mr. Jamieson, I'd appreciate it if you wouldn't drift too far away." He then directed his attention to the prosecutor's table. "Ms. Stevens, could you come back here also?"

"Your Honor, what is this about?" Dawes said. "My client has just been acquitted and has a right to know if this somehow involves him."

"By all means, Ms. Dawes, you should come with us also. And yes, bring your client with you. That will make it easier to keep an eye on him."

With that, Davenport wheeled around and headed back to his chambers. For the first time since the trial began, the smug look on Jamieson's face had disappeared.

Chapter 38

Davenport had the jurors and two bailiffs wait in his outer office while he, the attorneys, Jamieson, and Barker all went into his private office. As the others sat down, Davenport took off his robe and sat at his desk.

"All right, people, here's what's going on," Davenport said. "Detective Barker here has heard something about possible jury tampering. I'm not going to go into all the details right now. But jury tampering is a very serious charge, so I didn't want to talk about it in an open courtroom. But we are going to hold the jury here until we find out if it's true. Mr. Jamieson, you know anything about this?"

Jamieson had regained his composure, even though he was still feeling queasy inside, especially now that he had heard the charge.

"No, Your Honor, I don't know what you're talking about."

"Ms. Dawes?"

"Judge Davenport, I hope you're not implying I would have anything to do with something like this," Dawes said.

"I'm not implying anything. I'm asking you straightforward. Did you?"

"Of course not, Your Honor."

"All right, we're not in court now. You don't have to get all offended. Now, Ms. Stevens, what Detective Barker has heard is that somehow one of the jurors is not who they're supposed to be, that somebody has been planted on the jury pretending to be one of the jurors who was actually selected. Is that correct, Detective?"

Barker had gotten a chance to look at the text message from Dan while Davenport had been talking to the others.

"Yes, sir, Your Honor, and I've just received information that the fake juror is a white woman, probably under forty."

"Your Honor, if my client is under some suspicion here, could I ask who is the source of this information?" Dawes asked. She had also regained her composure.

"Right now, I don't know who to suspect, and yes, you can ask, but that's not important right now. The important thing is to find out if it's true. Ms. Stevens, or Detective, do you have any ideas on the best way to proceed?"

"Your Honor, this is just off the top of my head," Stevens said, "but we can start off with the jurors who are white females and ask them to provide a photo ID if they have one. I'd hate to make accusations against anyone we don't have to."

"Well, we're not going to accuse anybody right now," Davenport said. "But we're going to check all the jurors out before any of them leave."

"Your Honor, we could also run fingerprints on them, but as you know, not everyone's fingerprints are on record," Barker said. "I'd like to be the one questioning them, if you approve, since this would be a police matter."

"Of course, that's up to you and Ms. Stevens, but I want to be apprised of what's going on, because this is also a matter that concerns this court."

It didn't take long before the judge found a room for Barker and Stevens to interrogate the four white female jurors. They had quickly decided to try asking them all at once, and if that didn't work, try them individually.

"Now, ladies, I'm Detective Barker, there's been a claim made that one of the people on this jury may not be who they're supposed to be. I won't go into all the ramifications of this if it's true, but it would be a very serious charge. I think Ms. Stevens here would agree that the state would look a lot more favorably on you if you admitted at this point the truth."

"Yes, Detective, that's right," Stevens said. "If this allegation turns out to be true, the person we're most interested in is the person who arranged this, who paid you. I'm not saying you won't be charged with anything, but we'll certainly be more willing to deal with you. And just so you know, we'll find out one way or another whether this is true. So if you want to deal, this is your chance to do so."

Three of the women looked surprised, and one of the three started immediately denying knowing anything. The other one, a twenty-five-year-old auburn-haired, rather inconspicuous-looking woman with glasses, didn't look shocked, but did look rather disconcerted. Barker decided to go with his instincts.

"Okay, the three of you can wait outside now," he said, indicating the three women who had looked surprised. "We'd like to talk to you individually. We'll start with this young lady here."

When the three had left, Barker waited a moment to let the auburn-haired woman with glasses wait in silence for a moment. As he knew, silence could be a very valuable tool in interrogations.

"What's your name, ma'am?" Barker asked softly.

She paused, thinking. She looked at Barker, then looked at Stevens. After a few seconds, she sighed.

"Who's the one in charge here?" she asked Barker.

"What do you mean?" Barker said. "I'm in charge of questioning you, and Ms. Stevens is in charge of deciding whether to offer you a deal, depending on what you say."

She looked directly at Stevens.

"Well, you're whom I need to talk to," she said. "What kind of deal?"

"I can't say without knowing what you're going to tell me. Do you need a deal?" Stevens asked.

"Yeah, I guess so. I mean, you're gonna find out anyway, aren't you, whether I'm the person on this name tag?"

Barker nodded. Stevens looked at Barker. They hadn't really expected it to be that easy, but the woman had apparently weighed her options rather quickly and decided she was more afraid of jail than Jamieson.

"Now, why don't you start by telling me your real name?" Stevens said.

"And the deal?"

"I don't know specifically, but since we already know you're not who you've pretended to be, you'll be charged with impersonation of a juror and possibly jury tampering. I can say it will be better for you to tell what you know," Stevens said. Then realizing she could give her a little, she added, "I'll do what I can to make sure you get the least amount of time possible. That's all I can promise until I know what you can tell me."

"Okay, I guess I'll have to go with that. My name's Janet Clausson," she said, taking her glasses off. "And for the record, I never told anybody I was this juror woman. I just showed up with her juror ID tag, and since I looked like her, everybody assumed I was her."

"All right, that's not the most important thing right now," Stevens said. "We want to know who was behind this. Just tell us how this happened. Who approached you, assuming this wasn't your idea?"

"No, definitely not my idea. This guy, Bill Peterson, who's one of the guys that runs the club where I work, came by the place one night. He had some pictures with him, he kind of looked me over and asked if I would like to make a good deal of money to act like I was somebody else for a couple of weeks."

"And did you agree to it without knowing what exactly you'd be doing?" Barker asked her.

"No, I asked how much money first, then I found out what it was I was going to have to do. He told me most of it, and the amount of money got my attention. I made sure no one was going to get hurt. But I told him I was interested."

"And did this Peterson guy indicate if he was doing this for someone else?"

"Yeah, well, I told him I'd have to get off from work for several weeks and I had to make sure that was okay. And he said that would be no problem because the guy who owned the club was well aware of his offer and would let me take the time off."

"And who was the owner of the club?"

"You know already, don't you?"

Barker and Stevens both shook their heads no.

"Hilton Jamieson."

Barker and Stevens contained their excitement long enough to continue to get the details from Clausson. Stevens was so happy to get another shot at Jamieson that she offered her a deal where she could avoid jail time in exchange for testifying against Jamieson. They got all the details, but they had already heard the main one. Jamieson had overplayed his hand, and this time it would cost him.

Chapter 39

As soon as he could, Barker called Dan to give him the good news. It was days like this that made it worth all the hard and boring work and the mostly thankless job of being detective. The look on Jamieson's face when Stevens told him he was being charged with jury tampering was priceless. Then when the judge followed that up by telling him he was declaring the murder trial a mistrial, you could almost feel Jamieson coming out of his skin. He was fit to be tied, but he tried to regain his composure because that was what men like him did.

Dan received the news from Barker and let out a cheer. The others were watching him on the phone and immediately got excited also.

"They got him," Dan said exultantly after hanging up the phone.

The others then cheered as well. Carl and Dan gave each other high fives, and everyone started to hug each other. Shyanne kind of eased away a few steps from the others, not knowing whether she would be a part of the celebration. Simone hugged her first; then Shyanne looked expectantly at Dan. He hesitated briefly, then hugged her as well.

"Thanks for that," Dan said very softly in her ear as he hugged her.

"You're welcome," Shyanne said. "I'm really not a bad person."

"I know that," Dan said, looking directly into her eyes. He hadn't forgiven her, but he certainly felt a lot better about her than he did a few minutes earlier.

"Since this is our last night in Vegas, I'd say a celebration is in order," Carl said. Celebrations were what he did best.

As everyone but Shyanne discussed where they were going to celebrate, there was another awkward pause.

"Well, I guess I'll be going back across the street," she said. "I'll let you guys get on with your celebration. I don't want to intrude."

She started to leave, and Dan couldn't bring himself to stop her. There's an expression in the courtroom that you can't unring the bell, which means that when the jury hears some evidence or remark from a witness, you can't expect them to pretend they never heard it. Dan thought of that analogy and how he didn't think he could ever get past what she had done to him.

The others all stood awkwardly silent as Shyanne began to talk away, not knowing what to say. And then Simone took matters into her hands. She went over to Shyanne and caught her before she crossed the street.

"Wait a minute," she said to Shyanne. "Would you let us talk to Dan for a few minutes?"

"No, that's okay," she said. "I'm not really part of your group. Believe me, I understand. Besides, he's probably right. What kind of future could we really have?"

"You never know till you try," Simone said. "You do like him, don't you?"

"Yeah, but we don't really know each other that well."

"I'm not talking about getting married. I just know he's gonna regret it if he lets you walk away."

"Okay, I'll go change and get my stuff at the club. If you guys are here when I come back, fine, I'll give it a shot. If not ..."

"Thanks. Don't take too long."

As Shyanne walked away, Simone turned and went back to the others.

"Oh, she didn't want to stay, huh?" Dan said. "I didn't figure she would."

"She wants to, but she wants you to say it's all right," Simone said.

"I don't know, 'miga," Dan said. "She hurt me a lot. I know it was just one night, but I really fell for her. If I tried again, how could I ever forget what she did?"

Then Mattie took over.

"I'm going to say something to you that you won't like hearing," she said to Dan. "This isn't about her, it's about you."

"What? What happened is somehow my fault?"

"No, I'm not saying that," Mattie said, looking Dan directly in the eyes. "I've never told you this, but you're so good sometimes you're bad."

"Well, thanks, and no, I'm not. How do I respond to that?"

"What I'm saying is, you have this high sense of morality. You hold yourself to this code or belief or whatever it is of always doing the right thing."

"And that's a bad thing?"

"No, it would be good if everyone was like that. But you expect everyone else to be like that too. And as a result, nobody measures up. Even someone like Simone, who's about as close to perfect as you're going to find, disappoints you sometimes, doesn't she? And your poor brother—you're constantly disappointed by him."

"Hey, I'm standing right here," Carl said.

"Sorry," Mattie said. "I'm just saying, Dan, no one's ever going to live up to your standards."

Dan stood there, stunned by what he was hearing and not knowing how to react or what to say. Finally, he gathered his thoughts.

"All right, maybe I do expect myself to live in a certain way," he said, choosing his words carefully. "But I don't think I'm perfect or even all that good at it. And I'm sure not some holier-than-thou kind of person who thinks he's better than y'all. Sure I get disappointed sometimes by people, but I get over it. And I certainly don't expect any of my friends or family to be like me. 'Miga, do you think I'm like that?"

Simone looked at him and paused before speaking.

"Oh, great, you think I'm like that too," he said.

"No, no, 'migo," Simone said. "Mattie's not saying you act holier than thou. It's just you're a very thoughtful, considerate person."

"Again, not a bad thing as far as I know," Dan said.

"No, it's not. It's a great thing. But you don't understand it when we're not like you."

"Okay, that may be true, and I'll work on that. But this thing with Shyanne is hardly a case of her being thoughtless or inconsiderate."

"Of course not," Simone said. "She made a mistake, one that hurt you. But you liked her that night, better than anyone you've ever met, you told me. I mean, look at all the women I tried to set you up with, did you like any of them half as much as Shyanne?"

"No, but you said that was because I was looking for the wrong kind of woman."

"Well, maybe I was wrong. I'm not saying you have to forgive her right now, just see what she's like tonight, what she's really like. She's not getting paid to like you, or even talk to you tonight."

Mattie took over again. "Listen, one of two things will happen. Either you find out it was all an act and she's nothing like the person you fell for that night. In that case, you at least know what she's really like, and you can get on with your life."

"And the second possibility?"

"She actually likes you, and you like the real her, and the two of you end up getting married tonight at one of those sleazy wedding chapels with the ceremony performed by an Asian Elvis impersonator."

"And what about your theory that she's a stripper with a heart of stone?"

"Ah, that was just a theory," Mattie said smiling. "Maybe I was wrong."

"'Migo, we're just saying, give her a chance."

"Aren't you two the ones always telling me to look for someone more my own age and to not be so focused on good looks? And now you want me to go after some totally hot stripper who's fifteen years younger than me."

"Again, that was just a theory," Simone said smiling.

Dan turned to Carl. "Well, bro, you were the one that wanted to hunt her down 'cause no one hurts a Darwin. What do you say now?"

"Well, I hunted her down. It's up to you now."

"But what do you think I should do?"

"Hey, she's hot, I say, give her another chance. You'd never get a girl like that under normal circumstances. You've already gotten one shot at her, provided by Jamieson. And now she feels she owes you one. She might give you a sympathy roll in the hay since she feels guilty."

Dan turned back to Mattie. "I don't know why you would think I'd ever be disappointed by my brother."

"Yeah, what was I thinking?"

"Hey, I'm still right here," Carl said, feigning indignation.

"Well, if you're all in agreement," Dan said. "I don't want to be so good I'm bad, or so bad I'm good."

"No, that one's okay," Mattie said.

"Don't you want to know what I think?" asked Andrea.

"Uh, sure, why not."

"I agree with what everyone else said, but I like you just the way you are."

"Carl, you should marry this girl."

They waited a few minutes for Shyanne, who came strolling across the street looking a little surprised they were still there. She had changed from her stripper clothes to something more modest—that being a relative term. She was wearing a white T-shirt that stopped six inches above her pants, which were form-fitting blue jeans. And she still had on heels, but not as high as the ones she had on earlier.

There was an awkward pause while everyone waited to see what was going to happen. Dan realized everyone was waiting for him, so he went over and hugged Shyanne.

"Everyone seems to think I'm too unforgiving or something, so if you'd like to accompany us on our night of celebration, it would be okay with me," Dan said, turning to see what the others' reaction was.

Mattie was shaking her head, and Simone motioned for him to try again.

"It would be pleasing," he said, again looking for their response.

Simone gave him the same signal to try again.

"It would be … an honor?" he said.

"Okay, okay, that's enough," Shyanne said. "With such a heart-felt offer, how could I say no? Later on, you may have to actually come up with your own lines without any help."

As it turned out, later on, no one was needing any help with their lines. With the large quantities of alcohol being consumed, everyone's tongues became quite loose. They ended up going to a karaoke bar after Shyanne confessed she had always wanted to be a singer but had not had the nerve to get up and sing in front of a crowd.

"So let me get this straight," Mattie said. "You can get up in front of guys and take your clothes off, but you can't sing in front of a crowd."

"Stripping doesn't really take a lot of talent," Shyanne said. "If you have a nice body, you just get up there and let your clothes fall off. Besides, the first time I stripped, I was pretty well hammered."

"Well, are you pretty muchly hammered tonight?" Carl said, slurring his words.

"Pretty muchly so, yes."

"Then get up there and sing your little heart out," Carl said. "And if the crowd doesn't like it, let some clothes fall off. They'll like that."

"Strip-karaoke," Dan said triumphantly as if he had discovered penicillin. "It'll sweep the country."

Shyanne didn't seem that thrilled with the idea.

"Don't listen to them," Simone said. "You get up there and sing. You have to follow your dream. As Dan told me, if you don't follow your dream, you have nightmares or something."

"Man, every time you tell that one, it just gets worse and worse," Dan said, rolling his eyes. "Shyanne, forget the stripping part. If you're ever gonna do it, tonight's the night."

"I doubt they even have the song I want to sing," she said, still reluctant.

"Yeah, they will," Carl said. "This place is known for having songs nobody else has. What one is it?"

"No, no, it's a surprise," Shyanne said. "Okay, I'll see. If they have it, I'll do it. You guys wait here though."

She went over to the guy who seemed to be in charge and talked to him. She turned back to them and gave them a thumbs-up. She had to wait a few minutes for a fat guy to finish with his version of Rod Stewart's "If You Think I'm Sexy."

"Man, if that doesn't give her the confidence to do it, nothing will," Mattie said.

Shyanne got up in front of the crowd, and immediately guys started whistling. She sat on the stool and lowered her head. Finally, after a few seconds, she raised her head and spoke into the microphone.

"I want to dedicate this to someone here tonight whom I hurt," she said, deadly serious. "I hope this will make everything all right."

"Uh-oh," was all Dan could say.

As the music began, Shyanne seemed a little drunk, but enough in control to get the words out. When she started to sing, she had kind of a raspy, whiskey voice that men generally find sexy.

"Isn't it rich, aren't we a pair?"

Dan immediately recognized the tune and just laughed, shaking his head. It was the first line from the song "Send in the Clowns."

> Me here at last on the ground, you in midair.
> Send in the clowns.
> Isn't it bliss, don't you approve?
> One who keeps tearing around one who can't move.
> Where are the clowns? Send in the clowns.

The rest of the crowd didn't get the inside joke, but Dan and the group certainly did. After the others saw Dan wasn't hurt by the clown reference, they started applauding.

> Just when I stopped opening doors,
> Finally knowing the one I wanted was yours.
> Making my entrance with my usual flair,
> Sure of my lines no one is there.
> Don't you love farce? My fault, I fear.
> I thought that you'd want what I want, sorry my dear.
> But where are the clowns?
> There ought to be clowns.
> Quick, send in the clowns.

After the initial surprise of the song had passed, Dan suddenly realized she had quite a good voice.

"She's really good," he said.

"And with a sense of humor," Mattie said, "and really hot. You can totally see through her shirt with that spotlight on her.

"Mattie!" Simone said.

"I'm just saying …"

Dan tried in his inebriated state to listen to the words to the song more than he ever had before. Having never seen the musical by Stephen Sondheim from which the song came, he had never actually understood why someone was sending in clowns. But he was focusing on the words to see if Shyanne was trying to tell him something through the song.

> What a surprise, who could foresee
> I'd come to feel about you what you felt about me.
> Why only now when I see that you've drifted away,
> What a surprise, what a cliché.
> Isn't it rich, isn't it queer?
> Losing my timing this late in my career.
> And where are the clowns
> Quick, send in the clowns
> Don't bother, they're here.

Dan decided the words didn't have any particular relevance to the two of them, but the music itself was hauntingly beautiful, and Shyanne's rendition was much better than the usual karaoke fare.

Shyanne got a big ovation from the crowd, partly because of her see-through shirt and partly because she was good.

Before she came back to the table, Mattie said, "Hey, everybody, maybe she'll sing a song about Abe Lincoln now."

"There are no songs about Abe Lincoln," Dan said.

"Well, come on, comedian boys," she said. "Think of a song that might be about Abe Lincoln. Let's see how quick you are."

She knew Dan and Carl couldn't resist a challenge. Dan responded first, "How about 'Shot Through the Heart' by Bon Jovi?"

"Well, I don't think Abe Lincoln was shot in the heart, I think maybe the head," Mattie said.

"The Abe Lincoln I knew was shot in the heart," Dan said.

"The Abe Lincoln you knew was shot with blanks," she said.

Carl had been thinking while they were going back and forth. "If you two are through, I've got it. 'Hit Me with Your Best Shot' by Pat Benatar, although I guess that one would have to actually be sung by Abe to John Wilkes Booth."

"Okay, that's a good one," Mattie said. "How would the words go?"

"Let's see, it starts off with 'You're a real tough cookie with a bad history,'" Dan said. "What's next, Carl?"

"Okay, let's see, 'With a bad history of shooting guys named Abe …'" Carl said.

"'In the balcony,'" Dan said triumphantly. Then to Mattie, "And if he wasn't shot in the balcony, just keep it to yourself."

"No, I think he was. That's good," Mattie said.

"Very good, 'migo," Simone said. "I think I've heard that song before."

"Oh, I've got one," said Andrea, who was sitting at the end of the table.

Carl looked surprised and said, "Okay, what?"

"'Pour Some Sugar on Me' by Def Leppard," Andrea said.

The others all began laughing.

"What does that have to do with Abe Lincoln?" Carl said, still laughing.

"Oh, I couldn't hear what you guys were saying. I thought we were just doing songs from the '80s," Andrea said sheepishly.

Simone stopped laughing when she saw they had embarrassed Andrea, but the other three couldn't seem to stop. Finally, Dan stopped long enough to say, "You know, I'll never hear that song again without thinking of Abe Lincoln covered in sugar."

The laughter continued until Shyanne got back to the table. "I hope that's not about me," she said. "It was supposed to be amusing, but not that funny."

"No, it wasn't about you," Dan said. "You were really good."

"And totally hot," Mattie said.

"Do you want her to be Dan's girl or your girl?" Simone said.

"Oh, honey, I'm just drunk," Mattie said. "You know nobody's as hot as you, especially when you're being Raquel. Can Raquel come out and play?"

The group continued to drink and have fun into the wee hours of the morning. Shyanne seemed to be just as likeable as she had been that night, although in a less obvious way. She was naturally flirtatious, so it was hard for Dan to judge her actual intentions. Maybe that was what Mattie had been trying to say. He should stop judging people.

Chapter 40

That was about the last coherent thought Dan had that night. When he woke up, he wasn't sure where he was, but it didn't appear to be in his hotel room. He wasn't sure, but it sure seemed like the outside wall was at a slant. Had he really had that much to drink? No, the other walls seemed straight enough, but that one damn wall was definitely at about a sixty-degree angle.

He was on a sofa of what was a hotel room, but definitely not his hotel room. Surely he would have remembered one of the walls being at an angle like that. He heard the shower running, and the bathroom door was closed.

It was starting to come back to him. He remembered going out with the group and leaving with Shyanne. This must be her room, and Shyanne must be the one taking a shower. He didn't want to barge in on her to see, so he walked over to the slanted wall. He looked out the window, and damned if the whole side of the hotel wasn't slanted.

Ah, yes, the Luxor Hotel, the one built in the shape of a pyramid. If only the Egyptians had had the foresight to build a casino in one of those pyramids over there, then they would have had a real tourist attraction. He had seen this hotel from the outside, but this was the first time from the inside. That's right, this had to be Shyanne's room. He wondered what had happened in this room last night. He was dressed and had woken up on the couch, so probably just sleeping, he guessed.

Well, he would know soon enough. The shower had stopped. He hoped it wasn't the Janet Leigh character from *Psycho* that came out. Or worse, Tony Perkins. Come to think of it, he hoped it wasn't any dude coming out of the shower. It had to be Shyanne, he told himself.

It was Shyanne. She came out of the bathroom wearing a terry cloth bathrobe and a towel wrapped around her head. Damn, even with no makeup and a towel around her head, she still looked good. She saw him standing by the window as soon as she came out.

"Well, well, well, how are we feeling this morning?" she said.

"Um, fine, I guess, a little bit of a headache. This must be your room, huh?"

"Yeah, you don't remember much of last night, apparently?"

"No, not a lot. We didn't uh …"

"No, we didn't uh. You were quite the gentleman. You offered to walk me to my room even though you were having trouble walking, then when I told you that you could sleep here, you were gallant enough to offer to sleep on the couch."

"So even drunk, I was quite the gentleman, it seems."

"Yes, right up to the point where you threw up on my shoes."

"On your shoes? Why did I do that?"

"I don't think you meant to throw up on my shoes. I was helping you lie down on the couch, and then when you started to hurl, I jumped back. You missed me, but you got my shoes."

"And what part of that did you find ungentlemanly?"

She laughed. Dan looked over at the couch area.

"Don't worry. I already cleaned it up," she said.

"I'm sorry. And the shoes?"

"Threw 'em away."

"Can I reimburse you for them?"

"I'm not sure you want to. They cost $400."

"For shoes!"

Once again, Dan realized how he was missing that shoe-appreciation gene. He also thought about even with a loss of $400, Shyanne was still $24,600 ahead in her relationship with him. Okay, it was probably that kind of thinking he had to let go, according to Mattie and Simone.

"Don't worry about it," Shyanne said. "Right now, you better take a shower—a rather lengthy one, I'd say—and get ready. You've got a plane to catch in a couple of hours. I called Simone and told her you were here so they wouldn't be looking for you."

"Oh yeah, she probably loved that. What time is it?"

"Nine thirty."

As he thought about whether he should head back to his hotel or whether Shyanne had meant for him to take a shower there, he decided he might as well see what Shyanne intended to do.

"Uh, Shyanne, I don't remember whether we resolved anything last night, or if you even want to. But I was wondering, are you gonna stay out here awhile, or will you be coming back to New York, or do you know?"

"Well, we didn't really resolve anything last night, but you did call and make a plane reservation for me to leave on the same plane as the rest of you."

"I did?"

"Yes, you were quite insistent."

"So the drunk me apparently wants to let bygones be bygones."

"And the sober you?"

"I'm working on it. But if you don't want to go back to New York yet, I don't want to force you to do anything."

"No, that's okay, there's no reason for me to stay out here any longer. You didn't force me to do anything I didn't want to do. And as far as you and me, what I told you last night was that I'd like for us to go back to New York and try starting over. I mean, I know you said we couldn't have an Act II after our Act I, but maybe we can just start a new play and forget the old one."

"As long as last night wasn't the first scene."

"What, throwing up on my shoes is not how you want it to start out?"

"I can do better."

"We'll see. Maybe when we get back home, you can call me and we'll go to a movie or something."

"Really? You would like that?"

"Yeah, you don't think strippers go see movies?"

"Well, probably. I never have seen any data on it, but I would guess so. Can I take a shower here, or would you prefer I go back to my hotel?"

"No, go ahead and take one here. I promise not to peek."

"Yes, we certainly don't want to spoil anything for that first date thing later."

"Of course."

As he started to walk toward the bathroom, he stopped. "Hey, Shyanne, one other thing."

"Yes?"

"This time, if you would tell me where you actually live, I would appreciate it. I mean, there's only so many times I'm gonna fall for that fake address trick."

"We'll see."

Chapter 41

An hour or so later, they were all gathered at the MGM Grand with their bags. The limo driver put all their bags in, and they all piled into the back.

"You know, I could get used to this being-rich thing," Dan said. "Having a limo driver drop us off at the airport, that's the only way to travel. The fame thing, where people come up and want our autographs, I can do without all that."

"Not me, I want the fame part too," Carl said grinning. "Let our fans come over to us and ask for autographs. Snubbing the riff-raff would be half the fun."

"Andrea, how long you been with Carl?" Mattie asked.

"Six months."

"You are a saint."

"Hey, Mattie," Carl said, "you know how people always ask famous people if they will still remember their friends after they make it big? Let me just say right now, for the record, I will not be remembering you. In fact, you're already a little hazy to me."

Shyanne was seated next to Simone, and she leaned over to her.

"Is this pretty much the typical group dynamic?"

"Yes, quite charming, don't you think?"

"Ain't it though?"

Carl and Mattie were still going back and forth until Simone interrupted them to remind everyone they were going to be arriving in New York on New Year's Eve and the traffic was going to be a nightmare. Carl assured her they would be landing by five thirty and it shouldn't be that bad at that time.

"Yeah, 'cause five thirty in New York, there's never anybody out," Mattie said.

Dan had mostly tuned out the Mattie-Carl sparring battle. It all seemed so familiar to him. He was thinking about whether their careers were about to take off, or if the Vegas gig had meant anything at all. He knew Jamieson's grudge against him would be worse than before, but maybe his influence would diminish if he went to jail.

Then he laughed to himself at the absurdity of that. And he looked at Shyanne and wondered if she would be a part of his future, or if his doubts about her would always be there.

When they got to the airport and were about to enter the terminal, a tall man in blue jeans and a pullover shirt came up behind them and said, "Mr. Darwin?"

Dan and Carl both turned around and said, "Yes."

The man looked at Dan and said, "No, Mr. Dan Darwin."

Dan looked him over, didn't recognize him, and said, "That's me. And who are you?"

"I'm Paul Johnson, I'm a reporter from the Las Vegas paper here. I was just wondering if you were the same Dan Darwin who testified in the trial of Hilton Jamieson."

"Yes," Dan said. "And how did you recognize me or know I was going to be here?"

"I saw your show at the MGM the other night and started thinking about you being a comedian, and I remembered the guy who testified was a comedian with the same name. Seemed like too much of a coincidence."

Dan had wondered why no one had made the connection while they were out here. It wasn't like appearing in Vegas at a casino was part of a witness relocation program. But he was still suspicious about the man just running into him at the airport.

"So that explains how you knew me," he said. "How did you know I would be here?"

"Well, I've been trying to catch you at the hotel and hadn't had any luck. I saw you getting into the limo and grabbed a cab and followed you. Sorry, I'm not stalking you. Just wondered if I could get a quick interview with you before you leave. I assume you're going back to New York."

"No, we have to get inside here, and I don't have any comment to make anyway. As far as where we're going, unless you have a ticket on the same plane as us, I guess you'll just have to figure that one out."

With that, Dan turned his back on the man and went inside the terminal with the others going with him. As they went inside, Dan glanced back to see if the man was trying to follow them. He wasn't.

"Way to go, man," Carl said. "You're already getting the hang of this 'snubbing the little people' thing."

"Yeah, I don't know about that, but did you notice anything unusual about that guy?" Dan asked.

"He was kind of creepy," Shyanne said.

"Yeah, that too. But did you notice he didn't have a notebook or a tape recorder or anything?"

"He could have just had one in his pocket or something," Carl said.

"And he said he worked for the Las Vegas paper. A reporter always says what the name of the paper is. Even if he doesn't much like his job, he still says what the name of the paper is."

"So who was he, 'migo?" Simone said. "What did he want?"

"I don't know, but I'd say we're heading back to New York just in time."

"Yeah, 'cause it's always safe there," Mattie said.

"Be it ever so humble, there's no place like home," Dan said.

Their plane got delayed in Nashville for an hour, so by the time they landed at LaGuardia and gathered their bags, it was almost 7:00 p.m., not a good time on New Year's Eve to be trekking into Manhattan.

After a half-hour wait, they got one of those big cabs that all six of them could get into. It wasn't a limo, but it was the best they could do.

An hour and a half later, they were making their way at a snail's pace into the heart of Manhattan. The cabdriver, Angarwe, was from

South Africa and spoke English with an English accent. He had apparently been driving in New York for a while because he took them in one of the most circuitous routes into the city ever devised. But if he hadn't, they might still have been waiting in traffic.

Finally, when he got them within about a mile of where any of them lived, he threw up his large hands in disgust.

"That is it, people," Angarwe said. "This is as far as we can go for tonight. Either you can walk the rest of the way, or you sleep here in my cab."

Angarwe's cab smelled better than most, but the thought of camping out there didn't appeal to any of them. The thought of carrying all their bags for a mile or further wasn't too appealing either, but that seemed the only thing to do.

As they piled out and grabbed their luggage, Dan noticed for the second time that Shyanne seemed to have more bags than anyone else, ironic since she always seemed to be wearing less. Probably one of the bags was filled with $400 shoes, he thought.

She was the only one who had taken a couple of coats and sweaters with her, so she got those out and shared them with the other women, since the rest of the group had packed for Las Vegas and not the return home. They hadn't really thought they would have to walk any great length when they got back.

As they started walking toward Mattie and Simone's place because they lived the closest, Carl came up with one of his good ideas.

"Hey, the House of Hyenas is just two blocks the other way," he said. "Let's go leave our bags there, warm up for a few minutes, get whatever we need for the night, and we can come back for the rest of our stuff tomorrow."

Besides Carl, Dan was the only one who didn't have a coat or sweater, plus he was carrying two of Shyanne's bags, and his one, so he was the most enthusiastic in his support of the idea. But no one was having a lot of fun carrying their bags in the cold, so they turned left at Fifty-fifth Street and made their way to the comedy/music bar.

When they got within a block of the place, Dan stopped dead in his tracks and motioned the others to stop.

"Okay, I may be going crazy, but please somebody tell me they also see three clowns lurking across the street from the Hyena House," Dan said in hushed tones.

"No, I don't see any," Mattie said smiling.

"Yeah, me neither," Shyanne joined in.

Dan looked annoyed at them and turned to Carl.

"All right, all right," he said. "I'd like to pretend they're not there, but I'm the only other guy here, so I got to stick with you, bro. Yeah, I see three clowns."

"Well, I'm a woman, and I see them too," Simone said. "But why does that mean we have to stop? It's cold, and Shyanne's sweater has holes in it."

"Hey, that's the way it's designed," Shyanne said.

"I know. I'm just saying it's cold," Simone said. "'Migo, it's New Year's Eve, people dress up on New Year's Eve, some people probably as clowns. First the guy at the airport, now the clowns. Aren't you being a little paranoid?"

"That's what they told you to say, isn't it?" Dan said, looking around in a crazed fashion.

"Okay, enough with the jokes," Mattie said. "Let's get inside and get rid of these bags. See, the clowns aren't even there anymore."

"Or so they would have you think," Dan said.

Chapter 42

They all went inside and stashed their bags in Louie's office. Louie greeted Dan and Carl like long-lost sons. He told them he had heard things went great out in Vegas and he was hoping they would still deign to appear at his meager place after hitting the big-time. They assured him they would.

After they warmed up a bit and had a drink, the group was ready to head back out on the cold, raucous streets of New York. Carl was the only one who wanted to go down to Times Square and celebrate. The rest just wanted to go home.

They walked Simone and Mattie to their place first because they were closest. The group escort was not due to any more clown sightings, just the usual fruitcakes roaming the street on New Year's Eve.

They made it without incident to their apartment building, where Simone and Mattie hugged everyone and went inside. At that point, Carl said he and Andrea would go ahead and head to their place on their own if Dan thought he and Shyanne would be safe from fake reporters and clowns.

"That's right, go ahead and laugh it up," Dan said. "But don't blame me if you get squirted with water on your way home."

With that, Dan and Shyanne were alone, or as alone as two people could be on the streets of Manhattan on December 31. Dan realized this was the first time they had ever been alone without at least one of them being drunk. It was a little unnerving.

"So I'll walk you home then, and then we can say good night and try the new Act I sometime next year," Dan said, hoping to take some of the discomfort out of the situation, at least for him. "So where do you actually live, if you don't mind me being so bold? Is it within walking distance?"

"Remember that building you took me to before?" she said. He just stared at her. "Oh, I guess you do. I actually live in the building right across the street from there."

"Ah, good one. I would have never looked there."

With the difference in height, Dan was walking two steps for every one of Shyanne's, so he deliberately became more deliberate. He also noticed that she had on heels again, which didn't speed up her walking.

"You sure you don't want to take those shoes off?" he finally said to her. "It might be easier for you to walk."

"And walk barefoot in the streets of New York. Uh, no thanks," she said.

"Don't you have any shoes that are made for walking? Like sneakers or something."

"Yeah, they're back in one of my suitcases. But what's your hurry?"

"None, I guess. I was just … never mind."

As they walked along, there was a lot of activity on the streets which made it difficult to carry on a conversation, which Dan was kind of grateful for. This talking thing seemed a lot more difficult without alcohol.

Dan remembered he had told Detective Barker he would call him when he got back in town to find out what had happened with Jamieson. This seemed like a good time to do so. He asked Shyanne if she minded, and she said no, go ahead. When he called, he got his voice mail, not surprising on New Year's Eve.

"Hey, Detective Barker, or Sam," Dan said, deciding to leave a message. "This is Dan Darwin. I'm back in town, and I was just wanting to see what you had heard about Jamieson lately. You think he'll actually do time for this one? Anyway, I'm walking Shyanne back to her real apartment, and get this, she lives in the building right across the street from the one where I was at that night. I thought I saw some clowns out earlier, but everyone says I'm being paranoid. So call me back sometime. It doesn't have to be tonight. Talk to you later."

"Not answering?" Shyanne said.

"No, what in the world could he be doing at eleven fifteen on New Year's Eve? I hope I didn't wake him up."

About twenty minutes later, they were at her building. Dan turned awkwardly toward her.

"Well, I guess this is the part where you tell me to give you a call and pay no attention to the limo full of clowns around the corner," he said. He looked around. "I'm getting the strangest sense of déjà vu's for some reason."

He was about to hug her, and she stopped him. "Tell you what, why don't you just walk me to my actual apartment, so that you can see I really live there. I'll show you some pictures of my parents or something."

"Yeah, like I'm gonna fall for the old fake pictures of parents trick."

"So do you ever stop making jokes?" she said as she punched the entry code for her building.

"Yeah, sometimes."

"What's that like?"

"It's not pretty."

They got on the elevator, and she punched the button for the third floor.

"Hey, what about your apartment being too messy for me to see?" he said.

"Danny boy, I don't know how to break this to you, but not everything I told you that night was exactly true."

"Oh yeah, I'm a little slow sometimes."

"Duh."

As they were about to enter her apartment, his cell rang. He looked and saw it was Barker.

"Hey, Sam, sorry I called you so late."

"That's okay. I wasn't asleep yet. I'm not that old."

As Shyanne opened the door and went in, Dan's heart suddenly went up into his throat. They were staring at a clown pointing a gun right at them. The clown motioned Dan to come on in. He did so as his mind raced as to what he could say to Barker. Somehow it was easier to think of an ad-lib joke than it was an SOS warning that a gun-toting clown wouldn't understand.

Sam had asked him something on the phone, but Dan's concentration had been broken. As they entered the apartment, there were two other clowns waiting for them. Both of them were armed as well. The one who had greeted them at the door saw Dan was on his cell and motioned for him to hang up.

"Sam, I'm gonna have to go right now. I'll call you back. We've got reservations at that bar, Rossini's, and we've got to get there fast."

"Rossini's?" Sam said.

"Yeah, that place named for the Italian composer, or the Lone Ranger or somebody."

The lead clown moved the gun closer to Dan's face.

"Are you all right?" Sam's voice came through on the phone.

"No, not at all, see you later," Dan said and then pressed the End Call button on the phone.

"Get in here, and give me that cell phone," Clown Number 1 said.

Dan had been concentrating on the phone call, but now he looked at Shyanne. How did these clowns know he would be coming here? Had she set him up again? He had an awful sick feeling in his gut. He just couldn't have been duped again.

"Who the hell was that on the phone?" Clown Number 1 said.

"Nobody important. I just had to get rid of him."

"Yeah, well, I'm sorry to disrupt your plans at the whatever that place was, but you guys ain't going anywhere right now."

Dan looked at Shyanne, and she seemed as scared as he was. He figured these guns were not holding blanks, and these clowns were not just trying to scare him, although they were.

"Gino, call Mr. Jamieson and tell him we got lucky. We got two birds with one stone. We got the bitch who sold him out and the guy who ratted on him. Also, call Dennis and tell him he can quit staking out Darwin's place."

"Who's Darwin?" Gino said.

"That's this guy, dummy."

"Oh, he's the one we were looking for."

Gino called Jamieson and told him something, but Dan couldn't hear what he was saying. He looked back at Shyanne, who was looking at him. Well, maybe this wasn't her setup after all. And maybe he wouldn't mention what he had been thinking a few seconds earlier.

Shyanne looked at Dan, with probably the same look of fear in her eyes that he had in his. "I hope you don't think I had anything to with this," she said.

"No, of course not," Dan said as convincingly as he could.

"Okay, you two, shut up. Mr. Jamieson wants to come over here and see you two in person," said the head clown. "So why don't you two just make yourselves comfortable on the couch there and wait."

As they did what he said, the third clown got handcuffs and cuffed one of their arms to each other and the other to the table in front of the couch.

"How the hell did you guys get into my place?" Shyanne said, becoming angry despite her fear. "What do you want?"

"Well, little lady, you may have forgotten, but there's a Mr. Jamieson who happens to own this building you live in," said Clown Number 1 grinning. "And as far as what we want, I'll let Mr. Jamieson have the pleasure of telling you that. But you need not worry your pretty head about it. I don't think he intends to kill both of you. But then again, he's kind of pissed about having to go to jail. So you never know."

Those words made Dan's heart race even faster. He hoped his message to Barker hadn't been too obscure a clue. He really hoped he was not just a good guy but a great detective too.

Chapter 43

Dan looked around Shyanne's apartment and tried to get comfortable on the sofa, as much as he could, being handcuffed. He leaned over to Shyanne.

"You know, under different circumstances, this being handcuffed to you would be kind of a turn-on. Hell, even under these circumstances, I'm kind of excited."

"Danny, could you focus please?" she said. "We're in trouble here."

"I know. I know. I am focused. At least, we did manage to come up with an Act II to top our Act I."

"Yeah, I just hope there's an Act III."

"Oh, he's not really gonna kill us," Dan said as convincingly as he could. "I think he just wants to scare us a little."

"Well, tell him 'Good job, now let us go.'"

Dan lowered his voice to a whisper, "Follow my lead. I'm gonna try something."

"Hey, you two," Clown 1 said, "this ain't no talk show. Just be quiet till Mr. Jamieson gets here. He should be here in a few minutes."

"All right," Dan said. "You know, you seem like a nice enough guy. Do you really want to hurt us? Neither one of us ever did anything to hurt you."

Clown 1 just looked at him and laughed. Shyanne was glaring at him.

"That was it?" she said. "Appeal to his morality?"

"That's not following my lead."

Clown 1 held a finger to his lips and said, "Shh."

They both stayed silent for several minutes; then there was a lot of noise coming from outside. Dan glanced at the clock and saw it was midnight. Wow, what a way to ring in the new year.

"Uh, Mr. Clown, sir," Dan said politely. "If you wouldn't mind, since this is midnight on New Year's Eve and all, could I kiss Shyanne here? If it's all right with her?"

The clown leered at Shyanne and said to Dan, "Sure, as long as you don't mind sloppy seconds. I'm going first, and I'm planning on usin' a lot of tongue."

"Okay, never mind. The mood's kind of spoiled now."

"Thanks," Shyanne said to Dan. "What part of being quiet didn't you get?"

Just then, they heard a knock on the door, and one of the clowns went to open it. In walked a smirking Jamieson and his huge bodyguard, Bevo, who was not dressed as a clown this time.

"Well, well, well, isn't this a pretty picture," Jamieson said. "You two look so cozy there on the couch. It almost makes me regret having to make you get up and go out into this cold weather."

"If you'd rather not, sir, you can just leave us here, while you and your friends go back home," Dan said. "We'll figure out how to get out of the handcuffs by ourselves."

"Ah, yes, always the comedian," Jamieson said, still smirking. "You really think this is the best time to be making jokes?"

"Well, maybe not the best time. It's kind of late, you're probably tired, plus you've got the clowns here. Kind of hard to compete with a clown when you're trying for a laugh."

"Keep it up, funny guy," Jamieson said, not smiling anymore. "I've still got your brother's place staked out and those dyke friends of yours. Would you like me to send word out to have my guys pay a little visit to them?"

"No, sir," Dan said, suddenly serious. "I'm sorry. Don't take it out on them. Or Shyanne either. She didn't do anything except what you paid her to do."

"And the two of you just happened to be together tonight?"

"That is kind of a strange coincidence, sir," Dan said. "My brother and I were flying back from Vegas today, and as we're getting off the plane, I look and there's Shyanne getting off the same plane. We asked her if she wanted to share a cab ride with us, and then I was just walking her ..."

"Shut up," Jamieson said. "I'm not an idiot. I did some asking around, and I was pretty sure she was the one who told about the jury switch, and now that I see the two of you together, I'm real sure. What do ya say there, sweetie, you want to deny it? Maybe if you make it real convincing and take off your clothes while you do it, maybe I'll let you live."

Dan looked at Shyanne to see how she was going to respond. Instead of fear, he saw anger. He thought he better try to stop her.

"Listen, Jamieson, I'm the one you're mad at," Dan said quickly. "Now, I don't want to die either, but why don't you just leave Shyanne and everyone else out of this? In fact, why don't you and I just settle this man-to-man?"

Shyanne was not to be deterred. She stood up.

"Danny, shut up," she said. "Yeah, I'm the one who turned your ass in, and my only regret is I didn't do it earlier. And as far as taking my clothes off, you'll be the one doing the stripping soon enough, when you're in jail and you'll be stripping for your roommate, Raoul."

Jamieson laughed in an unamused way. "Ah-hah, the stripper has a temper. I better be careful before you take off your pasties and try to whip me with them. Listen, little girl, if you hadn't been such a whore and slept with this loser here when you were told not to, you would have never gotten yourself into this mess. All you had to do was take the money and run."

Shyanne lunged at Jamieson, but the handcuffs held her back. Dan stood up and tried to grab her. When she realized she couldn't get to Jamieson, she spit at him, hitting him right in the right cheek. Jamieson just stepped back, took out a handkerchief, and wiped his face. Then he slapped her hard. Dan managed to get ahold of Shyanne and get her back on the couch.

"Well, missy, you just signed your own death warrant," Jamieson said in the same tone of voice Dan had heard him use the night he killed the other woman. "I was going to let you live, but now I'm going to kill you both."

"Hey, you keep talking about killing us," Dan said. "Okay, big, tough guy, you got your muscle guys with you, you got the guns. But let me tell you, you kill either one of us, they're gonna know who did it."

"Yeah, well, let me worry about that," Jamieson said. "They may know you two are missing, but they're never going to find either one of your bodies. And this time, there ain't going to be any witnesses. Besides, according to your little stripper friend there, I'm already going to jail. What've I got to lose?"

Dan had gotten Shyanne to sit back down finally, but she had hardly calmed down any.

"Bevo, I'm tired of playing around," Jamieson said to his big bodyguard. "Make sure these two pieces of shit are handcuffed good and tight, and let's get them down to the limo. And make sure the cuffs are hidden so it looks like we're all just taking a stroll into the car. And if you two make a move when we're outside, I'm not gonna worry about witnesses. We'll just shoot your asses right on the street."

Dan got up and tried to help Shyanne up as Bevo uncuffed them from the table so they could leave. But Shyanne resisted.

"No, I'm not leaving," she said defiantly.

"I beg your pardon, slut," Jamieson said.

"Hey, if you're gonna kill us anyway, you might as well just do it here," she said. "At least you'll have to carry us out."

It had already occurred to Dan that even if Barker had figured out his warning, he wouldn't have known Shyanne's apartment number. He knew their best chance was out on the street.

"Shyanne, let's just go with them," Dan said, squeezing her hand. "Look at me. Do you trust me?"

She looked into his eyes. "Yes, but what does that have to do with anything? They're gonna kill us, he already said it. Let's not make it easier."

"Let's just go with them and do as he says. Please! I think you owe me that."

Again, Dan squeezed her hand. She continued to look at him. Finally, she sighed and nodded her head.

Bevo made sure they were cuffed securely and then put a coat over the cuffs so no one could see them. Dan moved as slowly as he possibly could, acting like it was hard to move with the handcuffs on.

Two of the clowns went down first to get the limo ready. Then Bevo and the clown they had been talking to stood on each side of Dan and Shyanne and held their arms. Jamieson walked in front of them.

The group made its way out the door and onto the elevator. When they got to the first floor and to the entrance of the building, Jamieson told Bevo to wait a minute while he went and got in the car. As he got in, he sent the other two clowns back where the others were leaving the building to make sure Dan and Shyanne didn't try to run.

As they began the walk toward the limo, there was a loud yell behind them, and out of nowhere came Carl, who let out another yell—this one a bloodcurdling one—and jumped on top of Bevo, who had one arm on Shyanne. Bevo took his free hand and grabbed Carl and tossed him aside as easily as he had the night he threw Dan into the slush.

Then another figure appeared from about twenty feet away. It was Barker, and his gun was raised.

"Hey, clowns, drop your guns and get those hands up where I can see them. You too, big boy."

The clowns dropped their guns and offered little resistance, but Bevo didn't want to go that easily. He grabbed Shyanne and put her in between himself and Barker, using her as a shield. Barker remained in a crouched position, ready to shoot, but not wanting to do so.

Dan's right arm was now free because the clown holding him had let go and still had his hands raised. The last time he had hit anyone, he had been eight years old, and the person he had hit then was Carl. So he figured he better make it good.

Bevo was not paying any attention to him, so he had a clean shot at him. He made a fist and punched him in the throat as hard as he could. He partially got the chin also, but he got enough of his throat that Bevo gasped and briefly let go of Shyanne. Instead of running, she stepped back, swung her right leg back, and kicked him right in the groin with the heel of her right shoe.

As all this was happening, Jamieson had rushed out of the car and headed over to where Bevo was screaming in pain. Apparently, Shyanne's heel had hit home, because Bevo had forgotten all about trying to grab Shyanne. But he had not dropped his gun, and he was still waving it around as he grabbed his groin area.

"Drop it, big boy," Barker yelled as he moved in closer.

Bevo seemed to be enraged and started looking for Shyanne whom Dan had dragged several feet away. He seemed to be aiming his gun at her when Barker fired.

The shot missed Bevo and went right into the throat of Jamieson, who was about three feet to Bevo's right. As blood started spewing from Jamieson's neck, Carl emerged from behind Bevo and took a big block of ice he had picked up off the ground and slammed it on top of Bevo's gun hand.

As the gun fell harmlessly to the ground, Barker came running up. One of the clowns had taken off running, but the other two were still frozen in time with their hands raised. Bevo had sunk to his knees and was holding his private parts with both hands now.

Jamieson had immediately grabbed his throat to try to stem the steady stream of blood coming out of it. He also sank to his knees, and he had the look of a dying man as he looked for someone to help him.

"Sorry," Barker said. "Shooting never was my forte."

Dan was so busy making sure Carl and Shyanne were okay it would be awhile before he realized he had broken his hand when he hit Bevo. But for now, he was not feeling the pain.

"Are you kidding me?" Dan said to Barker. "That was a great shot."

"Any more complaints about my shoes?" Shyanne said sarcastically to Dan.

He just hugged her as hard as he could. Whatever lingering feelings of doubt he might have had about her had all disappeared in the last few minutes. Nobody had made a move to see about Jamieson, who was gasping and calling for help.

"I guess we should call an ambulance or something," Dan said. For about the fourth time in the last hour, Shyanne just glared at him.

"That's my job," Barker said. "I'll call for an ambulance. First, I have to make sure the victims are all right and all the bad guys are immobilized."

"I'd say it'll be awhile before Bevo is mobile again," Carl said, grinning from ear to ear.

"Where the hell did you come from?" Dan said incredulously to Carl. "I sent out a code to Sam, but I never even talked to you."

As Barker took the handcuffs off Dan and Shyanne and put them on the two remaining clowns, he turned and said to Carl, "Yeah, what the hell were you doing here? I told you to stay home."

"Hey, this is my little brother. You called and told me he was in trouble. What am I supposed to do?" Carl said.

"I called you to see if you knew if your brother was okay," Barker said, halfway sternly but not really mad. "I didn't call looking for backup."

Carl shrugged, still grinning. "Well, lucky I didn't listen to you."

"Yeah, you almost had them all by yourself," Barker said sarcastically. "Don't know why I bothered to even show up."

"I had no idea whether you would catch the Rossini thing," Dan said to Barker. "That was the best I could do under the circumstances."

"Lucky for you, my wife knows every Italian restaurant in the five boroughs," Barker said. "And here I thought you weren't even listening when I told you about my book."

Shyanne looked at Dan, puzzled. "That Rossini restaurant thing. That was a code? How?"

"There'll be plenty of time to tell you all about it later," Dan said. "I'm not letting you get away from me again."

"Well, after all, you know where I live," Shyanne said grinning.

Again, Dan hugged Shyanne, and this time, he followed it with a kiss. She kissed him back. It was more of a romantic kiss this time than the one in the back of the cab. Dan pulled away to see Carl standing there grinning and staring at both of them.

"See, I knew you wanted to find her," he said.

Barker had been doing what he could to try to help Jamieson, but he seemed to be fading fast. Bevo had finally gotten Shyanne's heel dislodged from his testicular area, but he was just rolling around on the ground.

Dan reluctantly pulled back from Shyanne and said, "I guess that was our Act III."

"Yeah, can we go out for the curtain call now?" she said. "I don't need any more excitement."

Barker had stepped away from Jamieson, and the others looked down at him. For the second time in his life, Dan had seen somebody die. And even though he had hated Jamieson, it was still kind of a sickening feeling.

"Won't be a need for a second trial now," Barker said.

"No, you saved the taxpayers some money, Detective," Carl said.

"Well, we do what we can," he said.

"Hey, Sam, you think since Jamieson's not going to use that ambulance, maybe I could," Dan said. "I think maybe I broke my hand on that big lug's chin."

"Should have picked a softer spot to hit him," Shyanne said smiling.

Epilogue

And so it was that one of the most powerful men in America was bested by a pair of comedians, a stripper, and a cop with a bad aim. It may take a village to raise a child, but apparently it only takes a few people to bring down a bad adult.

And that's pretty much the end of the story. As the narrator, I've tried to stay out of it since I was just hired to write it, not interject my feelings into it. I did appear briefly as the cabdriver from South Africa, but other than that, I stayed out of it.

And what of our cast of characters, you may ask? Well, Big Bevo was not near as much in demand as a bodyguard after his voice went up an octave, so he quit that business and followed his first true love, painting.

There was the usual internal police investigation of Barker since he had killed somebody, and somebody pretty important. But his shooting was deemed justified since even the clowns and Bevo were ready to concede it had been an accident. It seemed nobody really liked Jamieson, and once he was dead, it was like when the Wicked Witch of the West died in *The Wizard of Oz*. Now that Barker had the ending of his book, he finished it and got it published. He did well enough with it to retire from the police.

As for Mattie and Simone, not too long after the beginning of the new year, they decided to take a little trip to Connecticut and get married. Dan, Shyanne, Carl, and Andrea went with them for the ceremony. Carl, never one to be upstaged, asked Andrea to marry him in Connecticut. It was not clear why he couldn't have asked her to marry him in New York, but with Carl, you didn't ask.

So with the four of them tying the knot or unionizing, Dan got to thinking he should ask Shyanne as well. She seemed to know what he was thinking and told him it was too soon.

For their first date, Dan had showed up at her apartment, and she was wearing sneakers. It was a nice beginning to a nice date—movie and a dinner. It seemed kind of mundane after what they had been through, but it was just what Shyanne wanted.

She retired from the ecdysiast business and found the nerve to try singing. Louie let her sing at his place, and it went quite well. It would take her awhile to get established, but it seems there's always a place for a really hot-looking singer who also has a good voice.

As for the Darwin brothers, with no one trying to hinder their comedy careers and with all the publicity Dan had gotten with the trial and shooting death of Jamieson, they became quite in demand. They even got to appear on Colbert. It turned out the call they had gotten from the Colbert show canceling them before hadn't been from one of the staff at all but from one of Jamieson's people pretending to be from the show.

And even though their careers were finally taking off, they still signed a long-term deal to appear at Louie's. After all, he had been the only one who stayed loyal to them.

As it turned out, Dan and Shyanne got along whether they were drinking or not. She made him feel fifteen years younger—not surprising, since that was what she was. She made him feel more alive than he ever had felt in his life. And he made her laugh. Sometimes life was just that simple.

So in the end, everybody lived happily ever after. Well, except for Jamieson.

He was dead.

THE END

About the Author

Mark A. Albright is a former sportswriter and newspaper reporter. He also taught creative writing. He lives in Little Rock, Arkansas. This is his first book.

CPSIA information can be obtained
at www.ICGtesting.com
Printed in the USA
BVHW071005250219
541082BV00003B/317/P